Chen, Justina

A Blind Spot for Boys

DATE DUE

PRINTED IN U.S.A.

a BLIND SPOT for BOYS

a
BLIND
for

SPOT BOYS

by Justina Chen

LITTLE, BROWN AND COMPANY

New York   Boston

Little, Brown and Company

Hachette Book Group
237 Park Avenue, New York, NY 10017
Visit our website at lb-teens.com

Little, Brown and Company is a division of Hachette Book Group, Inc.
The Little, Brown name and logo are trademarks of Hachette Book Group, Inc.

The publisher is not responsible for websites (or their content) that are not owned by the publisher.

First Edition: August 2014

Library of Congress Cataloging-in-Publication Data

Chen, Justina, 1968–
    A blind spot for boys : a novel / by Justina Chen. — First edition.
        pages cm
    Summary: After a bad breakup and the discovery that her father is quickly going blind, sixteen-year-old photographer Shana and her parents travel to Machu Picchu for an adventure, where Shana meets Quattro, a boy with secrets of his own.
    ISBN 978-0-316-10253-7 (hardcover) — ISBN 978-0-316-36438-6 (electronic book) — ISBN 978-0-316-36432-4 (electronic book—library edition)
    [1. Adventure and adventurers—Fiction.   2. Photography—Fiction.
3. Dating (Social customs)—Fiction.   4. Machu Picchu Site (Peru)—Fiction.
5. Peru—Fiction.]   I. Title.
    PZ7.C4181583Bl 2014
    [Fic]—dc23
                                                                            2013021621

10 9 8 7 6 5 4 3 2 1

RRD-C

Printed in the United States of America

For Steve Malk,
much, much more than a literary agent,
but an agent of love and friendship, faith and change.

The real voyage of discovery consists not in seeking new landscapes but in having new eyes.

—Marcel Proust

Part One

Nothing condemns a photograph more
than a blazingly bright sky.

—Annie Griffiths, photographer

Chapter One

I f you want to see the world with fresh eyes, haul yourself off to the Gum Wall in Pike Place Market. At least that's what Dad said twelve years ago when he brought me to the brick wall studded with spat-out, stretched-thin, and air-hardened wads of gum. Thousands of pieces. Hundreds of thousands. Both of us were armed with cameras for my first photo safari. His was a heavy Leica with a powerful telephoto lens, mine a red point-and-shoot I'd inherited from him, not some chubby plastic toy.

Back for what must have been my thirty-sixth trip to this weirdly mesmerizing wall, I still felt vaguely nauseous as I looked at all that petrified gum. I sighed, restless from fifteen minutes of positioning my tripod and another five waiting around for the perfect light. Last night, Dad had suggested the wall might make the perfect addition to my college application portfolio. He was right. After all, what's more unique and memorable than the Gum Wall? But then Dad begged off this morning—yet another panicked SOS call to our family business, Paradise Pest Control—leaving me to face the gum alone.

The morning sun had yet to trace its way over the alley. I shifted my weight and fiddled with my camera some more. Patience has never been my virtue, which could be a slight problem. My favorite photographers talk about being on constant alert for that split second when the ordinary transforms into the extraordinary. Until my portfolio review a few months ago, I thought I'd captured plenty of those moments: my grandparents holding hands, gnarled fingers interlaced, during their fifty-sixth and final anniversary together. The sunburst of disbelief on my mother's face a moment after her only game-winning goal in her adult soccer league. The first grin from the guy who stole my heart...

Stop, I told myself whenever my thoughts slid back to the boy who ruined me for love: Dominick Adler, Crew Boy, Mr. Yesterday. *Stop.*

As if my thought had conjured Dom himself, my heart lurched as it had done for the past year whenever I glimpsed a black Gore-Tex jacket. Always thinking, hoping, believing it might be—

I lifted my camera, tripod and all, and zoomed in on disappointment.

Not Dom.

Just a balding middle-aged man venturing down to the market for first dibs on fresh fish and flowers. Of course. Dom, a.k.a. Mr. Wrong—wrong boy, wrong time, wrong place—was in California, interrupting the best years of his post-college life, not to mention my love life, to create some rescue-the-rat cell phone game. A game, excuse me, I had inspired after telling him about an impossibly huge alpha rat that had outwitted Dad's traps and bait for months. A drop of rain hit my head as if I needed a reminder that Crew Boy had washed himself of me seven months ago. And that was precisely what I should do with this inscrutable Sphinx of a Gum Wall, all come hither but never revealing its secrets.

But I couldn't bail on the wall, not when I needed an iconic shot. The associate director of admissions at Cornish College had said as much with my portfolio laid flat in front of her. "Your photos of street fashion are really good, and good makes you pause," she had said after a close look at nine of what I thought were my best shots. "But a great photo knocks your heart open. So give some thought to that. What knocks your heart open?"

I didn't have to think; I knew. But it wasn't like I could exactly call Dom up and ask to take a series of portraits of him, not when he'd been black-ops incommunicado for more than half a year.

The Gum Wall, I figured, at least forced a reaction. So I spent another couple of minutes fussing with my tripod. The sky, though, remained stubbornly dark.

Time to face facts: This scouting trip, like every other boy after Dom, was a total bust. I was about to lean down to unscrew my camera off the tripod when the clouds parted. Through the cracked gray sky came a luminous ray of sunlight. The Gum Wall glowed with an otherworldly translucence. Right then, I could almost believe in miracles.

The decisive moment, that's what Henri Cartier-Bresson, who pioneered street photography, called it. The fractional instant when a moment's significance comes into sharp focus. And there it was at last: my decisive moment.

I crouched down to my tripod, perfectly and painstakingly positioned, already savoring my photograph.

"Whoa! Behind you!" a voice called above the whirring of bicycle wheels that turned to a squeal of mad braking.

Startled, I lost my balance, jostled the tripod, and only at the last second caught one of its legs before my camera could smash onto the asphalt. I wasn't so lucky. My elbows broke my fall. I gasped in pain. Not that I cared, because a cloud scuttled across the sky. The fleeting light vanished. The colors of the Gum Wall muted. My knock-your-heart-open moment was gone.

"Are you kidding me?" I wailed in earsplitting frustration as I scrambled off the ground and checked my camera— thankfully, fine. My elbows, not so much. They burned. Even worse, the fall had ripped a hole in my favorite sweater, cashmere and scavenged for three bucks at a rummage sale.

"You okay?" asked the moment destroyer.

Only then did I lift my glare to a dark-haired boy with Mount Everest for a nose, jagged as if the bridge had been broken and haphazardly reset. Twice. I pointed the tripod accusingly at him. Everest was about to see some volcanic action. "You ruined my shot. Didn't you see me?"

"I thought I had enough clearance, but then you...and your..." said the guy, waving at the general vicinity of my bottom.

4

"My what?"

"Well"—he cleared his throat and shifted on his mountain bike—"you got in my way."

My eyebrows lifted. I got in *his* way?

He rubbed the side of his nose. "Can you take it now?"

I jabbed the tripod toward the cloud-filled sky. "The sun's gone."

"It'll be back."

"You're not from around here, are you?"

"Not yet. I'm Quattro."

Quattro, what kind of name was that? Then, I guessed, "Oh, the fourth."

A startled look crossed his face as though he wasn't used to girls with healthy gray matter. I smiled sweetly back at him. *Hello, yes, welcome to my brain.* With slightly narrowed eyes, Quattro inspected me as though he was recalibrating his first impression of me. I stared back at him. Mistake. He swung one leg over the bike, propping up the kickstand as if he'd been invited to stay.

I sighed. Here we go again. Why does the right trifecta of hair, height, and hamstrings give me the illusion of being more attractive than I am? It was more than a little annoying, especially after last night, when Brian Winston—senior at a rival high school and latest post-Dom conquest—lunged at me as if three dates qualified him for a free pass to my paradise. Sorry, despite my ever-changing stable of guys, I am virginal as fresh snow. Shocking, isn't it? It was to Brian. And to Dom. And all the boys in between.

I quickly unscrewed my camera off the tripod, which should have been universal sign language for *Sorry, but this chicky babe isn't interested.* But did Quattro catch the hint? No. He said, "I'm visiting UW. What do you think about it?"

This guy was harder to lose than a case of lice. But thanks to hot summers toiling at my family business, deploying pest control techniques on rats, wasps, bedbugs, and other vermin alongside my twin brothers and Dad, I knew exactly how to handle this situation.

I assessed Quattro with an expert and clinical eye: nearly my height, at just over five seven. Brown hair streaked with gold. The poor guy must have been color-blind. What other possible explanation could there have been for pairing purple shorts with red sneakers from Japan and an orange Polarfleece pullover? It was almost tragic how much he clashed. My eyes widened. The pullover hugged the lines of his V-shaped torso closely. Much too closely for an off-the-rack purchase.

"You didn't actually have that *tailored*, did you?" I couldn't help asking him, as I gestured at his chest. His barrel-shaped chest.

Quattro had the grace to flush as he plucked at the fabric. "Oh, this? Let's just say my kid sister's life goal is to be on *Project Runway*. She raids my closet for"—he made quote marks with his fingers—"'practice.' You should see what she's done to some of my jeans."

In spite of myself, I laughed and watched his eyes slide down to my mouth as I knew they would. I could practically hear my best friend, Reb, teasing me: *Man magnet!* Quattro was more appealing than I had first thought. Just as I was trying to decide whether to retort or retreat, the sun reappeared.

"Lo and behold," said Quattro, his eyes gleaming with a

decidedly self-satisfied look. The light illuminated his cheek-bones, so chiseled Michelangelo might have used him as a model. I blinked, stunned.

Lo and behold, indeed.

Lifting the camera before the quirk in his lips could vanish, I zoomed in on hazel eyes that tilted at a beguiling angle that I hadn't noticed either. Hazel eyes framed in criminally long lashes. Hazel eyes that were rapidly narrowing at me.

I snapped a few shots in quick succession.

"Hey, who said you could take my picture?" Quattro demanded before he wrenched around to face the wall.

But he owed me. I moved in to capture his profile. He was the one who'd ruined my perfect shot, gone in a flash of an instant.

"I hate having my picture taken," he confessed, his steady gaze meeting mine through the viewfinder.

Damn it if I didn't see a hairline crack of vulnerability when he self-consciously rubbed his nose. His beakish nose. A flush of embarrassment colored his cheeks. Guilt flushed mine. I lowered my camera. I could empathize. When I was in second grade, my feet sprouted to women's size eights, which was traumatic enough since I kept tripping over them. I didn't need my older brothers to call me Bigfoot or joke that I had mistakenly swallowed one of Jack's magic beans to make me more self-conscious than I already was.

"I wasn't taking a picture of you," I said before adding guiltily, "per se."

"Really."

I held my camera in front of my chest. "It's for my blog."

"A blog? Don't you need some kind of a release form? Or my consent?"

"I've never needed—"

"What blog?"

"TurnStyle."

His expression began at startled and skidded toward fascinated. A girl could float away from an admiring look like that. The set of his lips softened. "No kidding."

Him? A follower of street fashion? Not a chance. He was obviously about to feed me a line. Even though I'd pretty much heard them all, I leaned my weight back on one foot and waited. Impress me, O Color-Challenged One.

But then Quattro said unexpectedly, "My sister reads you. Religiously."

"Really?" I frowned.

"Seriously. Kylie's going to think I met a rock star. But I wouldn't have guessed you'd be into fashion."

I crossed my arms over my chest, now acutely aware of the hole in my oversize sweater and the messy ponytail I'd tucked into a faded black baseball cap. While this was my uniform as a photographer, nothing flashy to draw attention to me, Quattro with his precious watch and designer sneakers would never understand that I had to go thrifting for my wardrobe. Trolling Goodwill and garage sales for clothes is much cooler when it's a choice, not a necessity. So I've made it my personal mission to help girls see that style has nothing to do with the shopping mall. Not quite a save-the-world ambition, but it was mine. I tightened my grip on the camera.

Lifting my chin, I clarified, "Street fashion."

"Okay."

I appreciated that he didn't ply me with a lame compliment, especially the one usually dropped on me: *You should be in front of the camera, not behind it.*

Instead, Quattro said, "Bacon maple bars."

"What?"

"My modeling fee." His expression was dead serious. "They've got to be on the menu wherever you're taking me."

"I don't pay modeling fees. And gross, you don't actually eat those, do you?"

"Well, yeah. Bacon. Maple syrup. Deep-fried dough. You know you want one. So...?"

"I'm not hunting for doughnuts with you."

"Nothing to hunt. Voodoo Doughnut in Portland."

Voodoo. A small smile played on my lips as I recognized the name. More accurately, I recognized their most infamous offering, shaped like a certain male appendage. Luckily, before I could point that out, Quattro jabbed his thumb southward and asked, "Want to go?"

"It's a three-hour drive each way. Seriously?"

He looked stricken. "It's not a drive. It's a pilgrimage."

Despite my best intentions, his words made me laugh again. Then I scrutinized him, really scrutinized him: His fashion taste was questionable, but he was funny, smart, and buff—his-muscles-had-muscles kind of buff. A sly whisper insinuated itself into my head: *And best of all, he's from out of town.* Which meant there'd be no possibility of a relationship, no drama, no trauma. I was officially between boys. So what was wrong with a little harmless flirting?

"Afraid?" he challenged me, lifting his eyebrows.

That did it. No boy was calling me a boot-quaker. So I said, "You're on. Voodoo Doughnut. Tomorrow."

That ever-so-slight shake of his head like he'd just been tackled was almost worth six hours of my time. For the record: There is absolutely nothing so satisfying as throwing a confident guy for a loop. My answering grin was powered by delicious smugness, just the way I liked it. That is, until I heard Dad call from down the street, "Hey, Shana!"

Not now.

My grin disappeared. Dad and his canine sidekick, decked out in their matching Paradise Pest Control uniforms, strolled toward us. I cringed—not just at the sight of so much yardage of khaki polyester but at the thought that Quattro would be condescending. I'd seen plenty of that from a few of the wealthier parents, who snubbed Dad at school functions once they learned he was in pest control.

But Quattro shook Dad's hand before scratching our dog in the soft spot behind her ears. Miracle of miracles, she didn't shy from him the way she did with most men. Quattro asked, "Who's this big guy?"

"Auggie," I said, before correcting him while our dog practically purred. "She's the world's best bedbug-sniffing dog."

"Wait, you weren't working at the Four Seasons, were you?" Quattro asked, glancing up at Dad. "Corner room. Fifth floor? My dad woke with a couple of bites."

"I can't say," said Dad, who may have had confidentiality agreements with all his clients, but his lifted eyebrows basically

10

confirmed that he had, in fact, been working at the hotel. Then he scratched his stomach like it was his skin that had become an all-you-can-eat buffet for bedbugs.

I coughed, because I knew what Reb would say about this synchronicity between his dad and mine at the Four Seasons, me and Quattro at the Gum Wall. She'd quote her psychic of a grandmother: *This is fate.* My heart raced as I rebelled against that thought. I'd had my fill of Don Juans and Doms. No more boyfriends, older or otherwise. I could have kissed Dad on the cheek when he told me that we should get going, since Mom was waiting for him.

Quattro shook hands with Dad again and stroked Auggie's head one final time before he hopped onto his bike. As Dad and Auggie strolled toward the street, Quattro raised his eyebrows at me, daring me to chicken out. "So, tomorrow?"

I snapped the latch on my messenger bag shut and told him, "Ten. I'll meet you in the lobby. Don't be late."

"I wouldn't dare."

Halfway down the block, I caught up to Dad and Auggie. The tiniest inkling of foreboding stirred inside my stomach. A six-hour road trip with a perfect stranger? What had I done? I breathed in a deep calming breath: Dad had talked to him, and Auggie had allowed Quattro to pet her. Those were two good signs. Still, I couldn't help glancing over my shoulder at Quattro as he pedaled in the opposite direction. Without turning, he lifted his hand to wave, as if he knew I would be watching him. I swung back around. After tomorrow, Quattro would be just another small, forgettable footnote in my love life, never to be seen again.

Chapter Two

Here it was, bright and early on a crisp Sunday morning, a time when most normal girls were hard at work on their beauty sleep. Me? Not only couldn't I sleep last night, since my traitorous mind kept rewinding to mental snapshots of Quattro, but then I had to go and download the pictures from yesterday's photo safari. Quattro's flaming orange Polarfleece added the missing vitality from all my previous shots of the Gum Wall. Stunned, I must have studied the series for a good hour. One photo was even portfolio worthy. Sleep was pretty much impossible after that, so I was awake when Dad switched on the overhead light, blinding me in my tiny bedroom.

"Good," he said, "you're up."

"Dad," I groaned, since awake didn't mean alert.

He waggled a glass vial enticingly as if it contained a magical elixir. I knew better: The stoppered test tube was filled with bedbugs—ugly, crawling bloodsuckers he had scooped out of an apartment complex two days ago. "You mind hiding this?"

From down in the kitchen, I heard Auggie bark, high-pitched and happy, which meant that my mom was up, fixing the first of her three daily Americanos sweetened with both chocolate and vanilla syrup. Before Auggie could eat her own breakfast, though, she had to complete her sniff-and-search exercise. She yipped again, raring to work. I hadn't been bragging emptily to Quattro yesterday: Auggie truly was the best canine bedbug patroller in the Northwest, a high-energy mutt we'd rescued from a pound two years ago.

"Hey, kiddo," said Dad, leaning against the doorjamb, "I'm really sorry about missing our photo safari. Next weekend, we'll go."

"Yeah," I said, nodding. He turned to leave. Given Dad's spotty track record, I had my doubts. If it weren't for his pictures hanging on our walls, I'd wonder if he actually looked for excuses not to photograph. His commitment to customers had trumped birthday parties, soccer play-offs, and even one of my cousins' weddings. My brothers had a bet riding on Dad missing our long-awaited climb of Mount Rainier this summer and wanted me in on it. But I hadn't answered any of Max's texts since my breakup with Dom, and I wasn't going to start now.

I yawned. Around four in the morning, I had done some serious online ogling of a professional-grade camera, the same one that my favorite National Geographic photographer had raved about in an interview. After three years of shooting senior portraits and children's birthday parties, I could finally afford to buy the camera, but I still hadn't. Couldn't.

Afraid? I heard Quattro ask.

Frugal and discriminating, I retorted in my head now, as I swung my feet to the floor.

"Hide it in a really good spot. She's been getting sloppy lately," Dad called on his way downstairs.

As hard as I tried to ignore the bugs inside the glass vial, I couldn't help looking. While you might think bedbugs are microscopic, allow me to educate you: They are not. Bedbugs aren't just visible to the human eye; you could go mano a mano with one as it plunged its outstretched pincers into a particularly succulent patch of your skin. So that flimsy silk cloth, cut from one of Mom's discarded scarves and clamped on top of the vial with a metal ring? That insubstantial barrier made me nervous, but Auggie needed to be able to sniff out their pheromones.

"Um, Dad, these are the dead ones," I called, frowning, as I trotted down the staircase. Dad usually kept a decoy vial to test Auggie, since she was only rewarded for finding live bedbugs. This was the second time in a week Dad had made that mistake.

He dug into his fanny pack for the right vial, shaking his head as we swapped. He said, "Old age."

I gripped the container tight because the worst thing I could do now was drop it. Do that, and bedbugs would infiltrate our home like an underground spy cell, lurking, lurking, lurking before attacking. Once entrenched, they were a pain to eradicate, even with a bedbug-sniffing dog.

While Mom took Auggie outside, I scouted the living room for a tough hiding place. Torrid romance novels—Mom's version of Prozac—teetered precariously next to her armchair, a sign that she was under extreme pressure at work. I swear, she must have been stressed when she was pregnant. That was the only logical explanation for how she'd managed to persuade Dad to name us after her favorite characters: Ash and Max for the twins, Shana for me. Always the lifesaver, Dad had insisted on altering the spellings of our names in case word ever leaked out about their steamy origins.

My gaze landed on the bulbous floor lamp that Mom had found at a recent garage sale. If I unscrewed the thick base, there might be room for the vial. . . .

"Okay, ready!" I called as I widened the front door, then retreated to the kitchen. Auggie darted into the living room, nose to the floor, with Mom holding her leash. In one minute flat, she parked herself in front of the lamp, head cocked to the side: *That's the best you can do?*

Training done, Mom sang out Dad's name—"Gregor!"— en route to the kitchen, where the table was already set with a neat stack of unopened bills and a platter of cookies for their biweekly budgeting ritual. Five years ago, on her fiftieth birthday, Mom had let her hair go silvery gray—*why fight it?* she had told her longtime hairdresser. But because her blue eyes sparkle as they did now, Mom is often mistaken for being years younger. "Guess what time it is?"

"Oh, baby!" Dad immediately drew to her side from where he was stretching in the hallway and planted a kiss on her lips.

15

"Dad! Shower!" I protested, waving my hand in front of my nose. "Mom, how can you stand it?"

Dad dropped his arm around Mom's shoulders and answered, "True love."

"Speaking of which..." Mom said a bit too casually. "Brian's mother called last night."

"You're kidding." I stopped midstride from going to the sink to get Dad and myself water. "About what?"

Mom's mouth pursed. "To discuss her 'concern' and 'dismay' over your 'pathology' of abruptly ending relationships."

"This," I said, wrapping my arms around myself, "is a nightmare."

"Just for the record," Dad said, grabbing a cookie before Mom moved the platter out of his reach, "we'd be more 'concerned' and 'dismayed' if you stayed with that mama's boy."

"Oh, that's good," Mom crowed, proud of their riff on my love life. "*Sine qua non*, honey!"

"I'm so glad you find my life amusing," I told them as I helped myself to a glass of water.

And my friends think my parents are cool? Really, Mom ought to have those Latin words tattooed on her ankle. It's her sweet nothing to Dad and cautionary tale to my brothers and me to hold out for that one necessary condition, that absolutely essential quality that we couldn't live without in a person. Without that *sine qua non*, says Mom, every relationship is doomed to fail, no matter how smart the girl is, how good looking the guy, how much attraction there might be in the beginning.

Dad's phone rang, and I plucked the cookie out of his hand as he walked past me toward the porch to take the call.

"So, honey," Mom said when we were alone in the kitchen, casting me a sidelong glance, "maybe you should spend some time thinking about your *sine qua non*?"

"Mom."

"Or take a break from boys for a little while."

"Mom."

"A no-boy diet for a couple of months. Really, you should consider it."

"Hang on," I protested, taking a large bite of the cookie. "You're the one who told me you'd shave my head if I got married before I'm thirty. So why should I get serious about anyone when I'm sixteen?"

With a rueful laugh, Mom said, "True, but maybe you'd go easier on their hearts if you knew what you wanted."

"I was wrong about Brian's mom. This is the nightmare."

Not a moment too soon, Dad returned to the kitchen, grinning as he held out his cell phone toward me. "You want to see what's really nightmarish?"

"No!" I rushed toward the stairs. "I don't!"

History had taught me that whatever disgustingness my father was going to share would rattle around uncomfortably in my head for days. Given a different life, Dad would have been a photojournalist for National Geographic, but he'd settled for photographing vermin, their dwellings, and his favorite subject: their droppings.

Dad closed the distance between us. "A hundred pounds of fresh bat guano."

"Dad, stop!"

"Odiferous piles..."

Luckily, his phone rang again before he could show me the mountain of bat dung, and I raced up the stairs, dodging the tall stacks of our library books, and retreated to my bathroom. As I stepped into the shower, more than water rained on me. So did Mom's words. Deep down, I knew she was preaching the truth about her *sine qua non* theory, which she had discovered from one of her self-help reads. Adventure first attracted my parents to each other when she flew past Dad on Mount Si, both of them on training runs. Kindness clinched it for them on their first real date when Dad sealed her house from future rat invasion. But it was their sense of humor that made them last twenty-six years of happily ever after.

I turned the water even hotter. As much as I hated admitting it, Mom was right: After seven months—count them, seven—of frenetic dating since Dom broke up with me, I was striking out on the *sine qua non* front. How hard could it be to find a replacement guy—one guy, that's all—who could make me fall even harder than I had for Dom? But no matter how fast I cycled through boys, no one came remotely close.

Overheating, I shut the water off, cracked the bathroom door open for fresh air, and toweled dry. Downstairs, I heard Dad telling Mom, "Looks like Auggie didn't find all the bedbugs at that new condo. I've got to go back."

"But it's Bill Day," Mom protested.

"I know, but we can't have them cancel the contract. Otherwise, Rainier will be a pipe dream."

18

And there it was again—the sound of another grand plan cracking under the pressure of reality. Dom breaking up with me because of our "age difference." Dad begging off yet another set of family plans. Legend has it, after Dad proposed, my parents committed to having fifty life-defining experiences and photo safaris before they turned fifty. Their Fifty by Fifty Manifesto was memorialized on a restaurant's napkin that now hung on our kitchen wall. They've ticked off exactly one and a half: mountain biking through Zion to celebrate Mom's fiftieth, and our plan to climb Mount Rainier this summer for Dad's. If the five-year age difference hadn't mattered for my parents, what were seven between me and Dom? At least, that's what I had told myself.

I shut my bedroom door and stared at my computer.

Afraid?

I didn't want to be the type of person who put her whole life on hold, waiting for perfect blue-sky conditions. So I opened the computer. The camera from my fantasy shopping expedition last night was still waiting in my cart at the online photography store. I had earned more than enough money, and the camera could be exactly what I needed to create the best portfolio possible.

I hit Buy.

—⟋⟍—

An SOS text from my other best friend, Ginny, led to a twenty-minute therapy session. Before she and Reb graduated, it would have been the three of us at one of our homes, dissecting this boy problem, preferably over raw cookie dough. But now it was too hard to coordinate a three-way call, with Ginny in New York and Reb wherever she was traveling these days. My phone chirped again before I could squeeze into my favorite jeans, which I had grabbed off the floor. Another text from Ginny: *So how do I get Chef Boy to notice me?* Right on cue, my stomach growled. Call it Pavlovian, but whenever I talked to her, I got hungry. She was, after all, an incredible baker, perfecting her skills at the Culinary Institute of America. Starving, I'd have to hurry if I wanted a snack before collecting Quattro.

I texted back: *Name a dish after him.*

Done, I turned to my closet to continue my own flirtation prep. Even if you're fishing catch-and-release style, you need the right bait. It took me a good five minutes to design an outfit that said casual yet shouted badass—skinny jeans, leather cuff, funky socks peeking over the top of motorcycle boots, all capped off with a boy's snug-fitting button-down shirt.

As soon as I made it to the kitchen, Mom filled two mugs of steaming coffee and handed me mine.

"You're the best!" I said, gratefully accepting the mug.

"Remember that," she said while tucking a computer cord into her yellow tote bag, "because I need the car today."

"Mom! I'm supposed to meet someone at ten....."

"I'm sorry, hon, but your dad had to take the truck for an emergency, and"—she shut down the PowerPoint deck she'd spent the last week designing for a CEO at a tech company—"my own client's having a conniption fit and needs me at the dress rehearsal after all." She checked her watch. "If you don't mind being about an hour early, I can drop you off, at least."

To be honest, I was relieved, since this provided me with the perfect excuse for nixing the long drive to Portland with Quattro. I was still hashing out the logistics of getting downtown with Mom when the doorbell rang. She frowned; I shrugged. Neither of us expected anyone, but there was Reb, standing outside the front door. It'd have been weird to see anyone but Reb at nine on Sunday morning, but who knew what time zone she had just been in?

"What're you doing here?" I asked, throwing my arms around her. Reb's so tiny, I'm always half-afraid I'll crush her, but from the way she squeezed me tight, I could tell she had packed on some serious muscles from lugging paint cans for her house-painting job.

"I got home a day early!"

The last time I saw Reb was two weeks ago. Juggling a part-time job and two internships during her gap year before college seriously ate into our time together. I said, "You're free? Today?"

"But you're not," she guessed before greeting Mom: "Hey, Mrs. Wilde!" Then, lowering her voice so Mom wouldn't over-hear, Reb asked, "So who's the new guy?"

"There's no new guy."

"Mmm hmm. So who're you meeting, then?"

"A guy," I mumbled.

"What was that? Did you say 'a guy'? As in 'a new guy'?"

"Sorry, I can't believe it, but I have to run," I said when Mom tapped her watch. "Mom's driving me to my non-date."

Without missing a beat, Reb told my mom, "I can drive Shana." A few minutes later, Mom sailed out the door, shoving a bag of cookies at us, and as soon as she was gone, Reb wriggled her fingers at me. "Where's your camera? Come on, show me the goods."

"I hope you're hungry, because I am," I deflected as my stomach rumbled again. In the kitchen, I plated the rest of the cookies Mom had baked yesterday, an excellent first effort at replicating one of Ginny's tried-and-true recipes. The cookie defense held Reb off for a good ten minutes, but then she brushed her hands together and settled down for some juicy girl talk.

"The Boy," she reminded me, as she leaned forward at the table.

"Fine," I sighed and powered the camera on, advancing to my favorite photo of Quattro. I wasn't expecting the excited little flutter in my stomach at his expression: searing. He stared straight into the camera as though daring me to look away. When I angled the camera toward Reb, her lips curved into a smirk. "Well, hello, New Guy. What time's the date?"

"This isn't a date," I told her, and glanced at the clock. Time had sped up the way it always did when we were together. It was now nine thirty. I sprang to my feet. "Oh, shoot, we gotta go."

I quickly ushered Reb outside as I grabbed my messenger bag and tucked the camera back in safely. After locking the front door, we dashed through my pocket neighborhood of fifteen storybook-size cottages, built on a plot of communal property adjacent to wetlands. My family had transplanted here after the twins left for college, seven years ago, downsizing so my parents could afford two tuitions and a mortgage. As we exited the gate to the street where Reb had parked her minivan, she asked, "And you met this mystery man how?"

"When he ruined my picture at the Gum Wall." I supplied the details about yesterday's fiasco as we settled into the minivan. Few people aside from Reb and Ginny could understand my frustration about losing the perfect shot for my portfolio. But after discussing a novel together every month for the past four years in our mom-and-me book club, we Bookster Babes knew virtually everything there was to know about one another, from smoking pot (why kill my few brain cells?) to self-starvation (Ginny's coconut chocolate-chip cookies; need we say more?) to sex. (Reb just lost her virginity to her longtime boyfriend, Ginny had come close, and I was the Virgin Queen.) Maybe I'd surreptitiously read one too many of Mom's relationship books—and I'd definitely heard one too many of Mom's *sine qua non* lectures—but I was holding out for true love. Anything less than that just seemed to make sex meaningless. And I, for one, refused to be meaningless.

Still, not even my besties knew about Dom. At least, I didn't think they did.

Hands on the steering wheel, Reb asked, "Where to?"

"The Four Seasons."

"Fancy."

"He's in town to scope out UW."

She waggled her eyebrows at me and put the minivan into drive. "An older man, huh?"

Don't you think you should have told me you were underage? I blushed at the memory of Dom's parting words, answering now more defensively than I intended: "He's just a year older."

At my combative tone, Reb's eyebrows furrowed. "What's up with you?"

"Sorry, just a little sensitive, I guess," I apologized, as I dug out the cookies my mom had pushed on us, handing one to Reb as a peace offering. "So Brian had his mother call mine yesterday."

"She did not call your mom."

After a therapeutic bite of butterscotch cookie, I gestured with the remnants. "She actually told my mom I was a pathological heartbreaker! Like I had some kind of disease!"

"That's just wrong, but..."

"What?"

"Okay, I'm not saying you're pathological or anything," Reb said carefully as she glanced over her shoulder to change lanes, "but what's with all these guys? I mean, it's like you've become some kind of Ellis Island: Give me your jocks and your losers."

"Reb, not you, too," I said. One analysis of my love life a day was more than enough.

"Well, what about that guy Doug? The one who used more product in his hair than I ever had."

"Or ever would." I shrugged. Three dates in a row full of excuses for why he was perpetually late, and it was good-bye, Doug.

"And what about that control freak? Mr. Texter Guy?"

I frowned, trying to remember. "Oh, you mean Stephen? Yeah, he was a mistake." After two dates, he thought he had the right to monopolize my calendar. So I voted him off mine.

"And Brian obviously lived in some kind of self-sustaining ecosystem of him, himself, and his mom," Reb said.

At that, we both laughed the way she, Ginny, and I do on late summer nights in Reb's treehouse, raucous and loud, when we're hyper from too much sugar and too little sleep.

"They're all nice guys," I said.

"Yeah, and they're all pretty good looking and can form complete sentences, but, Shana, no." Reb slowed when we hit the traffic going into downtown Seattle. "The longest you've been with anyone in the last—what? year?—has been a week."

"Two weeks."

Her hands clenched around the steering wheel like she was strangling someone. Then, she turned her gaze from the road to peer closely at me before looking away. "I'm not sure what happened, but when you're ready to talk..."

As used to Reb's spot-on insights as I was—after all, the women in her family had uncanny premonitions—I felt flustered and embarrassed. I clasped my hands together. According to my friends, I was the quote-unquote idiot savant of boys. Little did they know the truth: I was pure idiot. Eight dates over one summer with Dom back when I was almost sixteen shouldn't have slayed me. I knew that. I was Little Miss Rah-Rah Independence on the outside, chanting about seeing the world before settling down, but I had harbored a secret fantasy of me and Dom. He wasn't just older and wiser, and he didn't just have to-die-for biceps and superhero shoulders. He was turning his Big Plans for his life into reality, halfway done with business school and had already seen a huge chunk of the world. In other words, he was everything high school boys were not and he was everything I thought I wanted. I could so easily picture him in the future with his jet-setting career, and me with mine. It was a match made in *sine qua non* heaven.

Or so I thought.

I fidgeted with my seat belt, then switched the subject abruptly: "What're you up to this week?"

Reb's primary job was helping her grandmother lead tours to sacred places around the world, like Bhutan, where the gross national product is measured in happiness. I was envious—can you imagine the photos Reb could make in locales that most people never visit? But she was content with the camera feature on her cell phone. It killed me.

Reb took her eye off the traffic to stare at me. "Oh, my gosh, you know that treehouse builder I like?"

I laughed. "You mean, the one you're obsessed with?"

"Well, a new resort in Bend asked him to build a treehouse restaurant. Zip lining will be the only way to get in. And he wants me to join his team."

"That's so cool! So when are you starting?"

"In a few weeks, right after Machu Picchu," Reb said as she merged onto the exit ramp that would deposit us a few blocks from Quattro's hotel.

"Oh, just Machu Picchu," I teased with a careless wave.

She gasped so abruptly, I thought we were about to smash into the car in front of us. Instead, Reb reached over to grab my arm. "You should come! There're two spots left. You could take one of them. You'd be saving me."

"Reb." I gasped as her boa constrictor grip squeezed tighter. "My arm. Losing circulation."

"Oh, sorry." She released me. "Only two hundred people can be on the trail, you know. And all the trail passes have been sold out for the season. What do you think? It'd be an adventure."

Adventure. I could practically hear Quattro's echoing challenge: *I thought photographers leaned into adventure.* I sighed. "I really can't. Midterms. I can't even stand the thought of studying for them twice."

Nearing Quattro's hotel, I stole a surreptitious look at myself in the side mirror. Miraculously, my lip gloss was still in place.

"Okay, I know this is going to sound like whining," Reb said, glancing at me with an anxious expression, "but the trip's going to be rough. Grandma Stesha is really worried about some of the people who're going on it."

Who wouldn't be? Her grandmother's tours attracted a certain type of clientele, the kind who believed in fairies and water sprites, crystals and auras. Reb had told me once that Stesha was a rock star in spirituality circles, with some clients signing up for a new Dreamwalks trip every single year. So I guessed, "Repeat customers demanding to see impossible star alignments or something?"

"No. A couple of grievers."

Grieving. Now, that I understood. Time might heal all wounds, but here it was, mid-March. Seven months and three days after Dom broke up with me, I was still waiting.

Once upon an almost-sixteenth birthday, my brother Max was going to miss my big day because he was moving to San Francisco for a new job at a PR agency and wouldn't have the time or money to come home in seven weeks to celebrate. This, after being gone for two quarters in London already. So he promised we'd spend his last day in town together, only him and me, starting with a shot of espresso (so adult!) at a coffee shop near the university where he had just finished his MBA. I should have known better when he suggested I bring my computer "just in case." After we ordered our drinks, Max gave me the first of my presents: a shapeless UW sweatshirt. I hadn't even taken a sip of my espresso when he had to take an "important call."

"I'll pick you up in an hour," Max promised before he darted out of the coffee shop for a last-minute meeting with the professor who'd connected him to his job. "An hour and a half tops."

Three hours later, Max hadn't returned, and my coffee was long finished. Chilled from the overeager air-conditioning, I slipped on the sweatshirt. Still cold, I walked out into the hot July sun, lost in a fog of color, texture, and imagery from whittling a few weeks of photo safaris down to a single photo essay. Was the fall fashion trend in two months really going to be about long gloves, beanie hats, and boy trousers? Maybe it was going to be plaid paired with—

"You think you know everything!" a guy vented in the parking lot, his tone contemptuous. "You're always the teacher!"

My eyes jerked from the blue sky to a heavyset guy as baby-faced as the petite blonde in front of him. The Yeller's face was a bombastic red as he jabbed his index finger toward her. "You just can't stop!"

"I was just—" she started to speak, shaking her head.

"Just! It's always 'just' with you!"

Her lips clamped together. She wasn't allowed a single sentence, except for "Yes, you're right" and "I'm sorry, I'm sorry, I'm sorry."

"That's all you ever are. Sorry after the fact." The Yeller's next lacerating words were lost on me because I was staring at the wide-eyed girl who was caught in the hailstorm of her boyfriend's you-you-you rage. About a year ago, the Booksters had read Reb's pick, a novel about a girl who escaped an abusive relationship, each attack softened with a Judas kiss.

Then a black BMW screamed into the parking lot and jerked to an abrupt stop. A tall guy who filled out a black Gore-Tex jacket embroidered with UW CREW jumped from the car. He didn't bother to shut the door but ran straight to the Yeller.

"Do you know what I'm going to do to you if you ever so much as look at my sister again?" His voice was lethal and quiet. "Do you?"

"Come on, Dom. It's not what you think," the girl protested.

Without a thought to my own safety, I crossed the parking lot to place my hand on the girl's bony arm. She looked through me as if she were blind. How long had this gone on?

"Let me buy you a coffee," I said. When she didn't answer, I stared deep into those hurt-clouded eyes. "You need a mocha fix. Come on."

"Go," said Dom, his eyes focused on the Yeller. "Mona, go."

As the door closed behind Mona and me, Dom met my eyes through the window as though we were a couple who acted in wordless synchronicity. I shivered then, not from the air-conditioning but with knowledge. I had been twice gifted on my birthday: the college sweatshirt that camouflaged the high school junior I'd be this fall and the college boy who made me feel seen.

"Anybody can be charming when you first meet him," Reb said as we pulled up in front of the Four Seasons, the only mini-van in the brick-paved entry.

My head jerked to her. How did she know about Dom? But then I realized she was talking about the boy of the moment. I said, "Quattro was hardly charming, unless you call almost running me over charming."

"Where are you taking him?"

"I was thinking Oddfellows." Coffee shop by day, restaurant by night, the place had a great vibe: cool without taking itself too seriously. Best of all, there wasn't a whiff of romance about it.

"How's about I go ahead and wait there for you?" she asked as a valet in a tidy chocolate-brown uniform started to hustle to her side of the car until he noticed me. So intent on her question, Reb didn't notice him circling to my side first. "That way, if he turns out to be a total sociopath, I can be your personal extraction team."

"You're being paranoid," I told her. The valet opened my door. I unbuckled my seat belt. "Thanks for the ride, Reb."

"No, trust me," she said firmly and leaned over the parking brake to peer into my face. "You can never be too sure of anyone."

Reb should know: Her dad had up and left her family unexpectedly over the summer, not completely unlike Dom. I exhaled hard, as though I had been holding my breath.

"You're on," I told her, nodding. "Oddfellows in twenty-five minutes."

Chapter Three

I nside the wood-paneled hotel lobby, Quattro was hard to miss, dressed in a long-sleeved, traffic-stopping orange T-shirt. He rose from a cream-colored chair as soon as he spotted me. To be honest, he was better looking than I remembered, but that might have been the halo effect of the unexpectedly good Gum Wall shots I'd reviewed for way too long last night. Even before we reached each other, I bypassed the whole awkward do we hug or do we stand with our arms at our sides moment and cut directly to "Now about those doughnuts..."

"Bars, not doughnuts," Quattro corrected, then spread his arms wide. "Totally different."

"There's a difference in fried dough?"

"It's like saying golden retrievers and Labradors are the same breed."

"They aren't?" I asked, deadpan.

He laughed. Without waiting a beat, I sighed as sorrowfully as I could. "Hate to break it to you, but bacon maple bars aren't in your foreseeable future." I explained the car situation with my mom and proposed walking to Oddfellows instead.

"That's cool," he said with an easygoing shrug that I appreciated. Once we were outside, Quattro said, "Just as I predicted, my sister freaked out when I told her I met you."

"Really?" I smiled, flattered in spite of myself.

His realistic impression of a bubbleheaded middle school girl—"No way!"—made me snort from laughing hard. I blushed; it wasn't exactly the most feminine sound to produce.

"So Kylie had some questions for you, but I can't remember them. She's going to kill me."

"No prob, I'll give you my number so she can text me." Was I smooth or was I smooth? I made a mental note to tell Ginny how to slip her number to all the other Chef Boys in her future. As I started to unclip my messenger bag for my phone, I asked, "How about I just call your cell now so you have it?"

"I don't have a cell."

"For real?" Stunned, I stopped on the sidewalk to stare at him.

"I know, I know. Weird."

"Well, yeah." I dodged a piece of suspicious-looking garbage. The route to Oddfellows cut through a few sketchy blocks. "Oh, hey, did your dad recover from the bedbugs?"

"Yeah, they moved us to a new room, but once he found out that he got the job he was interviewing for on Friday, nothing would have bugged him. Literally."

"Wait, I thought you were here looking at UW?"

Quattro shrugged, then nodded at the crosswalk light that was about to change to red. We charged across the street together as I asked, "Your dad's actually following you out here?"

"He prefers to call it *relocating*." His face tightened. "But Chicago's our *home*. He and Mom...It's the only house I've ever lived in." His eyes flicked to mine, then down to the sidewalk like he was embarrassed.

Part of me wanted to tell him that the same thing had happened to Reb, and another part wanted to dig into what was bothering Quattro, but sharing led to revelations, which led to conversation and connection. Before long, if you weren't careful, you could be staring at commitment. No, thanks. It started to drizzle, and Quattro hunched his back against the light rain, his expression stark. The misty gray light made for perfect shooting conditions. I couldn't help breaking out my camera. What was a little impromptu photo session between new friends? So I wasn't paying attention to the street when Quattro grabbed me hard by the arm, yanking me back to the sidewalk.

"What the—?" I started to demand angrily before a BMW rounded the corner so fast, it nearly plowed into us. The driver didn't notice, too busy talking on his cell.

"Get off your phone!" Quattro shot at the vanishing car. Shaking his head, he loosened his grip on me. "Sorry, I hate that. You okay?"

"Whoa...we could have been hit," I said, only now measuring the distance between us and the speeding car. Mere inches. "Oh, my gosh, you saved me."

He breathed out, then said lightly, "Just add that to my fee."

"I owe you breakfast, for sure."

"And an entire box of bars."

I could only manage a halfhearted laugh, my pulse still racing. As if he knew and wanted to calm me, Quattro asked, "Where were we?"

After thinking a moment, I said, "Your dad's move."

"Right. I tried to tell him that I didn't need him ten minutes away from me."

"So how about a father-son adventure?" I suggested before we crossed safely to the opposite corner. This time, I was careful to look both ways. "Maybe he wouldn't feel like he needs to move with you if you did something epic together."

Quattro's wry smile returned from its brief vacation. "We've got that covered in a couple of weeks."

"Yeah? What?"

"Machu Picchu."

"No way! My best friend just told me she's going there, too."

"It's a popular spot."

"No kidding. My parents have always wanted to go." As we walked under the freeway overpass, I described my parents' Fifty by Fifty Manifesto, expeditions and photo safaris all rolled into one grand plan for an adventurous life. Machu Picchu topped their list.

"That's such a cool idea," he said, changing his stride so he wouldn't walk on top of a large crack in the broken sidewalk. He didn't strike me as someone superstitious—step on a crack, break your mother's back and all that—but I swept the thought away to focus on what he was telling me now: "We had to cancel our trip a year and a half ago, and the tour company's got a policy that trips need to be taken within two years. So it was use it or lose it."

Quattro brushed his hand through his rain-dampened hair. Some inner part of me that I thought had withered from Dom's rejection now wanted to reach for his hand. I fisted my own and thrust them deep into my jacket pockets, glad Quattro wasn't looking at me, uncertain what he would see if he did.

—⚬—

Damp and hungry, we finally reached Oddfellows. Quattro's gaze swept the brick walls, scuffed hardwood floors, and distressed tables. The scent of earthy coffee mingled with the aroma of fresh baked goods. Like half of the customers inside, the baristas and waiters wore the unofficial uniform of the Capitol Hill neighborhood: heavy army boots, funky T-shirts, and tattoos. Luckily, Quattro didn't notice Reb playing secret service chaperone at a window table, engrossed as he was in inspecting the vintage typewriter in front of the café.

"I like this place," he said, smiling at me.

That warm grin alone could be dangerous for a girl's heart. I vowed to keep our banter light and frothy and completely noncommittal.

"Just wait until you taste the desserts," I told him, pointing to the well-stocked glass case under the massive espresso machine.

After a quick but thorough glance, he said, disappointed, "There really aren't bacon maple bars. . . ."

"Well, yeah, because bacon isn't a dessert."

"To some people it is."

When I laughed, he refocused a hundred and ten percent back on me, as though we were the only two people here.

"Don't worry. I know just what to order for you," I said as I started for the register.

"Really?"

"Oh, yeah." As we passed Reb's table, she arched an eyebrow at me: *What are you doing?* I flushed and quickly diffused my flirtatiousness with a bland explanation: "That's what happens when you've got two older brothers. Twin older brothers. Trust me, I know guys."

Behind me, I thought I overheard Reb snickering. In case Quattro glanced her way, I drew his attention to the menu on the large chalkboard as we stood in line to order. "But on the small off chance that I might possibly be wrong—"

"Though you doubt it..."

"—you can check out what they have."

"Nah," he said, "I trust you."

"Good." So a few moments later, I ordered. "I think he'll want the breakfast panini. Extra bacon and a side of maple syrup, please."

He nudged my shoulder with his. "I like the way you think."

"I knew you would." I practically groaned at my knee-jerk flirtation. Maybe Brian's helicopter mom was right, and I had some kind of commitment disorder. Once boys bit, I fled. I asked the waiter manning the register, "How's the brioche French toast?" After he described the rich thick slice of fluffy bread dipped in vanilla-infused eggs, I groaned. "That sounds incredible."

The man's expression communicated all too clearly: *So do you.* If I so much as batted my eyes, he'd slip his phone number to me on the receipt. I lowered my gaze, glad that I could break the moment by insisting on paying for breakfast over Quattro's objections. "Fine," I said, "you can pick up my coffee."

"So guys pretty much fall all over themselves around you, don't they?" Quattro said as soon as we snagged the only open table, back in the dim corner. His eyes danced in amusement. I shrugged, lifted my coffee mug, then smirked at him over the top. He grinned at me and said, "Got it. You're the Genghis Khan of heartbreakers."

My eyes darted over to Reb, who was so busy drawing in her journal, she might as well have been in Peru already, which called into serious doubt not only her surveillance skills but her chaperoning ones, too. So much for Mission: Extraction.

"Not anymore." Time to self-police and keep this conversation on the friendship track. "I'm on a no-boy diet."

Quattro tilted his head in the direction of the waiter who was staring at me. "Yeah, so how's that going for you?"

"Really well."

"That's cool. I'm on a no-girl diet myself."

I couldn't help myself from asking, "Yeah, so how's that going for you?"

"How do you think?" He shot me a roguish grin that—I hate to admit—made me feel all quivery inside, as if I wanted to be the one to make him cheat.

Fortunately, our food arrived. But after our conversation meandered to safer territory—the Bumbershoot music festival every Labor Day weekend, hiking the Enchantment Lakes—why, oh why, did I have to return to his no-girl diet?

Shana, stop.

"With the move and college," he said, "I just don't want drama."

That, I understood. I wiped a stray drop of coffee off my mug. "I totally get that. You're so lucky. I've got an entire year before college. That's an eternity."

"But then watch out, Milan."

I raised my eyebrows. "How'd you know?"

"It's in your blog."

In the six weeks that Dom and I dated, I don't think he read my blog once, though he had a ton of great suggestions about how I could build my readership. I bit my lip uncertainly, so thrown off by Quattro's revelation I was almost glad that Reb was hurrying to our table. How'd she read my signal so quickly? But then I saw her pale face, and it didn't matter if Quattro figured out she was my backup plan.

I asked, "Reb, what's up?"

She blurted, "My mom just called. Your mom's been trying to reach you. Your dad's had an accident."

Dad, Mr. Strong and Sturdy, in an accident? Inconceivable. I slung my messenger bag onto my lap to retrieve my phone from the front pocket.

Five missed calls. Ten texts.

Worry trickled down my spine. My parents rarely texted. I skimmed the last of Mom's messages: *Come home.*

Home. I called home. No answer.

Chapter Four

*L*ater, I wouldn't remember how I left Oddfellows, just that Quattro placed a hand on my arm outside the café and asked me to call him at his hotel so he'd know I was okay. I remember him insisting on walking back to his hotel on his own. I had nodded distractedly before jumping into Reb's car and dialing my parents again and finally my brothers... even Max, who I'd been avoiding since Dom.

No answer, no answer, no answer.

At my front door, I hugged Reb a hasty good-bye, then slipped inside. Immediately, I noticed there was no Mom singing off tune, no Dad listening to his rock music. They were sitting beside each other at the kitchen table, their heads bowed, holding hands, and a space as wide as sorrow separating them. The halfhearted thump of Auggie's tail when she spied me was the only sound in the house. She lifted her large head but stayed at their feet, as though she knew my parents needed her more.

It may sound weird, but my first instinct was to document this moment. I fished out my cell phone and snapped their picture. So lost in their separate worlds, my parents didn't even notice me.

"Hey," I said softly after I pocketed my phone, approaching them at last.

Whatever they had been discussing had left an oily heaviness in our home. My parents sat back in their seats almost guiltily. Dad's hand lifted to shield the bandage on his right cheek. His lip was cut and swollen.

"What happened?" I demanded, alarmed at the drops of dried blood on his T-shirt.

"Oh, Shana, you're home," he said, sounding disappointed. Dad's fingers now tightened around his trusty camera. He looked dazed and disoriented.

"What happened?" I asked again as I drew closer with a sense of dread. The last time I'd seen my parents in such wordless despair was three years ago, when Grandpa toppled onto a restaurant floor, dead of an aneurysm. Dad couldn't possibly have a ticking time bomb inside his brain, too, could he? Still no answer.

My parents' Fifty by Fifty Manifesto scrawled on a white restaurant napkin rested between them on the table like an upended tombstone. I clutched the edges of my jacket around me.

"What is it?" I asked. My voice rose. "What?"

Dad met Mom's gaze, avoiding mine. An entire conversation

bookended with arguments and agreements had taken place while I blinked.

Mom started explaining, "Your dad was climbing a ladder and missed a rung—"

"You did?" I shot a quick look at him, frowning. Dad was one of the most coordinated people I knew. I'd seen him balance confidently on the top rung of a scary-tall ladder that no one's ever supposed to stand on, just to remove a hornet's nest.

"He hit his head pretty hard," Mom said, sliding her hand atop Dad's. "So we went to the emergency room and—"

"I'm going blind," Dad said bluntly.

"They think." Mom's voice was fierce. "It was just one doctor's opinion."

"She's right, Mollie. There's a black dot when I look out my left eye."

"But they can fix it, right?" I asked, shaking my head as if I was denying the diagnosis.

"Retinal neuropathy, that's the best guess," Dad said. He played with the corner of their legendary napkin, the list of all the adventures they'd promised each other to take: trekking the Inca Trail, canyoneering in Wadi Mujib, surfing at Puerto Escondido. "There's no cure."

"They'll know more once they get the blood work back," Mom jumped in.

"Six months." Dad folded his arms across his chest, rocking forward in his chair. "That's what I have left to see. To *see*."

"We don't know for sure, Gregor, until we get the second opinion."

Dad lifted his head to stare at Mom incredulously. "Mollie, come on." And then he proceeded to tell me about the genetic disease, which typically strikes men in their early twenties. "I've got all the symptoms."

"But it doesn't make sense!" I cried.

In what universe would it make any kind of sense for my dad, the ultimate photographer, to go blind? And besides, he was in better shape than men half his age. So how could he be getting a disease?

"Luck of the genetic draw. The only thing that matters," Dad said tiredly, "is that I won't be able to take care of anyone in six months."

"That's not true," Mom protested.

Dad ordered in an uncharacteristically harsh tone, "Mollie. Stop."

The room reverberated with Mom's hurt, Dad's hopelessness, my confusion. Mom bit her lip, chastened. For once, her cheerleader optimism failed her. Dad's tension was a beacon for Auggie, who lifted herself from Mom's perpetually cold feet to resettle at Dad's side. Her baleful eyes stared up at Dad until he rested his hand on her head. "It's okay, girl. God, I blamed the dog for missing the bedbugs over the last couple of weeks. It was me."

Dad dropped his head into his hands. His half-dollar-size bald spot—that vulnerable patch of bare skin—made my heart clutch. For the first time, I realized that Dad wasn't invincible. It was frightening, that thought.

"Wouldn't you know it? The twins are settled. Shana's almost

in college. Just when it was almost my time to do what I wanted...
I wasted my whole life killing rats. Trapping moles. Gassing spiders." A shudder of anguish passed over my father, and he wrapped his arms around himself, rocking back and forth. "'He killed bedbugs,' for God's sake; that's going to be my legacy."

"Dad! You were taking care of us," I told him.

Mom added passionately, "Providing for us."

"And what am I going to do to take care of everybody now?" Dad asked, his eyes wild. "You can't kill bedbugs if you can't see them."

Guiltily, I thought of all the times my brothers and I swore that there was no way in hell we were ever going to run Paradise Pest Control. Who cared if we were the fourth generation? My future, for one, was taking place in galleries and photo shoots. It had never registered that our paradise was Dad's purgatory, where he stayed out of duty to us.

Without warning, Dad scraped his chair back, gouging the hardwood floor.

"Gregor!" Mom called, standing up to follow, but the resolute bang of the front door made it clear: He wanted to be alone, wanted to be out of our home and this life.

—◆—

After some point, I couldn't stay with Mom, who stood guard at the bay window, waiting for Dad to return. I escaped to my bedroom to read up on his potential condition. Spinning around to grab the computer off my desk, I bumped against the

43

hope chest I had inherited from one of my great-grandmothers on Dad's side. The lid was lovingly carved with her name: Faith.

My own faith felt scraped raw. My knee throbbed. I slid to the floor, leaning against the bulky trunk, and rubbed the growing bruise. Then I waited impatiently for my computer to boot. As it did, I checked my cell phone in case Ash had called me back. Or even Max. Where the heck were they? If I were them, I'd be on the first flight home, but Ash was in Boston, probably awake for the twenty-third hour in a row for his residency, and Max was down in San Francisco, being a rock star publicist for a bunch of start-ups.

At last, the computer finished booting. After sifting through long articles with medical terms I couldn't understand, my worry spiked when I read one I could. Most people with Dad's potential condition can't tell that anything's wrong since the disease attacks only one eye at first. "Centrocecal scotoma," that's the official term for that stealth attack, more commonly known as a blind spot: *a permanent or temporary area of depressed or absent vision caused by lesions of the visual system.* When the remaining good eye starts getting a blind spot and people lose their central vision, that's when they finally notice their vision loss. Dad was right about one thing: There is no cure.

Rearing back from the damning words, my mind bounced to the thousand ways my parents were going to need me. College— was I even going to be able to go far away from home as I'd planned? How could I be off in Milan when Mom might need me here in Seattle to help take care of Dad? And my brothers— would they be willing to step out of their busy lives to pitch in?

On the off chance they had e-mailed me, I logged in to my account. But there, instead, was a message from Quattro, who must have gotten my e-mail address from my blog. For an insane moment, my heart rate quickened even before I skimmed his words: *Hey . . . You OK? Your dad? I'm in town till Tues, checking out high schools for Kylie: joy. Lmk if you need a bacon maple bar fix.*

Without hesitating, I started typing a response. Clever one-liners burst from my head to my fingertips until I jerked my hands off the keyboard. Dad was far from okay. I had told Quattro that I wanted a clean break from boys. And I was flirting? Confused, guilty, and slightly disgusted with myself, I abandoned my response and exiled the computer to the floor.

Across from my bed hung a photo of a blackened tree stump, scorched from last year's thunderstorms. I'd taken that photo right after Dom broke it off with me in mid-August. Unable to sleep, I'd gotten up at dawn, running hard through the wetlands behind our house. I spotted the stump and knew exactly how the tree must have felt: blissfully growing in the sun one day, then blasted into splinters the next. Now my parents were the ones fragmenting.

I never thought I'd feel this busted apart myself again. My gaze settled on my half-written e-mail. Here was a guy about to go off to college; I was shackled in high school. Hadn't I learned anything from history? Anything about dating an older guy? Maybe like a strain of superresistant bacteria, I had become immune to all the normal warning signs of a bad boy. Or worse—I'd developed a blind spot for all the wrong boys. I straightened, horrified.

45

If I were calling Paradise Pest Control in a panic about an epic infestation, Dad would recommend a complete purge. It was time to end this plague of Mr. Wrong, Wrong, and More Wrong.

This didn't require a no-boy diet; it was time for a total and complete Boy Purge.

Before I would even allow myself to be tempted, I blocked Quattro and powered off my computer. And then I went downstairs to wait with my mother.

Chapter Five

A couple of days after Dad's trip to the emergency room, a neural ophthalmologist confirmed the diagnosis that Dad would be blind in a measly six months. In the week since then, we'd been on a yo-yo diet of denial, bouncing between Mom's manic optimism and Dad's stoic silence. Case in point: Dad had insisted on trail running with me this afternoon like everything was normal. Not that I would ever tell him this, but I kept worrying that he was going to trip on some tree root he couldn't see and knock out his teeth or worse.

Then, as luck would have it, our next-door neighbor Mrs. Harris—beloved resident watchdog—spied my dad and me returning from our run. Her warm gray eyes disappeared into a frown that compressed her double chin as we walked past her house. A few weeks ago, Mrs. Harris had questioned our goal of climbing Rainier this summer with a "Why on earth would you do *that*?" Today, she questioned our sanity: "Why on earth would you *still* want to do that?"

Who knew that concern could be so suffocating? At her question, I felt the wild rush of colossal unfairness. Here was just one more way our lives would change, one more plan being stripped from Dad. I made a hasty excuse to leave, but in my hurry to get away from her prying eyes, I almost tripped on a box left on our doorstep. My irritation was two seconds away from boiling over until I noticed the logo of my dad's favorite camera supply store on the label.

My camera had arrived.

I cast a guilty glance at Dad, who was still chatting with Mrs. Harris on her porch. How could I have wasted a fortune when he was worried about earning a living once he was blind? I rested the box on my hip as I opened the front door quietly. Without a word, I crept upstairs like I was stashing contraband drugs inside our home.

"Shana, that you?" Mom called.

"I'll be down in a sec!" I answered, leaving the box on my bedroom floor. After I shut the door with a firm click, I trotted downstairs toward the tantalizing scent of garlic. Foil-wrapped baguettes rested on the kitchen counter alongside a pan of roasted Brussels sprouts and crispy pancetta. "Wow, Mom, you went all out." I examined the half dozen types of cookies tucked in plastic bags.

"Ginny sent another care package," she said.

"That's so Ginny."

Mom leaned down to peer into the oven. "I thought I should start freezing some meals for later."

"Later," I silently translated, meant "after blindness."

"Mom," I said, "we still have months. . . ."

"Maybe."

Half of Mom refused to believe that Dad's sight was moving from endangered to extinct; the other half seemed to be hunkering down for war. At the sound of the front door opening, Mom called out eagerly, "Gregor!" But there was no returning "Hey, hey! Where are my best girls?" Instead, we got a sepia version of Dad, bled of color: "Hey."

Mom chirped, "Hope you're hungry!"

Dad managed a limp smile. In the dim kitchen light, I couldn't see the last traces of the bruises from his fall, but there was no missing the dark bags pleating the skin under his eyes. Never a great sleeper, Dad looked like he hadn't managed more than a few hours since his diagnosis.

"So lasagna and burritos. We might get tired of eating them," Mom babbled, "but they freeze really well."

Few people are immune to the call of Mom's four-cheese lasagna, the one dish she can cook reliably well. But tonight, not even this could cajole a real smile from Dad, not when he spotted his camera and their Fifty by Fifty Manifesto alongside a new guidebook, 1,000 *Ultimate Adventures*, on the kitchen table.

"Mollie . . ." Dad sighed and bypassed the table for the living room, where he all but fell into his old, fraying armchair, imprinted with his shape.

If he thought he could escape Mom, he was wrong. She

followed and perched on the coffee table in front of him. "Gregor, listen. I think we should cash out our retirement."

Dad stood, shaking his head, and sidestepped around her to the kitchen, where he reached for a beer in the fridge. Now didn't seem like a good time to remind him that we'd been told alcohol might accelerate his blindness. Mom couldn't care less that he had his back to her. She plodded on. "Let's take the next six months and travel. You can do your photography. We've got forty-nine places left on our manifesto. So let's choose the places you want to see the most. And just go."

Finally, Dad turned and took her hand, leading her to the kitchen table as though she were the one going blind. He sat at the head of the table and said, "Mollie, I love you for suggesting that, but it's totally impractical. You know that."

Mom's eyes burned with evangelical intensity. "No, you listen to me, Gregor Wilde. I don't want us to look back on life and regret that we didn't do more before it was too late. I'm not going to just sit around for the next six months playing wait and see."

"So to speak." Dad laughed so grimly that I flinched.

"Aside from money, what's keeping us?" Mom argued.

"What are we going to do about Shana, for one? Junior year's the most important year. We can't exactly pull her out of school and take her with us."

"Why not? We can homeschool. She's only got three more months of junior year. Colleges would love that she went traveling, and just think of her portfolio. Right, Shana?" Mom's gaze slipped over to me as she nodded her head vigorously, willing me to agree. "Right?"

But I was stuck on Mute.

It was one thing to declare to Reb and Ginny and anyone who would listen that I was done with high school. College couldn't come any faster. And another to pull out halfway through junior year.

Mom urged, "Let's choose one trip, then."

"We're already climbing Rainier," Dad said. "Isn't that enough?"

"That's three months from now. . . ." Mom's voice trailed off as each of us filled in the blank. It might be too late in three months. Her face brightened. "Machu Picchu." Mom held up their frayed napkin of dreams, stained with age, and pointed at its primo spot at the top of the list. "We've always wanted to see Machu Picchu."

"Reb said the trail passes have already been sold out for the season," I murmured.

Dad latched on to the excuse. "See? This is so slapdash. It'd be a total waste of money."

"So okay, maybe not Machu Picchu. What about Patagonia? Or Kili? *Something's* got to be in season now." Mom held the thick guidebook out to Dad, but when he didn't take it, she opened it randomly. "Or a month from now. We have enough saved for three big trips. We could take each of the kids on one. Spend some quality time with each one alone."

"I won't do this," Dad said firmly. "Not to you, not to the kids. I won't be selfish."

Selfish.

"The boys haven't needed our money for years, and I'll work

full-time...." Mom's voice faded. We all knew Mom's refusal to travel for work because she wanted to stay close to home had limited the projects she was offered since so many executives required on-site support for their keynote speeches. How could she travel when Dad would need her soon? She glanced at me like I might betray her again by sharing that thought. "Shana, why don't you give your dad and me some privacy, okay?"

Unable to think or breathe, I was only too happy to leave my parents, as they began to talk about how Dad had had to take over the family business. And set aside his own college education. And then the twins arrived. And then unexpected me.

Selfish.

My heart tilted as I rounded the main stairs and stopped at the second set of narrower steps, which led to Dad's attic office. As always, the treads were stacked with travel books that Mom collected from around the house for him to reshelve. Where other girls got bedtime stories, I got death-defying stories from memoirs filled with the epic adventures Dad had intended to have...before the diagnosis ground his dreams to dust.

Once in my bedroom, I banished the package to the corner, still unopened. I couldn't bring myself to unpack the camera. How on earth could I possibly be a photographer when Dad had sacrificed that same dream career to take care of us?

The eggplant dark of early evening shrouded the room. I was glad for it. The presence of my new camera felt reproachful, but I didn't know where to store it—my microscopic closet was already crammed with shoes, books, old art projects. Then I glanced at the hope chest and knew I'd found the perfect coffin. When I opened the lid, I caught the familiar whiff of cedar along with the expensive perfume Dom had given to me on our third-to-last date. I had tucked that bottle away along with every gift Dom had given me because they were too painful to see out in the open. As I nudged aside the boxes filled with other childhood mementos that Mom had saved, I touched the plastic container that held my first camera, bright red, inherited from Dad. My hand recoiled.

Selfish.

The night after the ophthalmologist confirmed that Dad was going blind, Mom had come into my bedroom to check on me. Sitting beside her on the bed, I asked, "Is Dad going to be okay?" Mom's answer had been an emphatic "yes," but she had worried her bottom lip.

Dad would never be okay if he didn't take this chance to travel and photograph. I knew that. I lay down on my bed now, my eyes tearing. I was selfish to stand in his way. What was the worst thing that could happen to me? Repeat junior year because I bombed Chem?

Selfish.

My entire life of the best still lay in front of me; Dad had spent a life settling for second best because of us. Me.

Selfish.

I finally opened the package, labeled with my name, and withdrew the brand-new camera from its plastic bag. Once it was freed, I blew a speck of dust from its sleek black exterior. The weight of the camera felt right in my hands, but I knew which hands would appreciate it more. Which hands should have been documenting life. Which hands were empty now.

So I picked up the phone and dialed a number I knew by heart: Reb.

"Hey, are there still two spots left on your trip?" I asked.

"Oh, my gosh! Your parents actually want to go?"

"Pretty sure."

"Then I'm pretty sure there's room for them." Reb continued in a breathless rush, "You have to go with them."

"How? You said there were only two spots left."

"There are. But if you're okay helping Grandma Stesha out during the trek, I'll ask her if you can take my place."

"I can't do that."

"This is probably going to be the only time you'll ever photograph Machu Picchu with your dad."

My eyes overflowed with tears at her offer. I bit my lip. "I know."

"So just say yes."

—✳—

Down in the living room, my parents were sitting on the couch, the flames in the potbellied stove banked low. I lifted the dream camera and took their photo. The flash startled them.

"Shana!" Mom said, hand to her heart. "You scared me half to death."

Into my father's hands, I placed the new camera, the next best thing to lifelong sight.

"Dad," I said. "We're taking you on a photo safari to Machu Picchu."

Part Two

But the eyes are blind. One must look with the heart.

—Antoine de Saint-Exupéry

Chapter Six

If anyone had told me that my parents were capable of mobilizing for an international trip in two weeks, I would have bet an entire year of rat removal with me doing the rat-removing honors that they weren't. How many of our travel plans had been canceled due to last-second emergencies and panic attacks over the impending cost? But there was Mom, hauling home three sets of rain gear she'd found on the extra-reduced clearance rack, placed there for good reason. Honestly, compared to the puce-colored rain jacket and matching pants, the Paradise Pest Control uniform was haute couture.

"Ta-da!" Mom cried, holding up the rain gear like hard-won trophies. "Try them on! Come on!"

"Mom," I complained, frowning at myself in the mirror, "we're going to look like our own paramilitary troop."

"Shana's got a point, hon. This gives new meaning to 'dressed to kill,'" Dad agreed.

"Double O Seven would rather be shot than be seen in this," I retorted.

But as Mom pointed out sharply over our snickers, "Who are we going to know on the Inca Trail anyway?"

My parents decided that it was only fair to take my brothers on trips, too. So the plan was for me to fly home on my own from Peru while they met Ash in Belize for some scuba diving. Then, Max would pick up the third leg of the trip, intercepting our parents in Guatemala to climb a couple of Mayan pyramids. My lucky brothers, their adventures didn't involve military-grade outerwear.

So five thousand miles and seventeen hours after our travel day started in Seattle, Mom, Dad, and I set foot onto the Southern Hemisphere, backpacks stuffed with trekking pants, flip-flops for sketchy showers, and our questionable rain gear. After a five-hour overnighter in Lima, Peru, we'd catch a dawn flight to Cusco, the ancient capital of the Incas and gateway to the Inca Trail.

As exhausted as we were when we stumbled into the airport hotel in Lima, Dad still insisted that we check our room for bedbugs.

"Dad," I groaned, "for real? Do we have to do this tonight?"

"Well," said Dad, as he paused while inserting the key card into the hotel room door, "did I ever show you the pictures of that lady whose face ballooned with a hundred bites, not to mention her torso—"

"Fine." With a resigned sigh, I took my assigned role in the drama that repeats itself in every single hotel, motel, and friends' home where we rest our heads for a night. I flung our backpacks one after another into the bathtub. (For the record, bedbugs cannot climb porcelain.)

When I came out of the bathroom, Dad was approaching the side-by-side queen beds as though he were a medical examiner, sleeves rolled up and headlamp on his forehead. He wrested one of the headboards off the wall, leaned into the space between, then took a deep whiff.

"You know, some people might think we're a little strange," I said.

"Don't smell blood here," Dad said, and rehooked the headboard onto the wall.

"That's reassuring, Mr. Cullen," Mom said. "I'll be sure to let the Volturi know."

She yanked the sheets off the corner of one mattress and motioned me to do the same on the opposite end. I was about to protest—I'm the official lampshade inspector, since bedbugs adore snuggling into those seams—until I realized that Dad probably couldn't make out the telltale sign of bedbug droppings: tiny speckles that could double as black pepper.

"I wish Auggie was here," I said before I tucked the sheets back under the mattress.

"That makes two of us," Dad said, sighing.

Bless Margie, my aunt who worked as Dad's office manager. Dad is famously picky about dog care for Auggie, barely trusting anyone with her. So Aunt Margie had come prepared yesterday with freshly roasted chicken. One bite of that succulent bird and Auggie had practically leaped into Aunt Margie's car.

Morning came much too soon for another bleary-eyed flight, and I was grateful that Reb's grandma Stesha was awaiting us in Cusco.

"*Hola!*" Stesha cried and threw her arms first around me, then my parents. I had met Stesha once before but had forgotten how much she and Reb looked alike: the same pixie body build, the same joyful smile, the same mischievous glint in their eyes. It was a little odd to see what Reb might look like in fifty years.

With one dramatic wave that jangled the bright bracelets on her wrist, Stesha ushered us toward a waiting van. Her walk was a girlish bounce barely touched by the gravitational pull of adulthood. Who cared that we were in a boring airport parking lot? I trained my camera on Stesha.

Afterward, I tried to relieve Stesha of her massive tote bag, but she brushed me off with a "You need both hands free to photograph." Clearly, "helping" Stesha was going to be a challenge; I didn't need Reb to warn me of that. In my initial call with Stesha, she had told me, "Everyone signs up for a Dreamwalk for a reason and a purpose." She went on to describe how some people came to get closure on unresolved relationships, others to understand their lives. Case in point: An older woman named Grace was on this trip to grieve and let go, emphasis on the "let go." Stesha had assigned me to be her walking companion.

A couple in their late twenties was already inside the van. The pale man could have been auditioning for an Indiana Jones flick, dressed as he was in a fedora, multipocketed safari shirt, and khaki pants. All that was missing from his outfit was a gun belt and bull-whip, but he wielded his iPhone like a munitions expert. Stesha had mentioned that a couple of grievers would be joining us, not just Grace. But neither the Indy wannabe nor the petite brunette with him looked particularly grief-stricken until she lost whatever game they were playing on their matching phones. Even when she threw back her head in defeat and he pumped a triumphant fist in the air, I doubted they were aware of us until Dad introduced himself.

"Oh, hey, I'm Hank," the man said with a friendly grin. He nodded to the woman beside him, who looked up at us shyly through a massive halo of dark brown curls. Her long hair occupied nearly as much space as her entire body. "This is Helen. We're from the Bay Area. What do you do?"

"Pest control," Dad answered frankly as we maneuvered around the front row to reach the back two. Draped across Helen's lap like a blanket was a Gore-Tex jacket, embroidered with the logo of Dom's favorite game: Field of Fire. Had he been here, Dom would have gone into full fanboy mode. Dad must have noticed the logo, too. "So are you into gaming?"

"I'm just in finance." As Helen tucked her hair behind her ear, her massive diamond ring caught the sunlight. She looked proudly up at Hank. "But he is gaming." Hank shook his head modestly, though he smiled widely. "No, really," she said, tapping the embroidered logo, "that's his game."

"Really?" I cringed at my squeal, the one that told me I wasn't completely, one hundred percent over Dom. I remembered all too well Dom rattling off Hank's bio—a Stanford dropout who banked his first million before he was legally able to buy beer. Dom intended to make sure that that start-up lightning struck him, too.

Turning to Dad, Hank asked, "So pest control?"

"It's a family business," Dad said.

"Well, good thing you're here, because whenever I travel, it's like bugs have a vendetta against me." Then Hank told us about the scorpion infestation he had encountered in a remote village in India and the one cockroach that had nearly ruined his first trip to the Great Barrier Reef with Helen. "I never thought I'd see anyone walk on water until scaredy-pants here"—he gestured at Helen with his thumb before fluttering his hands in the air—"ran screaming bloody murder from our villa all the way into the sea."

We all laughed, even Helen despite flushing a deep rose. She ducked her head so that her hair hid her face and mumbled sheepishly, "It was huge."

Mom murmured sympathetically, "I'm sure it was."

"Hey," Hank said to Dad, his head bobbing up and down enthusiastically, "we should create the Mario Brothers of pest control. I bet that could be hot."

My mouth opened to say that I knew someone who had already come up with that concept, but I clamped my lips shut and stared out the window at the parking lot, wondering yet again when everything would stop reminding me of Dom.

"You promised you wouldn't work on this trip," Helen complained lightly to Hank, now shaking his phone as if to drive the point home. Her ornate ring caught my eye. Two "H" initials, each outlined with diamond chips, flanked an enormous round diamond. Hank noticed me ogling, which wasn't hard to miss—drool may have been a dead giveaway—and told me, "I designed it. H and H, see?" He lifted Helen's delicate hand for our better viewing.

"It's beautiful," I said simply. Talk about understatement. The ring had TurnStyle blog written all over it, but I didn't have the heart to gush over the stone or the setting.

Here was the It Couple that Dom and I were supposed to be. We were supposed to be the ones at the top of our careers who'd travel the world together in the midst of our crazy busy lives. We were supposed to be the ones with funny stories and inside jokes about our trip mishaps. And I'd really thought we had all that, starting the moment Dom told me he knew I'd love his grandmother's favorite perfumery in Paris, which blended a unique fragrance for each and every client. "Yours would have to smell like nights in Bali," he had said on our first date. "Have I ever told you about the week I spent there? No? You would love it." Then four weeks later, he returned from a family reunion in Paris, bearing a tiny bottle of perfume crafted just for me.

Stesha walked back to the van with her phone in her hand and the paunchy driver at her side. She sighed with regret as she climbed into the passenger seat up front. "The last couple couldn't make the trip after all. Family emergency."

"Oh, no," Mom said, frowning. "That's terrible."

"Well, things have a funny way of working out for the best," Stesha said philosophically. "Grace has already been at the hotel for two days. So we'll be a small party. Plus Ruben, Ernesto, a few other porters, and myself."

On the drive to the hotel, Stesha warned us, "Be careful not to overexert yourselves as you acclimatize to the high altitude." With a pointed look at my big, strapping father, whose knee was bouncing up and down impatiently, she continued in a stern voice, "I mean it. We're at eleven thousand feet—almost as high as your Mount Rainier. So drink a ton of water in the next two days, take a nap as soon as we get to the inn, and make sure to eat lightly. As appetizing as roasted guinea pig may sound, hold off on it until your body adjusts."

"Guinea pig?" I repeated weakly, as Mom twisted the cap off a water bottle and handed it to me.

"A local delicacy."

The thought of eating one of my elementary school pets pretty much obliterated all my appetite and jet lag. I didn't protest when Dad suggested a short run while we scoured the hotel room for any and all telltale signs of bedbugs. Despite Mom's meticulous packing, it took her another good fifteen minutes to get herself ready. So I cracked open the manual for the new camera I'd given to Dad. Since there was only so much a travel-worn person could process about f-stops and shutter speeds, I abandoned that effort and retrieved my old camera. I thought I had wiped the SD card clean of photos, but of course, there he was: Quattro, glowering at me in front of the Gum Wall, with all the staying power of a cockroach after a nuclear blast.

"Oh, who's that?" Mom asked, spotting Quattro's photo when she leaned over me to snag her deodorant from the backpack. "He's rugged looking."

Dad ambled over. "Hey, that's the kid from the Gum Wall. He's got quite the schnoz."

"Dad!"

"Oh, he'll grow into that," Mom said with the same easy confidence that she had when she assured me that I'd grow into my large feet. Unbelievably, she was right, as I'd discovered in ninth grade, the year when boys started pursuing me with off-putting enthusiasm. "And besides, never underestimate the beautifying power of a good personality. So who is he? When did you meet him?"

"We better go if we want to be back on time," I said loudly. Dad must have agreed, since he hustled to the elevator bank before our hotel room door could even shut behind us.

"You sure about this?" Mom asked as we landed in the lobby, looking guilty for disobeying Stesha's orders.

"This'll be the perfect training run for Rainier since we're already at altitude," Dad said, ignoring the employees at the front desk, who stared at us while my parents stretched. Of course, people stared. I'm sure they were wondering how we'd pay the hotel bill if we had to be medevaced back to the U.S. "We'll just take it a little slower."

But slow for Dad was race pace for most humans. His guiding principle for exercise was to train hard and train often. My lungs protested every step for the first quarter of a mile. There was a reason why all the other tourists lollygagged at a slow, dazed pace. Can you say "oxygen deprivation"?

"Sorry, I can't keep up," Mom huffed.

Did that slow Dad? No, he and his lungs of titanium kept on going. After ten minutes, Mom grabbed Dad's arm and tugged him to a stop. "Honey, please."

Dad may have nodded in reluctant agreement as he checked his watch, but it was like he heard a different clock ticking. The next few weeks with me and the twins weren't just family vacations but his last epic adventures with sight. No wonder he wanted to squeeze in as much as he could. Mom must have guessed that, too, because she said, "Gregor, we've got seven days here to see everything."

At that, Dad sidled away from Mom. She flinched at the slight. I felt so bad for her, I actually asked her to tell us what she had read about Cusco. We wove through the labyrinthine streets back to the hotel with Mom (still) talking about the first order of Catholics who built a monastery on top of the foundation of an Incan building, supposedly to show the superiority of Christianity. But then an earthquake in 1950 toppled the monastery. The only thing left standing was the Incan stonework underneath. As I walked in between my parents, I only wished that our family would be so lucky in the aftermath of Dad's diagnosis.

—∿—

Despite our being showered and wearing fresh clothes, Stesha divined that my parents and I had disregarded her suggestion to power-nap: "Well, you three better drown yourselves in water to rehydrate, then some *coca de mate*." She gestured to the tea service in the middle of the lobby. "Coca tea. Really. Have some."

Guilty as charged, I obediently hightailed it to the beverage table. There, Hank was filling his teacup from a large dispenser. He lifted his cup to me in a toast. "Say hello to liquid cocaine."

"Cocaine?" Mom practically lunged for my cup until Stesha said, "Mollie, sheesh, the tea's brewed from such an insignificant amount of leaves—"

"Which is why it's been banned back in the States," interrupted Hank with a large grin. "Down the hatch, right?"

Stesha continued despite Mom's shocked expression. "And it's absolutely harmless. Plus it helps with altitude sickness."

"So when in Rome..." said an old woman who acted anything but elderly as she tipped back her head to catch the last drops in her teacup. She smacked her lips, then grinned impishly up at us from the well-worn couch. "Whatever it is, it's kept me refreshed these last couple of days. I'm Grace. Grace Hiyashi."

So this was Grace, the woman I was hired to accompany during the trek. I lowered my hand to shake hers, but Grace scooted to the edge of the sofa, placed her hands next to her hips, and hoisted herself up. My parents and I obviously weren't the only ones to ignore Stesha's advice. Grace didn't exactly move like she'd exercised an hour a day the way Stesha had advised as preparation for the trek. Even with a few inches on Stesha, who barely scraped the five-foot mark, Grace was tiny as she stood before me.

"So I hope everyone took the packing list seriously. If you have any problems with your hiking boots, we'll have just enough time to take care of them before we hit the trail tomorrow," Stesha said, waving us to follow her out of the hotel, but not before she cast a worried glance at Helen's and Hank's boots, so new they couldn't have seen much action beyond a store aisle. I recognized them as the top-of-the-line mountaineering boots that Dad had coveted but quickly reshelved when he saw that they cost more than a camera lens.

Once outside, Stesha added ominously, "The restored

section of the Inca Trail may be just twenty-four miles long, but it's quite uneven. Quite."

Mom's concerned gaze flicked to me before it planted on Dad. From her pre-trip reading of every published guidebook about Machu Picchu and her hours searching the Web for photos of the steep and rocky trail, we knew this trek would be rough. But it was entirely different to have it confirmed by someone who knew the trail well.

"Okay, so everyone ready for a tour of Cusco?" Stesha asked, but without waiting for our response, she began rattling off details about the Temple of the Sun, which had once been the most important building in the Incan empire, then repurposed by the Catholics. I was beginning to sense a theme with dominant cultures.

In front of me, Helen confessed to Hank, hand over what must have been her overworking heart: "Oh, gosh, I'm not sure I'm going to be able to make it on the trail if walking here is this tough."

He said in a supportive undertone, "Don't worry. If that old lady can do it, so can you."

Grace's expression didn't betray whether she overheard him as she untied the shamrock-green raincoat from around her waist. She paused on the sidewalk, breathing hard, while she struggled into her coat.

"Here," I said, holding it so she could slip her arms through the sleeves.

I had to agree with Hank, though: If Grace lagged behind now, panting from the altitude even with two days of acclimatizing, how was she going to keep up with us on the trail? The Gamers distracted me from my thoughts. Out of shape or not, Helen was acting pretty spry up ahead of me, nudging Hank playfully. I had to wrestle down my envy, and not just over their flirting; they were snapping pictures with their matching cameras, so state-of-the-art, our new model looked like a toy. I was only too happy to test Hank's camera when he asked, "Hey, could you take a picture of us?"

I took so long framing the shot that I blocked the flow of traffic on the sidewalk. But honestly, it was a thrill to handle a camera I'd only ever read about.

"Sweetie, this isn't for the cover of *Time*," Helen teased me with an easy smile that turned doting when she blinked up at Hank. "Yet."

Apologizing—"Sorry, I get kind of carried away"—I returned the camera reluctantly. As we followed Stesha on a whirlwind tour of Cusco, my eyes kept finding the Gamers. Maybe it was a little stalkerish, but I couldn't help but study how easily Hank draped his arm across Helen's shoulders. How they walked in unison, stride matching stride. How I was walking behind everyone with an old lady who was cute, but not Dom cute.

Right then, Stesha stopped dramatically in the middle of the plaza. With her arms spread wide, she announced, "You are standing in Huacaypata, the Square of War and Weeping."

War and weeping. That, I understood. Just the idea of my final conversation with Dom was enough to make me want to war and weep against the memory of it.

"If you believe the Incas, this is the navel of the entire

earth." Stesha jabbed her finger at the ground. "Literally, you can draw a straight line to connect all the sacred spots in the Incan empire to this point right here."

"All roads lead to you," Hank crooned to Helen behind me.

Just like that, I realized that the next four days with the Gamers were going to be my own personal purgatory. Their perfect-couple company would only remind me of what I could have had if I were just a couple of years older or Dom a couple of years younger. Doomed by our birthdays; talk about unfair.

With no time to lose, Stesha ushered us toward the cathedral, an imposing and ornate building better suited for medieval Spain than the Incan empire. No photographs were allowed. Even if I had been able to shoot, I don't think I could have lifted my arms. They felt weighed down and strapped to my sides in the oppressive space, which made it easy to imagine blood-thirsty priests and ruthless conquistadores.

"This entire cathedral is a subversive rebellion fought with art," Stesha told us, pointing to a painting and telling us that the rumored model for Judas's face was none other than Francisco Pizarro, the Spanish conquistador who pillaged the city.

"I should do that with our competitors in the next game," Hank murmured to Helen.

To put more distance between me and the Gamers, I trailed behind everyone, even Grace, down an aisle. Elaborate art was crammed into every square inch, making me feel claustrophobic. Before Stesha stopped in front of a statue in an alcove, my heart began pounding in double time. But why? Why would this supplicating saint make me feel anxious, as if I were late

70

for a final? My family wasn't Catholic, just part-time Presbyterians who made it to services only on Christmas Eve and Easter morning.

"Meet Saint Anthony," Stesha said, her eyes on Grace, not me, thankfully. "Women of all ages come here first thing in the morning."

"Why?" Grace asked.

I knew why.

Once Ginny, whose mom is a devout Catholic, found out that I was going to Cusco, she told me about Saint Anthony, the patron saint of missing people and possessions. In this particular cathedral, the faithful believed that he paid special attention to the lovelorn. So Ginny had begged me to leave a note for her. I knew she meant business when she sent me that note, signed, sealed, and delivered in a FedEx envelope. Obviously, Chef Boy needed a massive prod of the divine intervention kind.

Stesha explained, "To leave prayers for a *novio*."

Novio. Boyfriend, soul mate. I knew that word from years of Spanish classes. Still, I wasn't prepared for Stesha to gaze at me—me!—with so much empathy, I could have been one of the lovelorn making a special pilgrimage to petition Saint Anthony. I took a hasty step back to distance myself from that mistaken identity. Nope, just an innocent messenger. I was of the no-boys-allowed order of girlhood, thank you.

"It's been ten years, Grace," Stesha said quietly.

"Some men are irreplaceable," Grace murmured. Her fingers flew to the man's wedding ring that rested on a chain above her chest, rubbing it as if it were a rosary.

Stesha may have placed her hand between Grace's shoulder blades, calming her, but a stern directness replaced the warm glow in her eyes. She told Grace flatly, "You have a second chance at love. You told me that you really cared for Henry. You can't be afraid to love again."

That statement tore into me, threatened to reopen the scar tissue from my breakup with Dom. As much as I wanted to join my parents, who were examining another alcove, I was frozen in place.

"I miss Morris so much." Grace's husky confession welled up from a grief so deep, plumb lines couldn't scrape the bottom.

The sound of this heartbreak scared me. It was bad enough missing Dom, bad enough having every little conversation and every little black-jacket sighting remind me of him—and this was after dating him for only six weeks. So how do you even move on after an entire lifetime together? Grace's face crumpled. Who'd ever want to risk being buried alive under that kind of grief? Not me.

"He was my life," Grace continued softly. "I'm almost seventy. And Henry's even older than Morris was. So why bother? If I want companionship, I could get a dog."

"Grace Hiyashi!" cried Stesha, placing her hands on Grace's shoulders. "I refound the love of my life and I'm almost exactly your age. There's no age limit to loving. And have you even considered that maybe there was a reason why you met Henry where you did? You've always wanted to go to Bhutan."

Unable to breathe, I needed out of this gloomy cathedral with its burden of gold. I was only too glad when Stesha glanced at her watch and said enthusiastically, "Oh, good! We've got just enough time to look at some ruins today."

And here I thought we had already looked at ruins.

All I wanted to do was follow Stesha along with everyone else out into the plaza. But a promise was a promise, and I had promised Ginny I'd deliver her note. How could I place her prayer on the altar with Grace still standing there, practically guarding Saint Anthony? Finally, Grace lifted her head. Finally, she walked away with heavy footsteps. As soon as she did, I tossed Ginny's prayer onto the pile ringing the saint's feet. Just as I turned to escape, a name flew into my head before I could grab hold of it and bury it so far down that even my subconscious couldn't tap it: Quattro.

What the heck?

A single candle in the alcove flickered, a sudden bend in the flame, as though Saint Anthony himself had chuckled.

Wait a second. I whirled around to face the statue. *That was so not a prayer.*

After Reb came home from a trip to Hawaii, she talked about certain places being able to rearrange you. I hadn't understood until now. My survival instincts shifted into such high gear, I felt the power burst of cortisol pulsing to my nerve endings. I rushed out: out of my memories, out of the cathedral, out into the afternoon sun, where everyone was waiting. Unused to the bright equatorial light, I squinted and saw a blur of orange. Orange, the all-too-familiar color used to flag emergencies. Orange, the signature color of a certain boy with a beak for a nose and a taste for bacon maple bars and who had told me he'd be at Machu Picchu, too.

Chapter Seven

My heart couldn't have thudded harder after an hour of wind sprints up stadium stairs. Alarmed, I scanned the crowds of tourists in the plaza for another sighting of that impossible-to-miss orange, but saw nothing except blue jeans and earth-colored trekking clothes. Relief collided with disappointment. Disappointment? What was with that? Pushing that unwanted feeling aside, I plowed toward my tour group. What was I thinking—that I'd run into Quattro just because he said he was coming to Machu Picchu? From the moment we landed, my eyes had felt desert dry, and my muscles still felt sluggish after our halfhearted run. So obviously the hallucination was just another game the high altitude was playing on my body.

"There you are!" cried Stesha when I reached the safety of our group. Before I could breathe a sigh of relief, the sea of tourists parted. And there he was, Quattro in all his blazing orange glory, staring at me, stunned. Alongside his father, he now approached, loose limbed in well-worn hiking boots.

Five feet away, Quattro's lips curved into a confident smile I remembered too well, and he said, "Fancy meeting you here."

My vocabulary was suddenly, unmistakably, and embarrassingly reduced to caveman grunts: "What...? How...? Why...?" Worse, the more I stammered, the more amused Quattro grew, as if he were used to girls losing command over speech in his presence.

Pull yourself together, Shana Wilde.

You are the Wilde Child.

Remember?

But all I could remember was Saint Anthony, and I shot a swift wordless glare over my shoulder in his general direction. A staff position at the *National Geographic*, an internship during Milan's fashion week, an A in Chem—those were the sorts of practical miracles I could have used. Not this.

When I faced everyone again, Dad was smirking at me like I was some kind of Pied Pipress of boys. That is, he did until he clued in that this wasn't just any boy but one he had met. One immortalized in some of my photos. His mouth gaped comically before he leaned down to whisper in Mom's ear. Her "No way!" was a yodel that bounced off all the building walls around us. Great, so much for acting blasé.

"You know each other," Stesha said, looking between me and Quattro, all statement, no question. I knew the conclusion

Stesha was drawing, because it was no different from what Reb would blurt out if she were right here: *Fate!*

Thankfully, Dad shook hands with Quattro's father right then, so there was no room for Stesha to say that word aloud. "Christopher, good to see you again," Dad said, grinning. "No bedbugs here, I hope?"

"So far, so good," Christopher answered, a small smile lifting the edges of his mouth and accentuating the deep circles under his eyes. When had the man last slept? It didn't look like anytime recently. But tiredness and graying hair aside, he looked like an older, darker, and much, much thinner version of Quattro. Gaunt came to mind.

"How's Auggie?" Quattro asked, forever endearing himself to my father by bringing up our dog. That rat.

After Dad filled Quattro in on Auggie's dog-sitting situation, Hank stopped fiddling with his camera long enough to say, "Small world."

"I suppose that's what some people might think." Stesha's dubious smile made it all too clear where she stood on that theory.

But Hank's statement set off a chorus of similar stories about people running into friends in the unlikeliest places. I felt like I was trapped inside It's a Small World at Disneyland with all the same nightmarish, head-exploding repetition.

From Grace: "Bumping into friends happens to me all the time! Once, when I was in Paris, I ran into a long-lost college friend. I literally thought I had read her obituary in the alumni magazine just a week before. But there she was, back from the dead, sitting at a café, calling out my name. I nearly had a heart attack right then and there."

From Helen, nudging Hank: "And remember the time when we were in Scotland, walking across Saint Andrews?" For our benefit, Hank clarified, "The golf course. Anyway, we ran into one of Helen's former colleagues who she hadn't seen in what? Five years?" Helen nodded triumphantly, saying, "I had a feeling that I was going to see her all during the trip, right? Didn't I keep saying that?"

Of course, everyone had a small-world story; this was a Dreamwalks tour, after all, the one that attracted people who sought out the weird and the woo-woo. What I didn't expect was Dad to join in on the fun. He said to Mom and me, "Remember the time when I kept meaning to call that client with that huge alpha rat? And then who do we see at the gym the next day? And he'd never worked out at five in the morning before?" Mom lit up because old Dad was back: joking, grinning, teasing. Right on cue, she piped in: "Alpha rat guy!"

While everyone else kept chattering around us, one-upping each other with more stories about coincidences that were too coincidental to be coincidences—go figure that one out— Quattro sidled up to me and said, "Hey, you didn't tell me you were coming to Machu Picchu, too. Oh, that's right. I wouldn't know because you haven't answered a single one of my messages. I was beginning to wonder if you blocked my e-mail."

Busted. I flushed.

Where was that quick-witted banter that intrigued boys and had girls lining up for private tutorials? Three weeks on a Boy

Moratorium couldn't have rusted my flirting skills, could it? Before I could embarrass myself with another series of one-word Neanderthal gruntings, Quattro placed his warm hand on mine. Not even a strangled "what?!" could have passed my paralyzed lips when a corresponding jolt twanged in the back of my knees.

With a shiver that I knew he felt, I finally looked up into Quattro's eyes. Mistake. They were much warmer than I remembered. So warm, a girl's icicle-spiked defenses could melt if she weren't prepared. I yanked my hand away, then covered it up by scratching the back of my neck vigorously.

"Hey," he said, "fate or small world, I'm glad we bumped into each other here."

Me, too. Given my subpar bantering response, it was miraculous I didn't actually blurt out those betraying words.

"So your dad's okay?" Quattro asked.

"Only if you call six months of sight left okay." I softened my words with a slight shrug.

Quattro looked at me with such sympathy, I had to blink away tears. My response was completely unexpected. I hadn't realized that my emotions were that raw. If he could tap into that vulnerable part of me so easily, then he could hurt me without even trying. I needed the safety of space and quickly hunted for a nonthreatening topic.

"Are you leaving or going to Machu Picchu?" I asked.

Quattro said, "Going tomorrow."

"We are, too."

I thought I overheard Stesha's knowing mmm hmm. I definitely heard Reb's *There's no such thing as coincidences.* But when

I glanced over at Stesha, she only smiled sweetly before asking Quattro and his father, "Who's guiding you?"

"Andean Trekkers," Christopher answered.

"Oh, them." Hank tipped his fedora back with one finger. "I wanted to go with that outfitter, but Helen's mom insisted on this tour."

"Mama thought Dreamwalks would be the perfect pre-wedding present," Helen explained, her lips parted as though she had more to say, but Hank spoke right over her. "If you're an athlete, you go with Andean. They do real trekking."

"I'm sure everyone on the Inca Trail will experience real trekking," Christopher said mildly.

Stesha beamed at him, and to my horror, she offered, "We've got two empty spots in the van if you'd like to join us for a walk through some ruins right now."

Before she was even done speaking, Christopher was shaking his head. "I don't want to be an imposition."

"No imposition at all." Stesha's voice lilted as if each syllable were a different, decadent temptation of a chocolate truffle: "Sacsayhuamán."

"Really?" Christopher said now, a reluctant smile knocking ten years off his face. He had already retrieved his wallet, opening it to withdraw some cash. "You should at least let me pay you for us."

In answer, Stesha looped her hand through Christopher's arm, saying, "Nonsense! Those spots were already paid for by two people who couldn't make the trip. So put that away. Everything happens for a reason!" as she steered us back toward the hotel, where the van awaited.

Wait a second.

Wait.

A.

Second.

I stared accusingly at Quattro, party crasher. He was joining my group? Who cared if it was just for the afternoon? These were my people, and this was my trip. It didn't matter that up until a couple of hours ago, I'd never met Grace or the Gamers before. My rapid heartbeat when I glanced over at Quattro had nothing to do with altitude and everything with my stupid, boy-attracting attitude. Not now. I grasped for an excuse, any excuse, to leave his side. I found a ready one in Grace, who had fallen behind everyone again.

"I have to hang out with Grace," I told Quattro lamely, not caring anymore that I sounded rude and didn't make any sense, so long as I was safely away from him. But if I thought I'd find a nice, quiet oasis in Grace where I could just walk and be, I was wrong. The first thing she said to me when I joined her was a cheeky "Talk about synchronicity. When things are meant to happen, they do."

I jerked my gaze off Quattro, unsynchronizing from him.

Grace chuckled, but because her breathing was so uneven, it was more of a smoker's wheeze. Worried that she was going to keel over from a heart attack, I slowed down. That was harder than it sounds given her sloth pace. She continued to puff. I continued to shuffle. Even so, we gained on Helen, who was studying a window display of handwoven blankets, a few shot with the same moss green as the designer sunglasses Dom had given me on our first date. As if I needed a reminder that boys were dangerous for my battered heart.

When we reached Helen's side, Grace smiled at her reflection in a storefront window, then fluffed her hair and said, "Since the Inca Trail is pretty much a straight shot to Machu Picchu, you'll probably bump into that boy plenty as it is."

The thought hadn't occurred to me. Me, Quattro, Inca Trail. I blinked at Grace.

"And by day three," she said, "you'd really have to be in love to find each other attractive."

"Day three?" I squeaked. I couldn't even begin to process the "in love."

"Oh, that's a tough way to begin a relationship," said Helen. She actually shuddered at the thought.

So stuck on "day three," I couldn't muster the energy to deny wanting, starting, or having a relationship with Quattro. Now, I'm not a vain girl, the kind who parks herself in front of a mirror for hours, applying and reapplying mascara to each and every eyelash. But still. I couldn't help but frown at my reflection alongside Grace, who primped at hers, and Helen, who sucked in her nonexistent stomach. I had four days of trekking ahead of me. Four days of camping. Four days of no showering. Four days of using nature as my facilities, which was going to be awkward enough with Quattro who knows where on the trail, but potentially in plain sight? I groaned, ran my fingers through my hair, my clean, grease-free hair. No shampooing my hair that went greasy after two days?

Day three?

"Don't worry," said Helen with a sympathetic pat on my shoulder. "I brought extra hair product."

—⁂—

With my gaze fixed out the van window, I refused to engage in any conversation with Quattro, who had managed to slip into my row. As the van lurched and swayed, I made sure to stay on my side of the seat. Not so much as a stray thread on my clothes was going to brush up against the boy.

Stesha spun around in the front passenger seat to inform us, "What we're going to visit is a temple, but as soon as you see Sacsayhuamán, you'll understand why the Spanish mistook it for a fortress. It's very well fortified."

Just like me. I stared pointedly out the window, pretending that Quattro's "Sounds cool, huh?" was intended for his dad, who was sitting on his other side and checking his phone.

Not soon enough, Stesha hustled us off the van for a mini-excursion to our first real Incan ruin, rescuing me from a conversation I didn't want to have with a boy I didn't want to know. As much as I tried paying rapt attention to Stesha's history lesson, I was all too aware of Quattro walking a half pace behind me toward the mammoth stone ruins. Self-consciously, I tucked my hair behind my ear until I remembered reading in one of Mom's love guru books that women toy with their hair as a primal way of displaying good health to a potential mate. My hand couldn't have dropped from my hair faster if it was infested with head lice.

Needing a distraction, I held on to my camera and focused on the site. The scale of these ruins was nothing short of awe inspiring. Enormous walls ran the length of two football fields, cutting tiers into the hill. Many of the boulders were easily five times as tall as Dad. Some, Stesha informed us, weighed more than an entire airplane. And to this day, no one knows how the temple was constructed.

When everyone filed forward, I took the opportunity to frame the group against the ruins. As I did, Quattro slipped out of the shot to join me. Ignoring him, I zoomed in on a massive gray stone that had somehow been cut to fit around another large boulder like this was a jigsaw puzzle for giants. I was so awestruck, I wasn't even aware that I marveled out loud after I lowered my camera: "How?"

Quattro answered, "How, what?"

"How on earth did they get these boulders here? I mean, really, how?"

"I read that the Spanish literally couldn't believe that Indians could build anything like this. So they gave the credit to demons."

"I read that some people actually think space aliens made this."

Just like that, his answering grin could have placed us at the Gum Wall, at Oddfellows, halfway up the Andes—the location didn't matter. That instant connection scared me more than the fluttering in my stomach. To regain my balance, I focused on the dirt path as though it were the most entrancing creation on the planet. Just when had Quattro's smile become a special occasion that could warm me?

I needed to scare him off and fast. In my humble experience, I've found that a girl with serious brain wattage can intimidate a certain kind of guy. So watch me show off my superior knowledge.

"The Greeks thought stones this big could only be moved by Cyclops," I said, then added for good measure, "Cyclopean architecture." I gave silent thanks to Reb for sharing all things architectural ever since I've known her. Who knew that her ramblings would come in so handy one day?

"You're the only person I know who's ever used 'Cyclopean' in a conversation," Quattro said. Unexpectedly, the expression on his face turned into something close to respect, the tone in his voice intrigued.

"You must not hang out with very interesting people."

"That's something I'm about to change."

I flushed. What was I supposed to say to that? If anything, his easy response only confirmed what I thought: He was a player. And I wasn't a girl who could be played with one day, discarded the next. Honestly, I should have walked away, but a part of me relished the company of a guy who could actually banter. Maybe—just maybe—we could be friends if enough boundaries were established. If I enforced the no-boy zone around my heart.

"Well, good luck with that." I tested him with a practiced half smile, "I'm still on my Boy Moratorium."

"That's a relief."

It *was?*

"I'm still on my Girl Moratorium."

He was?

"Friends?" He held up his hand to fist-bump mine.

That's it? Just friends?

A tiny smidge of disappointment poked its ugly head out of my asphalt-covered resolve to stay boy-free. And that betraying emotion was a pest that needed to be eradicated. Right now, this minute. Automatically, I returned the fist bump, then needing the safety of numbers, I strode toward the rest of my group. Their backs were turned to us as they listened to Stesha telling them, "Before we all know it, we'll be finished with the Inca Trail, Machu Picchu, Cusco, Lima. So just how open are you to being changed in five days? Radically changed?"

In front of me, I overheard Hank mumble to Helen: "Remind me again why your mom gave this to us for an engagement present? And don't tell me it was because of her trip with Stesha to Varanasi."

"It was. India totally changed my parents," Helen answered softly.

"Radically changed?"

He barely muffled a snort.

She nudged him with her shoulder, brushed her hair behind her ear. The diamond on her ring gleamed. "You know, Mama just wanted us to have that same experience."

Meanwhile, over their side conversation, Stesha finished her mini-lecture: "You can't walk the Inca Trail without knowing yourself and each other inside out."

All thoughts of anyone and everything else evaporated the moment I felt Quattro's gaze land on me as if he wanted to know me inside out, Girl Moratorium or not. What I wanted to know was this: Why had he sworn off dating? Clearly, my Boy Moratorium needed some reinforcement. Flirt now, clean up later, I reminded myself. A flirtation gone bad, and the next couple of days on the Inca Trail could melt down into one awkward disaster. Grace was right. I was bound to bump into him sooner or later on the trail. I stepped to the side of the Gamers, darting out of his sight line.

As Stesha guided everyone forward, Mom walked slightly ahead of Dad, scouting all possible obstacles. She warned him, "There's a sharp drop here."

Dad sighed heavily, his frustration obvious. "I can see," he said before backtracking to a different outcropping of stone. With his arms crossed and hunched shoulders, he couldn't have been clearer that he wanted to be left alone. Mom wisely joined Stesha and Christopher at the front of our group.

Quattro's empathetic expression reminded me of how I'd pitied Dom's little sister when she was lambasted in a public parking lot almost a year ago. *This isn't how my parents usually treat each other,* I wanted to tell him. Besides, it wasn't like his family was all picture perfect either. Over by Stesha, Christopher was obsessively checking his phone. Had he even noticed that Quattro wasn't walking with him?

I was about to join Mom as she told the others, "I read that this place became a quarry for the Spanish. They pillaged it to make some of the buildings in Cusco."

"This poor temple," crooned Grace, and without warning, I stopped midstride, already lifting my camera. My fingertips could feel the impending moment. As I waited, Grace pressed her age-spotted hands on the wall and leaned her forehead against the stones as if this was her private wailing wall, a sacred place to pour out her grief. While Jerusalem was yet one more photo safari that Dad had planned and put off more times than I could count, I would have refused to budge even if aliens and demons rained on us now. Finally, I understood what Dad meant about making a photo, not just taking one. All the thought that went into telling a story. Every ounce of me thrummed with the need to make this photo.

I felt Quattro's presence near me more than I heard him or saw him. More than anything, I liked how he didn't distract me the way some boyfriends had, jealous that my photography required my full attention.

Then I tuned everybody out—Quattro, my parents, other tour groups milling around us. I allowed myself to lose all sense of time as I fell under the spell of color and texture and feeling and moment. I waited, waited, waited. At last, Grace tilted her face to the blue-lit sky, her expression beatific.

"Yes," I breathed as I made my shot. Slowly, I lowered the camera.

"Beautiful," Quattro said equally softly, his eyes on me.

Chapter Eight

*E*arly the next morning, I woke, excited, before dawn even had a chance to bleach the sky. Today, our trek to Machu Picchu would officially begin, the lifelong dream my parents had spoken about in reverential tones. I turned to check the other double bed, where Mom was miraculously sleeping through Dad's avalanche snores.

Apparently, the combined effect of altitude and one too many pisco sours last night had knocked Dad out. Even though he'd had so many sleepless nights after his diagnosis—his midnight pacing in his attic office above my bedroom was difficult to miss—I tried waking him, first with a low "Hey, Dad. Dad!" That was followed with an equally useless nudge. He snored loudly. I gave up.

Dad or no Dad, I was heading out for the photo safari we had planned over dinner last night. Quickly, I slipped into the hiking outfit I had laid out the night before, grabbed my camera, and tiptoed out of the hotel room. According to our calculations, we'd have exactly an hour and a half before our group was supposed to meet in the lobby. The grand plan was for me and Dad to photograph the awakening town. But instead of staking out the main plaza, I found myself drawn back toward the cathedral.

I had a pretty good guess where a few women were speed-walking to this early in the morning: the statue of Saint Anthony. As for me, the saint and I were about to have a private chat: *Now, I know you meant well and all. And I don't mean to be ungrateful. However. Could you please retract Quattro and help all these other women instead?*

The heavy doors opened, and the last two people I expected to see staggered out into the gathering dawn: Stesha and Quattro. What were they doing here? Together? As soon as Quattro spotted me, he flushed. That momentary lowering of his self-confident guard made me yearn to photograph him again: Quattro, unplugged.

"Well, fancy meeting you here," Stesha said, smiling as if she had anticipated this very encounter. "You're up early."

"I was just going to take some last pictures," I said lamely, holding up my camera as proof that I wasn't here to petition Saint Anthony. No, not me. No help needed in the boy department. I babbled on, "I thought I'd get a picture of this at dawn."

Stesha waved at the entry of the cathedral. "We'll wait."

"No, you don't have to. Really."

"It's not safe for you to be out alone. Do your parents know you're here?"

"This is a small town," I said, shrugging. "What could happen?"

"Anything!" Quattro retorted hotly, as if he were furious at me. I blinked at him. What was his problem?

"What he means is that tourists have been known to be robbed or kidnapped even here," said Stesha smoothly. She nodded in the direction of the plaza. "We were just going to hunt for some coffee, but we can wait for you, right, Quattro?"

Feeling self-conscious and embarrassed, I could already hear my mom's lecture once she found out that I had snuck out alone.

"Nah, I need caffeine, too," I told them quickly, and swung my backpack around so I could stash away my camera. "I'll grab the shot with Dad on our way home."

Stesha studied me intently, just like Reb does when she feels compelled to tell me the hard truth in the most loving way possible. Whatever it was that Stesha wanted to say about safety, I didn't want to hear any more, not with Quattro beside me. A girl can only look like so much of an idiot before any guy.

"It's better this way. Dad would hate to miss out on this," I said. Then, desperate to fill the growing silence, I found myself babbling about how my parents are so careful with money, we rarely go to coffee shops, much less restaurants, except on Sundays. "That's when my brothers and I were treated to hot chocolate, and my parents got themselves their lattes," I said, laughing. "We went to a different coffee shop every week."

"An expedition at home," Stesha translated.

I blinked at this reinterpretation of what I'd always seen as nothing more than a weekly treat.

"We used to do something like that, too," said Quattro.

"Only it was hiking. Our Saturday morning hike. My mom says her church was in the mountains." A fraction of a second later, Quattro corrected himself, "Used to say."

"I sometimes think people forget that they can have adventures without even leaving their homes," Stesha said, leading us across the street.

As I followed, I cast a curious glance at Quattro, wondering what had happened to his mom, but his inadvertent slip wasn't an opening for a deeper conversation. Instead, his mouth clamped tight, as firmly locked as the shuttered cafés lining the streets.

Defeated, Stesha sighed. "Well, there's always the hotel, I suppose." But when we reached the hotel, Ernesto, our driver, flagged her down from outside the van, where he'd been waiting for her. Whatever he needed to discuss, it looked urgent.

"Oh, dear," Stesha sighed. "You two go on in."

A good five feet separated Quattro and me before I even stepped foot in the lobby. If he'd hustled any faster toward the elevator, he would have set a world record for racewalking. Just before the door closed in front of him, Quattro mumbled something about needing to wake his dad for coffee—at least that's what I guessed since I could only make out the words "wake" and "coffee" and "dad" before he left me standing there, alone.

My head rattled back and forth between disbelief and confusion. Waking his dad to join us for coffee was only a slight variant of my rarely invoked but highly effective "Oh, my parents have always wanted to try that restaurant! You mind if they come?" Plus, yesterday, I had seen with my own two eyes his father's megalithic watch, which had more instruments than an airplane's cockpit. Waking his dad up, my foot. I bet his father's watch could have blared an alarm that could scare the entire hotel awake.

From behind me, I heard Stesha—my best friend's grandmother, the woman who had committed to taking care of our needs this next week, the tour guide who vowed to transport us safely—chuckle. At me.

"I bet that doesn't happen to you every day," she said, not even bothering to hide her smirk. "That boy *ran* from you."

"Whoa, for a second there, I thought it was Reb speaking."

"Oh, thanks for reminding me. She said to remember that she met Jackson on a trip. Good karma, these trip romances."

I blushed and informed Stesha that Quattro and I were both on relationship moratoriums. "So nothing's going on."

"But, honey, romance or not, there's a reason why you're both here. Together. Whenever things like that happen to me—sitting next to someone at a movie theater who knows exactly the person I need to talk to—well, there's a reason. And a purpose."

Synchronicity, reason, purpose—those words reminded me of my first phone call with Stesha: "Sometimes, you got to get out of your daily rut to get clarity about your life. That's why a lot of people go on Dreamwalks."

Safer territory, that's what I needed. I gestured in the direction of the slumbering street. "Is everything okay with Ernesto?"

"Well," Stesha began heavily, "the government mandates that you have a specially licensed tour guide to take you on the Inca Trail. Ruben can come, thankfully, but we like to have extra help for our guests. His second in command broke his foot in a soccer game yesterday." Stesha frowned at the empty tea cart with so much desperation that the receptionist saw her and pantomimed that caffeine was coming. After a joyous "*gracias!*" Stesha plunked herself down on the sofa and patted the space next to her.

"So what does that mean?" I asked, lowering myself to her side.

"Well, I've been meaning to talk to you about Grace. You know, I had asked you to keep her company. But now, even though we'll have a guide and a few porters, they'll all be busy. And...she's not moving around as well as she did on our last trip together."

I nodded even as I replayed my observations about Grace yesterday. "I can stay by her all the way. Well, at least for as much as she'll let me. She seems pretty independent."

"That's all you can do."

"Can I do anything else?"

"That's helping a lot." Stesha breathed out, releasing her tension.

"It's pretty amazing that someone her age is going on this trek," I said carefully, thinking about my neighbor Mrs. Harris, who couldn't have been much older than Grace or Stesha, but an outing for her was a ten-step stroll to her porch.

"We can usually do a lot more than we think. Isn't that how it works?" Stesha said, visibly relieved when the tea service arrived. I followed her to the serving cart. Instead of handing me a cup, she held my hand, her face softened with a bemused smile. "So forget about Quattro." She shrugged, squeezing my hand tightly before letting go. "Figure out why you yourself are here."

—✺—

The van descended into a seascape of gritty brown clouds that looked like millions of sand grains magically suspended in air. The sight was so spectacular, it knocked me out of my regret that I didn't even get to say good-bye to Quattro before we left the hotel and transported me right back to Stesha's final advice this morning. I hadn't even considered that there might be a reason outside of my father for me to be on this trek. I was already unpacking my camera. This shot alone could have been the reason.

"This," Stesha said in a hushed voice from the front passenger seat, "is the Sacred Valley."

"Can we pull over?" I asked eagerly, even though I heard the Gamers' medley of impatient sighs. They were already irritated that we'd been late to load into the van this morning, and stopping now would only delay our reaching the trailhead, still an hour's drive away. But when were any of us going to see this mirage of a floating beach ever again in our lives?

"I think so," Stesha said, leaning over to Ernesto, who immediately pulled off to the side of the road. "Two minutes, okay? Ruben will be waiting for us."

My parents followed me as I hopped out of the van. I

quickly found an interesting angle and framed the shot. A breeze dragged the clouds down into the valley. Trees pierced through the clouds so they looked like stubborn sentries determined to remain on high alert. I got my photo, then on a whim, spun around to capture my parents, standing on the cliff edge as if they were planning to take flight. Dad was staring hard at this sandy veil as if he were memorizing it, Mom breathing in so deeply, she could have drawn every molecule of air inside herself.

"Look, Dad," I said, as I pointed out the misty line where the clouds converged with clear air. "Do you see that?"

Dad flinched.

I mirrored his pained grimace. No matter how careful Mom and I were, our word choices themselves were unintentional land mines. "Look" and "see" had become the ticking bombs of reality.

But Dad recovered with his usual easy grin for me and agreed, "Beautiful."

As he left my side for the van, I swallowed the lump of guilt in my throat. Why was this happening to my father? Our family? Only now that my parents were about to board the van did Hank lumber out with his camera. He said to me, "This looks like something that could be straight out of a game, doesn't it? You know how much money I could make off of this?"

"Yeah," I said faintly, knowing that if Quattro were right here with me, he'd appreciate this view, not for what it could earn him but just for what it was. Where were he and his dad now?

Hang on a second. What was I doing, wrapped around thoughts about Quattro, wishing we'd said good-bye to each other when we hadn't? I hurried inside the van, frustrated with myself. If there was one thing I wasn't going to do, it was waste my vacation obsessing about a boy, particularly one who had all but fled from me this morning. Been there, done that for the better part of a year. No matter what I told myself, though, it was hard to ignore the empty space in the back row where Quattro had sat with me just yesterday.

At last, Hank finished his photo shoot, beaming when he clambered into his seat. He crowed to no one in particular, "*Halo* is going to look so old school."

"See?" said Stesha once Ernesto had pulled back onto the road. "Nothing is wasted."

Chapter Nine

U sing holes dug into the ground and enclosed by concrete stalls, I'll admit, was a bit of a shock to this suburban girl. (Apparently, years of backcountry camping in the Cascades did nothing to break my dependence on indoor plumbing.) But watching my sure-footed father stumble over a rock he didn't see at the start of the trek? That was heartbreak, plain and simple.

"Gregor!" Mom cried from where she and I stood with the rest of the women for a female-power photograph at the humble wood signpost: WELCOME TO INKA TRAIL. We sprinted to where Dad had tumbled just ahead of us on the path.

"I'm fine," he said shortly, ignoring Mom's outstretched hand. He dusted himself off as he sprang to his feet. "Go on. Really. Go on."

Mom reared back from his harsh tone, one step, then two.

Her lips tightened as she tried but failed to stem her hurt and humiliation. Automatically, she glanced at the other women who were busy cooing over a small herd of llamas. Her cheeks flamed red when the Gamers shot meaningful looks at each other as they passed us. I could almost hear them revising their wedding vows: *We'll never be like them.* But my parents had never been one of Those Couples either—that's what I wanted to scream at Hank, Helen, Grace, and most especially, Stesha, who was watching not my parents but me.

Without a word, Dad hoisted his backpack higher on his shoulders, then strode forward purposefully. I'd never been afraid to talk to my father about anything, but this wounded-lion routine made me wary around him. Fortunately, Grace provided me with a ready-made excuse to stay far from Dad today; she lagged way behind everyone else. Mom hung back with us, muttering regrets and second guesses: "This was a mistake. Maybe we should turn around now and just go home."

Grace smiled gently. "Then you don't know men. He's got to do this."

"But he couldn't even see that rock. The entire trail is rocks and cliffs," Mom fretted.

"He'll manage," said Grace.

"But—"

"He's losing his sight, Mom, not his legs," I told her.

Both Mom's and Grace's mouths curved into shocked Os at my flat statement, but I wouldn't want Mom to be hovering over me any more than I knew Dad did. All further conversation was cut off when Stesha introduced us to the team assembled near the warden's hut.

"Okay, everyone, I want you to meet Ruben," Stesha said with an arm around our barrel-chested guide, whose black vest was embroidered with his name and well-worn pants were frayed at the bottom of each leg. Then she gestured at the six men lined in a row. "And these are our porters."

Wiry and muscular, the men had been hired to haul our food and tents along the Inca Trail while we carried our own backpacks filled with clothes and supplies. Their legs were so corded with muscles, they looked more than capable of sprinting up and down the trail, regardless of the number of bags they were already lugging on their backs. One was wearing flip-flops, most of them in shorts, which made me feel like a wimpy, overdressed tourist in my sturdy hiking boots and new trekking pants. I could only imagine how Hank felt in his Indiana Jones getup, the fedora topping his head.

Once each of us had signed in with the guard in the hut, Ruben led us to a rickety bridge that spanned the fast-moving river, much more dangerous and alive than what we'd seen from above in the safety of our van. He stopped in the middle of the bridge, raising his voice to be heard over the wild rush of water: "It's been raining nonstop for the last week. Today's the first day we've seen the sun." He joked, "I almost thought we'd need an ark."

"Let's hope this flood doesn't destroy the universe," Mom whispered to me before she moved to stand next to Dad. He didn't even look at her, as indifferent as a stranger.

"Okay, this might be a good time to tell you that we think of the Inca Trail as a pilgrimage," Ruben said, turning serious. "There are definitely easier ways to get to Machu Picchu. Most tourists go by train, then take the bus up to the ruins. If we really wanted, we could just follow the river." With a finger, he traced the bend of the cascading river in front of us. "And be at Machu Picchu in six hours."

"But where's the fun in that?" Grace asked. Dressed in her green raincoat, she looked like a leprechaun.

"So we're going to see Machu Picchu the way the Incas did," said Stesha.

Ruben scrutinized each of us as if calculating the odds that we'd make it to our destination. "The next four days of walking through pretty difficult terrain will make you appreciate the site even more."

"And by the time we get to the Sun Gate," said Stesha, "I think you'll have discovered things you've never known about yourself."

Almost immediately, our group divided into four sections— Grace and I bringing up the rear. The porters, who'd disappeared about two minutes after we began walking. Ruben at the front with Dad, Hank, and Helen. Stesha in the middle with Mom, the better to answer all of my mother's thousand questions. The last I heard before Grace and I trailed behind everyone, Mom was peppering Stesha with questions about all the plant species we encountered even though she had no interest in vegetation. Mom couldn't even keep a cactus alive if she tried, which was why we didn't have any plants, but she was obviously determined to wring every last bit of learning from this trip.

After four hours of what Grace dubbed "trudgery"—trudging that was pure drudgery on soggy ground—I confirmed what I already knew about myself: Can you say impatient? The trail ascended so slowly, you could barely call it an incline. So why did everyone describe the Inca Trail as challenging? But then the trail taught me a fast lesson about faulty first impressions. Too soon, I had to stop every ten feet or so to catch my breath.

If I thought I was dragging myself up the mountainside, Grace's pace was even more sluggish, inching forward while bent over at the waist. How was she going to trek for four days if an hour of hill climbing taxed her? No one was in sight, just the two of us poking along.

"You doing okay?" I called up to Grace after deciding that it was safer to walk behind her in case she lost her footing. From back here, I could at least break her fall.

"I'm fine," she said, her tone sharp.

One cantankerous father was more than enough to deal with, but now I was latched to an old lady who should have known better than to join a long trek? For this, I had given up my brand-new camera and come to Peru?

"You can go up ahead," Grace told me in a gentler voice, casting an apologetic glance at me over her shoulder. She looked as winded as she sounded, which pushed aside my irritation to make room for serious concern. "I'll go at my own pace."

"You know what they say about slow and steady," I shot back.

Grace may not have fallen into silence now, her labored breathing preventing that, but she plowed on, only stopping at our first view of Patallacta, gray-stone ruins atop banks of terraces. At our last break, Ruben had told us that these ruins were rediscovered in 1911 by Hiram Bingham, the real-life explorer who was the inspiration behind Hank's favorite fedora-wearing movie hero. Hearing about the site was a completely different experience from seeing it, just like writing about Ginny's chocolate soufflé was way less satisfying than eating it, especially straight out of the oven.

All misty and gray, the ruins could have been a watercolor painting. They begged to be memorialized in a photo.

Just as I crouched down for a better angle, Grace howled to the skies: "Girls!"

Worried, I hurried up the hill to her side. Was she having a mental breakdown? Maybe she'd succumbed to some kind of altitude sickness that induced delusions.

"Girls! You seeing this?" Grace spun around in a slow circle. In an even louder voice, she called, "Check it out! I'm here. I'm really here."

"Ummm... Grace. Who are you talking to?"

Grace grinned before she wheezed, "The Wednesday Walkers."

"Who're they?"

"My walking group. There were five of us. We started hiking together almost exactly forty years ago."

"Really? Where?"

"Vermont. If you weren't burying a husband or dead yourself, you were walking." She laughed lightly. "Rain, snow, or shine."

"Every Wednesday?"

"Every single one. I'm the last of the bunch. The last of the Wednesday Walkers." She sighed deeply, then brushed her bangs out of her eyes. "Bertie died back in October, right after our walk. Bless those girls, they talked a good talk about wanting to trek abroad. We had such grand plans, too. Following in Alfred Wainwright's footsteps in the Lake District. Doing the Appalachian Trail. The Cinque Terre. But we never made it out of Vermont together. Life called. If there weren't children, there were husbands to take care of. And then there was always the issue of money. But you're too young to understand all that."

"I get it. We're here for my dad. He's going blind." I followed Grace as she started up on the trail again, thinking about all the life and living my parents had forfeited.

"I heard."

"You did?"

Grace stopped. Turning to face me, her eyes scanned mine. I didn't know what she was searching for, but she said, "You mentioned it earlier."

"I did?" I said, dismayed. I hated sharing our private business, having seen too much pity in people's eyes over the years when they learned how cash-strapped my family sometimes was.

"You know, our Wednesday walks gave us midweek exercise, but it was so much more than that. It was being there when breast cancer took Olivia. And Kat lost her baby, and then her husband turned to the bottle. And..." Grace waved her hand in the air as though conceding to an entire lifetime's heartache, then blew her breath out. "When terrible things happen to us, it's so easy to think that our lives are nothing but rubble."

"I know."

She gestured to the ruins in the far-off distance. "But here we are, looking at broken rocks! We're admiring these ruins like they're artwork."

"It's a little weird when you put it that way."

"And you know what the biggest shame is? All the people who are alive but aren't really living because they're still trapped in their own ancient rubble! Me included! Right before Kat died, back in 'ninety-six, Bertie and I promised that at least one of us would make it here. But then there was this excuse, and that reason..." Unconsciously, Grace pressed her hand to her husband's wedding ring. "So after Bertie's funeral, I said to myself, 'Enough, Grace. This is the year.' And then Stesha called."

"She did?"

"On our last trek together, Camino de Santiago, she told me the exact same thing." She straightened her backpack on her shoulders. " 'This is the year, Grace Hiyashi. You aren't getting any younger.' "

"It's Wednesday," I told her.

"It is."

As we continued walking, I couldn't help but think about Reb and Ginny. I said, "I have my own Wednesday Walkers, but we're called the Bookster Babes, for our mother-daughter book club."

"That's great, honey! And I bet you girls know each other's secrets."

"Pretty much." But that wasn't the whole truth. Instead of pretending that I had it all together, I should have told my friends the truth: I had a secret boyfriend who had dumped me, the girl everyone thought did all the dumping. The girl who adopted a Boy Moratorium to stop all the boyfriend drama when really, she was just afraid to be hurt again. The next best thing was to tell Grace now. So I confessed, "Well, they knew everything except a guy I was dating. He asked me not to tell anyone about us."

"Why on earth would he do that?" Then Grace guessed before I had a chance to answer. "How much older was he?"

I gaped at her. "How'd you know?"

"Why else would he need to keep you a secret?"

"He didn't know that I was only fifteen until the very end. Well, I was almost sixteen, not that it really matters. He was twenty-two."

"Trust me, Shana," said Grace, her eyes unwavering as she stood her ground. "He knew. You don't get to be twenty-two and not be able to tell when someone doesn't have much life experience. I mean, really!"

This time when we started walking, I was the one dragging behind. It was as if the stone-enforced fortress that I'd erected around myself since Dom was crumbling with my every step. Dom knew? There it was, the nagging memory of him sidestepping the waiter who asked to see my ID on our second date, a dinner at a romantic seafood restaurant at the edge of the lake. "No wine for her tonight," Dom had said smoothly. "She's training for a marathon." I had felt so special because Dom had tracked our conversation from the first date in a way that virtually none of my high school boyfriends ever had, never mind that I had said I was thinking about running the Seattle Marathon. He had actually listened and remembered—and was proactive!

Our conversation must have energized Grace, because she picked up the pace. For the first time since the last rest break, we were within view of Stesha and Mom, though they were still pinpricks in the distance.

"How about if I take your pack for a little bit?" I asked Grace.

She turned to me then, placed one wrinkled hand firmly on my arm. "Shana, you are a dear. If I need your help, I'll ask. But I'd rather have your company than your concern. Deal?"

"Deal," I said, nodding. I could respect her independence. "Tell me more about the Wednesday Walkers."

—⁓—

Peanut butter slathered on bread or handfuls of trail mix would have been called a gourmet lunch on one of my family's hikes. But here, our amazing porters had prepared hot quinoa soup by the time Grace and I caught up to everyone. I saw Hank shake his head impatiently: "Finally." Embarrassed, I cast a quick glance at Grace, who looked chastened until Ruben threw his arm around her shoulders.

"Good job," he boomed loudly, then gestured to me. "Shana, can you take our picture? My mom needs to see what she's missing."

I could have hugged Ruben right then, and was only too happy to take a series of other shots: Ruben helping Grace with her backpack, Ruben leading her to a chair-shaped boulder, Ruben calling it a throne. Perfect timing, too. Grace's body drooped in desperate need of a rest. She gratefully accepted a cup of soup from me and absently rubbed her knee.

Mom was sitting alone, tense, her usual expression these days. When I settled next to her, she cast an annoyed glance at my father, who sat by himself at a distance. Neither of them had spoken more than a few words to each other this morning, and neither appeared grateful that we were on this once-in-a-lifetime family trip now—the word "family" felt like a joke. Grace looked happier than they did, hands wrapped around her cup for warmth.

"He's going to kill himself on this trail," Mom said, her words sharp.

"Mom, he can still see." *Sort of.*

"It's not even that. He's intent on proving to Hank that he can keep up the pace. No, not even keep up. *Set* the pace. I just don't understand him."

I averted my gaze from Mom's tight frown and focused on my soup. But then I heard a snippet of Spanish, the voice familiar. My head shot up to find Quattro crouching down to chat with the porters. Our porters. How had I missed him, wearing that unfortunate orange Polarfleece jacket? Another few phrases of Spanish wound their way to me, and even though I couldn't understand Quattro's words, I knew the tone: teasing. The porters burst into laughter.

"What's Quattro doing here?" I hissed at Mom, nodding over at him. The last thing I wanted was another encounter with him. First, the guy sprinted from me. Then, there was the

107

parental factor. Who knew what Dad might do or say within Quattro's earshot? And you could never be too sure whether Mom might spring some kind of *sine qua non* lecture on him.

"Oh, he's still here?" She winked at me. "Take a guess."

"Mom."

"His group was already here when we arrived. Hank wasn't kidding. All the guys on that Andean Trek looked like Navy SEALs." She fanned herself. "Oh, boy, I think I'm giving myself a hot flash."

"Mom, I know this is going to be a shock for you, but there are some things mothers should never share with their kids."

"What? All I'm saying is that if I were a romance novelist, I would be on that trek."

"Mom."

"For *research* purposes. Anyway, looks like they pushed on ahead."

"Don't sound so disappointed," I told her as I spooned another mouthful of quinoa soup.

"Well, I better go see about your dad," Mom said, straightening like she was venturing into the lion's den.

As I cleaned off my cup, I caught Grace sneaking onto the trail, as if to get a head start or make a break for freedom. Either way, I grabbed my backpack and started after her, telling myself that my leaving had nothing to do with dodging Quattro. Nope, this had everything to do with my job. What I hadn't counted on was Grace asking for privacy when I caught up to her.

"But—" I started to protest.

She raised a finger. "Remember what we talked about?"

So I fell back, giving her enough space for alone time but still remaining in view in case anything happened. One by one, the rest of the Dreamwalkers passed me, Dad nodding at me with a "Great job, kiddo," and Mom grinning at me. Even more humbling, our porters sprinted around first me, then Grace, on the steps despite being weighed down with so many bundles that only their legs were visible from behind.

"Talk about in shape," a familiar voice called up to me. "Those guys are humbling, huh?"

I spun around, my eyes focusing on Quattro as he ambled up the steps toward me, acting like he had never done his ninja disappearing trick into the elevator early this morning. Way back in Seattle and again in Sacsayhuamán, he had told me that he was on a Girl Moratorium, but a small part of me had dismissed that as a throwaway line you tell people for one and only one purpose: to win them over. It was no different from Ginny to her Chef Boy: *Whoa! You're into blowtorching food, too?*

"Where's your dad?" I asked now, more gruffly than I intended.

"Probably trying to find cell phone service up ahead," said Quattro.

"How come you aren't with your group?"

"I want to walk with you."

That single statement burrowed into me further than I liked, secreting into the soft places in my heart that I thought I had barricaded successfully. No more boy drama; no more boyfriend trauma, I reminded myself. But I could lash myself with a thousand memories of breakups past, remind myself that I'd instituted a Boy Moratorium for good reason, and still, my pulse sped in response to Quattro's answer.

"I'm not sure you could keep up," I told him now, lifting my eyebrow. As I've coached Ginny, a little challenge every now and again is good for a guy.

Just as I knew they would, his eyes glinted. "Oh, yeah?"

"Yeah. My job's to walk with Grace, and I bet you couldn't go this slow without going crazy."

"I don't think speed is the point of the Inca Trail."

He was right, and that was the whole problem. Just one more confirmation that where this guy was concerned, it was much better to draw a distinct boundary line, clear and stark: You on this side, me on the other.

Even so, I found myself telling him, "I wish my dad got that. I'm worried about him."

"I bet," Quattro said sympathetically.

That understanding unleashed a flood of pent-up confessions. I couldn't stop myself if I tried: "He's going blind, but he needs to be Mr. He-Man, I Own This Trail! It's like his whole entire personality has changed. I don't even recognize him. Or my mom. My mom! I still can't believe that she cashed out their retirement account to make this trip happen. I mean, who are these people?"

Instead of changing the subject, Quattro said, "I think it's cool that your family would actually do something like this— pick up and go. Your parents are just getting adjusted."

I mounted the steps faster. "But what if this is the new normal? Dad's perpetual grouchiness?"

"Well, he's going blind.... That's huge. Who wouldn't be angry about that?"

What Quattro was telling me was all true, but that wasn't the point. He wasn't supposed to *empathize* with me. He was supposed to say one or two perfunctory words, clear his throat uncomfortably, change the subject, and then flee at the first chance from high-maintenance, mentally unhinged me.

"But what if my mom can't stand it anymore?" I found myself wailing. "You know, she's totally used to Dad doing almost everything manly man around the house. If it requires the toolbox, it's Dad's job. If it needs a ladder, it's Dad's job."

"They'll figure it out."

"And then what if their relationship totally falls apart and they get divorced? My best friend Reb—"

"The one waiting to rescue you at Oddfellows?"

I shot a look over my shoulder, then blushed. "Yeah, about that..."

"I get it, but you can trust me."

I wanted to! That unexpected thought almost made me lose my footing as I continued up the steps without looking where I was going.

"Careful!" he called just as I righted myself. Then he prompted, "So Reb? Is she the one who's coming to Machu Picchu, too?"

I stopped and frowned at him. How the heck did he know about Reb's travel plans? But then I had a vague recollection of mentioning her Machu Picchu trip to him just to keep one of our first conversations flowing.

"My memory can scare people," Quattro admitted with a self-conscious shrug.

"I like it," I told him, then flushed, feeling vulnerable, as if I'd just admitted that I couldn't stop thinking about him. Quickly, I began walking again and commented over my shoulder, "So Reb was supposed to be on this trip. Stesha is her grandmother."

"No kidding."

"Yeah, but she insisted that I take her spot. Anyhow, Reb thought she had the perfect happy-happy, all-American family, too. And then, boom! Her dad's splitting because he's having an affair. And I like my family! I like my family exactly the way it is. Was. The way it was."

I hadn't realized that I had stopped again, that my hands were on my hips, that Quattro was watching me with sympathy as he closed the gap between us. I should have ended my rant then, but it was as if my fears had their first taste of freedom and refused to be imprisoned for a moment longer. Why—why?—did I find myself babbling about how my parents had done everything they could so I could live the life I want?

"And Dad totally gave up his dream to be a photographer. He should have been one! For *National Geographic*." I would have shaken my camera at high heaven, but I was trembling too much to retrieve it from my pocket. "So how fair would it be for me to be a photographer? I mean, wouldn't that be rubbing it into my dad's face that, hello, you'll never get a chance to live your dream. But look at me: I'm going for it, thanks to your support?"

"It's what your dad would want. Plus, Beethoven was deaf, and he composed music."

"But a photographer needs to see."

"Monet painted his most famous pictures when he had cataracts."

"Yeah, but photographers need to *see*." I was panting, wild eyed. A sight to behold, I'm sure. "You should see the pictures he used to make, not take, but make. I never got it until this trip. All the hours waiting for the right moment to tell a story."

What was I doing? This wasn't emotional flooding but a thirty-foot, crushing tsunami. No one—and I mean no one—wants to experience the ruins of anyone's family this up close and in person.

"Shana," Quattro said softly. I could tell he was going to reach for me, touch me. I backed up, my heels hitting the next step. I stared down at my scuffed hiking boots, embarrassed about losing control. And then he wrapped his arms around me, which was awkward given my backpack, but I didn't care. I tipped into his chest, resting my head on his shoulder. How long had it been since I had felt safe?

"Why do you always have to wear orange?" I sniffled.

Quattro laughed, then after a moment pulled away to open his water bottle and urged, "Drink."

As I tipped my head back, I wondered whether Dad was taking care of Mom now. Or were they walking alone?

"Sorry," I mumbled. Without looking at him, I whispered, "It's just not fair."

"I don't think life's about being fair." After a moment, Quattro added, "If it was, my mom would still be here."

I jerked my head up to study Quattro, really study him. There was a hollowing in his face, which made him look vulnerable. But instead of meeting my eye, he stared hard at the wispy trees. "She was killed in a car accident."

I cleared my throat. "I'm so sorry, Quattro."

"It happened."

"When?"

"A couple of years ago. Two. You'd never know it from the way Dad acts like this shadow of himself. He wasn't ever like your dad, rock climbing, skiing in the backcountry, and all that. But Dad...he used to be pretty adventurous. He'd get out there." But now, as if he was the one who had revealed too much, Quattro changed the subject when the overhead clouds released a light drizzle. He held his hand out to feel the rain-drops. "Hopefully, it won't pour."

"Otherwise Ruben's going to break out the ark."

"Remember what the Flood was supposed to do, though?"

"Kill everyone?" I said.

"Be a fresh start."

Chapter Ten

C onsidering how tired I was from trekking at altitude,
I should have fallen asleep instantly, but snippets
of my conversation with Quattro kept replaying in
my head that night. Grace wasn't the only mourner on the Inca
Trail; if Quattro looked haunted by his mother's death, then his
father had one foot planted squarely in the otherworld. The next
morning, I woke groggily to a conversation I didn't understand
and raucous laughter that I did. Our porters.

Did they think it was odd that tourists from around the world
paid good money to look for ruins hidden deep in the jungle? I
was wondering that myself after unzipping the tent to find grim
skies and mud from last night's deluge. There was nothing to do
but retrieve the ugly paramilitary rain gear from my backpack. I
sighed as I yanked the rain pants on and half-hoped that I wouldn't
bump into Quattro on the trail today. My hair already felt lank

from a day of sweating without bathing. Why hadn't I packed even one measly tube of lip gloss? And had I really dumped all my messy emotions on him yesterday? I groaned.

"You don't look that bad," Dad said. When he gazed at me as affectionately as he had the year Mom dressed me as a bedbug for Halloween, I knew the rain gear was worse than I imagined. "Here," he said, "I'll take your picture."

As if, I was about to retort until I remembered the campfire last night. All of us were stretched out before the heat of the flames when Hank had suggested that we trade cameras to check out what everyone else had shot.

"These are all blurry," Hank had said, holding up the camera I recognized as my splurge purchase. I tried to stop him from asking whose it was by reaching for it.

Dad said flatly, "It's mine."

"I bet a little Photoshop will fix them," Helen said kindly after a damning silence.

Until that moment, I hadn't understood what Dad's loss of vision was going to be like for him. He wasn't just losing his vision; he was losing a part of himself. Wherever he went, he wouldn't be Gregor or the twins' father or even the pest control guy but the guy with the bad luck. The blind guy.

Now, as if Dad were remembering last night, too, he said abruptly, "No, never mind. Let's get breakfast."

Over quinoa sweetened with raisins, Ruben revealed the plan for the day. The morning's trek up to Dead Woman's Pass would be divided into three ninety-minute segments. Helen slumped and shut her eyes wearily, already exhausted.

"We'll take ten breaks, each a couple of minutes long," Stesha said cheerfully. How she had managed to look adorable in pink socks that peeked out from under her rain pants, I don't know. I pretty much doubled as an overstuffed sausage squeezed into a casing of nylon.

"Everybody ready?" asked Ruben, reminding us that we had a strict schedule to keep if we wanted to make it to the next campsite at a reasonable hour. Naturally, Grace chose the exact moment of our departure to heed the call of biology.

"Oh, geez, she's going to take a million years," Dad complained, readjusting his backpack as he glowered at Grace's receding back. He had a point; with all our layers, going to the bathroom was a long, multistep ordeal.

"You go on ahead," I said quickly. "I'm walking with her anyway."

"You're not being paid to keep her company."

"Actually, I am."

"But you're not a trained guide. If anything, Stesha should have hired you to be the trip photographer." Shaking his head, Dad held the new camera out to me. "Here, take it, kiddo. I can't see well enough to use it."

I backed away, frowning. "Dad, it's yours."

"Look." His tone may have been mild, but that word was scalding. He pushed the camera at me so I could see for myself that Hank was right. The image in the viewfinder was blurry, an impressionist's rendering of the landscape. "It's wasted on me."

I was about to suggest that he just default to autofocus, but I knew better. Dad would rather leave the camera behind to be ruined in the rain. Mom nodded at me, silently ordering me to take the camera already and stop making a scene. Everyone at the campsite was watching us. So reluctantly, I accepted the camera, no longer a friendly weight in my hand but a cold, heavy anchor, weighing us down to our reality. If Dad couldn't take photographs, neither would I.

—⚊m⚊

The rest of the day was nothing but one lesson in humility after another. As soon as I congratulated myself for being in excellent shape and managing the trek so well, the stone-paved path that the Incas had laid down five hundred years earlier turned into a waterslide. Stones that were already large and uneven now became slippery from the rain. I kept expecting to twist my ankle. I glared at the swirling rain clouds overhead. What next?

"Sorry," Grace said as she stopped again, this time to wrestle her water bottle from her backpack.

After I drew the bottle out for her, I said, "What are you apologizing for? If anything, I should be apologizing for my dad. He's not normally like this."

Instead of answering, Grace studied a branch so gnarled it looked like a witch's deformed finger. I wondered where her mind had taken her. Finally, she identified it: "Polylepis."

"That's so cool looking." I started to pull out my camera only to remember my vow: I wasn't taking photographs, not with my old camera, and definitely not with the new one.

"Survival does that, doesn't it?" she mused.

"Warps us?"

"Shapes us." She paused, letting the branch go so it sprang back. "You know, if my husband were standing here, I'd tell him that I was beginning to wonder whether he loved me."

"Why?"

Grace swept off her wide-brimmed rain hat to wipe the sweat off her brow. "We loved to travel, Morris and I. But this"—she jabbed her hat accusingly down at the rain-slick stones—"this isn't about travel anymore. This is beginning to feel like a *suicide* mission. I mean, I am going to *become* the Dead Woman's Pass."

The truth was, the Inca Trail wasn't as romantic or fun and definitely not as bonding as I had imagined it would be. What had I been thinking? That we'd be the von Trapp family, trilling melodious harmonies as we skipped single file through majestic mountains? It wasn't just Grace I worried about but Dad and his he-man pace to prove to Hank and everybody else that a twenty-year age gap and impending blindness meant nada when it came to his physical fitness. And then there was Quattro, who was disrupting my much-needed, much-wanted Boy Moratorium. I hadn't seen him at all today, and I didn't like missing him. Really missing him.

"Do you want to turn back?" I asked Grace, studying her intently. Less than halfway to Machu Picchu, now was the time to retreat if we were going to backtrack.

"Absolutely not," she said, her mouth tightening. "I made a promise, and by God, I'm going to finish."

But we still had the entire descent, never mind all the

elevation gain ahead of us. I needed to get my mind off the trek. So I asked, "How long were you married?"

"Fifty-two years." She stretched backward and groaned.

"Fifty-two! The longest I've ever been with anyone is four months, and that was back in freshman year."

"Up until today, that didn't feel nearly long enough." Grace raised her eyebrows. "You know, he refused to die in the hospital. So our sons transferred him back home. And our last kiss... oh, I'll never forget that one! I leaned down to peck him on the lips. But he French-kissed me instead."

"No, he didn't!"

"French. Kissed!" She yelled the words as she spun around toward me. "He was sexy to the end!"

We both laughed so hard, we couldn't have taken another step if we tried.

"And then he sighed, the two most beautiful sighs in the world, like he was reliving our life together. You know, he always made me feel so beloved." Grace's eyes shimmered with tears.

Always beloved. That was so far from how Dom made me feel during the last weeks we were together, even before the breakup. Try nuisance. Try pest. Try anything but beloved.

"You must miss him," I said softly.

"More than you know. Or maybe you do."

"I thought I missed Dom—that was his name. But now I sort of wonder if I missed the idea of him more."

"Why do you say that?"

I flushed. It was hard to admit the truth to myself, let alone to another person. But I had kept my heartbreak a secret for too long. "He had a big presentation, and it must not have gone well. He didn't get the funding he was expecting."

"And he blamed you," Grace guessed.

"Yeah! It was so unfair, because we hadn't even seen each other for a week. And then before that, he was on vacation with his family." I peered up at Grace on the step above mine. "How did you know?"

She shrugged. "At first was he charming? Complimenting everything about you?"

"Yeah," I said, so astonished that the slight breeze could have knocked me off my feet. For our third date, I had asked Dom to join me for a long run, ending with a three-mile loop around Green Lake to his rental house. His roommates had been tossing around a football on the lawn. Thanks to my two older brothers, who had trained me well in all things sports, I'd intercepted the football and thrown it back in a beautiful spiral.

"Whoa, you found the perfect woman," one of his roommates had said, tossing the football to me.

"Hands off," Dom had said, knocking the football out of my reach. "This goddess is all mine."

With her hands on her hips, Grace asked, "Did he tell you that no one had ever understood him the way you did? That he'd never been able to talk to anyone the way he could with you?"

"Yeah! How did you know?"

Grace's lips pressed together. "And what happened after the first time you disagreed with him?"

"It was our fourth date," I said, remembering the day clearly because I had kicked myself for a full five days afterward when

Dom didn't answer a single one of my texts or calls. I knew I had blown it, but I couldn't understand what I had done wrong. "He asked me what I thought about the website for his game. So I told him I didn't think it was unique enough."

"Let me guess. He took it as a personal insult that you criticized it, right?"

"How did you know?"

"And then after that," said Grace, "I bet nothing you could do was right or good enough."

I remembered how Dom's criticism had begun to creep into our conversation, so subtly, I could never point it out to him: *You really don't know about f-stops?* Whenever I bristled, he said I was being overly sensitive. I demanded, "Really, Grace, how do you know all this?"

"My daughter was married to a narcissist, and he just picked and picked and picked at her. She thought she was living in crazy town, but it was just him, diminishing her to make himself feel more important. Thank goodness they got divorced before they had kids. How long were you together with Dom?"

"Six weeks."

"You should be grateful that you got out as soon as you did," said Grace, drawing her hood over her head as the rain restarted.

After months of blaming myself for the breakup, the world might have spun off its axis, Grace's answer was that startling. It was shocking to consider that even though Dom went to the right school, knew the right people, drove the right car, aspired to the right career, he may never have been my Mr. Right.

We walked in silence for such a long time that Grace misread my quiet. Without warning, she spun around to apologize. "I'm sorry, honey! Did I offend you?"

"No!" I told her emphatically. "I think this might be the first time that I've thought straight about the whole thing. I mean, I was so wrong about Dom, what if I find out that my next guy is a narcissist, too?" I grimaced. "Maybe I should just go solo forever."

"You can't shy away from love just because you're scared and—" Grace stopped suddenly with a sharp intake of breath.

"Grace! You okay?"

"Okay, I get it!" She called up to the sky. "Girls, I get it."

"What?" I looked heavenward, too, as if the answer were written up in the clouds.

"I'm such a hypocrite!" Grace tapped her heart, then nodded firmly as if making a pact with herself and her Wednesday Walkers. "I'm telling you to get out there and love when I've been Chicken Little myself: He's older than I am, and I don't want to be widowed twice!"

"Well, that's scary!"

"But no more being afraid. Especially when you finally meet the right guy who's worth the risk," she said, and nodded in the direction of the trail.

"What—" I started to ask even as I followed her gaze up the trail to Quattro, who was loping nimbly down the long flight of hand-carved stairs toward us.

—⟡—

Call it a miracle, call it a cosmic shift in the universe, but Quattro wrangled Grace's backpack from her with two measly sentences: "I'll just carry this up to the next rest stop. Your group's ready for lunch, but they wanted to wait for you guys."

Honestly, I didn't think Grace was capable of releasing a single burden, dead set as she was on carrying her own weight. So when she shrugged off her backpack, my eyebrows shot up so fast, they could have launched off my forehead.

Grace explained rather lamely—"I need a little alone time"—then flew up the steps. Flew as if she had sprouted wings. I didn't know who to glower at: her for playing Cupid, or Quattro for tucking her forty-pound backpack easily under his arm while I strained under the burden of mine.

Show-off.

But to tell you the truth, I rather liked this male display of strength.

"From up above, it sounded like you guys were having a party," Quattro said as he unzipped his rain jacket, opening it to a T-shirt that hugged his chest.

No matter how often I declared my Boy Moratorium and how hard I fought my attraction to Quattro, my mouth went dry in a way that had little to do with dehydration. I zeroed in on his pecs. *Sexy to the end!* I cleared my throat now. "Just some girl talk."

"Dare I ask?"

"Do you speak girl?"

"Obviously not. Kylie's a mystery."

"Why didn't she come here with you guys?" I asked.

"Nationals for her dance team fell this week. But Dad and I had to come."

Now was the moment to change the subject, redirect our conversation to a safer, surface-layer zone. Instead, I deep-dived and asked, "Why?"

"Mom's birthday. Her heart was set on Machu Picchu." He shot me a wary look, then waved me ahead of him on the trail. "A couple years back, she said it was time to tap into her Scottish ancestry, but Dad was too busy working to go with her. So she and some of her friends went to Scotland. The Isle of Skye. They wanted to see their roots and the fairies."

I inched closer to him now, unsure I had heard him correctly. "Fairies? As in—"

"Yup." He mimed fluttering wings with his hands and looked somewhere between adorable and dorky.

I burst out laughing. Just watching his face light up made me want to photograph him—to capture him in this misty light. But I pictured Dad's withdrawn face just as Quattro's closed.

"Anyway," he said, "right after she came home, she told Dad to book this trip."

"Why?"

"She wanted me and Kylie to get in touch with our roots. We're a quarter Scottish, part Chinese, some black, and the rest Peruvian. We've got some real ground to cover."

"So her last wish was to come here?"

"It was." His words may have been soft, but they rang with finality. Just as I knew he would, because it's exactly what I would have done to keep things light, Quattro deflected. "I hear the last leg of this trek is a killer. So how's about we make it a little more challenging?"

"As in..."

"You know the Sun Gate in Machu Picchu? The two stone pillars on top of the mountain?"

"Yeah..."

"So how's about if I touch it first, you drive me to Voodoo as soon as I move to Seattle?" Quattro said.

I placed one hand on my hip. "And what happens when I get there first?"

"I'll drive you."

"And that's supposed to be my prize?"

"Maybe it's more of a consolation prize," he conceded.

"Fine," I said, surprising him. He cocked his head suspiciously just as I continued, "It's the least I could do for including your picture in my college portfolio."

"Wait—"

Before I could fashion a smirk, I had to lick my dry lips. His eyes were arrested on that slight movement. The mood shifted. He stared at my mouth with a distinctly appreciative look.

Quick, now, deflect.

But I didn't want to deflect anymore. My girlfriends would have been shocked. I know I was. I'd changed boys as frequently as some girls change nail polish, finding one excuse after another to erase any boy who might make the slightest inroad into my heart. But I wanted Quattro to *see* me. To *like* the real me. Me, the girl who worried about her parents. Me, the girl who planned to be a photographer. Me, the girl who found Zen in her lens. Me, the girl who wanted to be loved for herself.

Instead, in a classic deflecting move I had perfected myself—see, we're just friends—Quattro stuck out his hand and said, "So? Deal?"

"Deal," I answered, shaking his hand.

Electric shock. I knew he felt it, too. I could almost feel his breath. I definitely heard my own gasp, a sharp intake, as I wished we were running straight to the Sun Gate this very day.

"We should go," he said abruptly, as if he'd heard my thoughts and didn't like them. Not at all. He charged around me, fleeing like this was the scene of a crime.

Chapter Eleven

Maybe it was because I was shivering—feeling imminent hypothermia or heartache, it was hard to tell the difference—but I couldn't have been happier at the sight of the flickering campfire at the end of the day's trek. The awkwardness of wordlessly following Quattro was over at last. That is, I was relieved until I noticed Dad sitting sullenly by himself on one side of the fire, opposite the Gamers and Mom. It would have been hard to miss him, considering the scalding blast of his scowl at Grace. These days, the slightest comment could change the weather pattern of his moods.

Preempting Grace's apology, I announced loudly so everyone could hear, "Sorry we took so long. It was my fault."

"No, it was mine. Shana kept having to help me balance all of this," Quattro said as he placed Grace's backpack carefully on the ground.

Once again, Quattro's bigheartedness blindsided me. But if he had stayed with me—and with Grace, once we caught up with her—out of some weird misplaced sense of obligation, he could have just left us now. He was taking the bullet of blame for us. Now, as I started to shuck my backpack, he actually slid it off my arms. Layers of water-repellent polyester and microfiber may have separated us, but I still shivered at his touch. What was his deal?

Dude, you don't know how to break up with a girl.

Dad stalked off to our tent like a sulky toddler. Since I was such a bundle of irritation, too, I staked out an outcropping away from everyone else so I wouldn't have to make small talk or worse, do a Dad and lash out at an innocent bystander. But who came toward me, bearing a steaming cup of quinoa?

Without a word—big surprise there—Quattro handed my dinner to me.

So grateful for the food, I wove my hands tight around the hot metal cup as if it held all my scattershot thoughts from the day: the cataclysmic insights from Grace about true love and Quattro about his mom, to be precise. Softening, I held the cup out to him. "Want some?"

"You first." Sitting down, Quattro waited for me to take the first bite. Why was he hanging out now?

Confused, I lifted the spoon to taste the familiar nutty grain that I knew I'd forever identify with this trail. But I wasn't hungry after all, at least not for food.

"You didn't take a single picture today," Quattro said, turning his full attention on me.

Trust him to notice. I cleared my throat, trying to think of an excuse. Over our silence, I heard Dad snap at Mom, "Fine, you go live your big life." He didn't need to go blind: He had already stopped seeing anything good around him. I shifted just in time to watch Mom reach out a conciliatory hand, but Dad jerked away from her.

I could only hope that Quattro hadn't overheard them. But of course, he had. Everybody had. And now everybody was resolutely admiring the sunset and focusing on the meal. Even the porters, who didn't speak a word of English, had fallen silent. Quattro was looking at me with pity. I had to do something, anything, to stop him from staring at me like that.

"Don't you need to go?" I asked him. We had passed the Andean Trekkers campsite a good quad-burning ten minutes earlier. He had done his duty, carried Grace's backpack, and deposited us safely with our group. So bluntly that I verged on rude, I demanded, "Why are you here?" It was hard to be vulnerable, but I added, "With me? When you clearly didn't want to talk to me?"

He scratched the side of his nose and dropped his head, his shoulders hunched. Then he angled his head to look me straight in the eye. "Sorry about that. It's just that I never talk about my mom."

Yet he talked about her with me. *Interesting.*

I couldn't follow that intriguing line of thought because Quattro switched the topic: "All parents bicker."

"Not mine. They've always been a united front. Always." Needing to prove it to Quattro—or maybe to myself—I finally salvaged my camera, then quickly cycled through the snapshots

I'd taken. Sea-Tac Airport, my parents holding hands. I lifted the camera up to him. "See?"

But then he forwarded to the Inca Trail, where Mom fell farther and farther behind my father until they stepped out of the same frame. Perfect twenty-twenty vision wasn't necessary to observe the meltdown in my parents. It was as if their bonds, spoken and unspoken, had snapped, flinging them into separate stills. Frustrated, I frowned over in Dad's direction. Couldn't he see that his life wasn't the only one that was going to change from his blindness? I took the camera back, shut it off, buried it deep in my backpack.

"You know..." Quattro paused as if weighing his words. Then, he plunged forward. "Your dad's not just pissed. He's scared."

"But Dad isn't ever—"

"I don't blame him. I'd be scared if I were going blind, too. I mean, try walking for five minutes with your eyes closed."

"But that doesn't excuse what he's doing. He's taking it out on Mom. Reading all kinds of stuff into every little thing she says." Dad, at least, was still pretty normal with me, but who was going to be the buffer for Mom when I went to college?

"It's natural—not cool, but natural—to be pissed. At least that's what my mom would say." Quattro blew out his breath. "I wish my mom were here now. She was a counselor."

"What do you think she'd tell me?"

"Your parents love each other. That's a good start."

Sine qua non, I thought, and held those rescuing words tight.

"What?" Quattro asked, leaning closer to me. "You were thinking something."

So I told him about my mom's love mantra, her belief that every single relationship had one must-have, deal-breaker quality. Without that, there was nothing.

"My parents had that," said Quattro, leaning back so he could look up at the velvet-blue sky. "They could always make each other laugh, no matter what. You know, they could be having a fight, then all of a sudden, both of them would make monster faces at each other like they were three or something. They'd crack up and everything would be okay."

All I wanted, right that second, was to throw myself into Quattro's arms. It was as if I knew with bone-deep knowledge what being together with him would feel like: absolutely right. But if my parents were in an official state of disaster, what chance did anyone have? I didn't care if I was being Chicken Little, running around seeing thunderstorms where there were only blue skies.

"What's up?" Quattro asked after a few minutes of silence, elbows on his knees, leaning toward me.

That's what I want to know.

At the same time, I didn't. He was the first boy I had seriously liked since Dom, and being rejected by him—look how I felt with the silent treatment—was going to hurt more than I thought I could stand. Listening to the urgency sweeping inside me to push him away, I retrieved my old camera, found the photo I wanted, and thrust it at Quattro. "Look."

For a long, silent moment, he studied his image at the Gum Wall, then zoomed in. Finally, he lifted his eyes to mine. What I saw in them—surprise, disbelief, and admiration—tugged at the seams of my stitched-up heart.

"How did you do it?" Quattro asked, his eyebrows furrowed, genuinely perplexed. "I've never liked any picture of me before."

"The light loves you," I said before I tightened my lips. No more encouraging a guy. I needed him to go. Now. "Your dad's got his computer, right?"

Quattro nodded.

I ejected the SD card from my camera and held it out to him. "Take it." It wasn't like I was going to be shooting any more pictures, and this way, I wouldn't even be tempted, not with photography, not with him.

Quattro placed the postage-stamp-size card carefully into a plastic Ziploc bag that held a couple of granola bars before sliding it back in his pocket. At last, he said, "I better get going before it's pitch-black." But before he hiked back to his campsite, Quattro told me one last thing: "I doubt your dad would want you to give up photography just to be in some kind of solidarity with him."

Chapter Twelve

Y ou know what a good daughter would do right now, don't you?" Mom whispered as she laced up her hiking boots the next morning. The air was so cold that her words left breathy traces inside the tent.

In response, I managed a one-note grunt that spanned sigh, question, and groan. Freezing, I wished I were burrowed deep in my sleeping bag, but I pulled on another layer of fleece before shaking out my rain gear.

She yawned widely before narrating what must have been a really great dream: "A good daughter would go and forage for coffee for her feeble mother."

"As if you're feeble—"

Out of nowhere came an immense roar. The thunderstorm of the century. The snapping of bones. Hundreds of bones.

"Get out!" Dad flung open the tent flap from where he had

stood outside to step into his rain pants. In a blur of movement he yanked Mom and me up, but Mom's feet got tangled in her bag. He all but hoisted her into his arms and lugged us out of the tent.

She protested, "Wait! Our stuff!"

"Leave it," Dad ordered, dragging us.

"Mudslide!" I heard someone yell, the alarm echoed in other languages.

Outside was dawning chaos as trekkers from other groups ran through the shared campsite. Another angry roar erupted from the earth. Dad's grip around my wrist was bruising tight. He glanced left, right. I looked up. And then I saw the dark mass of mud flowing down the cliff, plowing a forest of trees, devouring everything in its path. Quattro had been up there, somewhere. He hadn't been caught in that mudslide, had he?

"Over here!" Dad barked and tugged us toward safer ground. We stumbled toward an outcropping of boulders. Once there, he stared at Mom, who was wild eyed and shivering. He shrugged out of his raincoat and handed it to her. "You'll be okay here."

Mom clutched me to her side as though she would protect me bodily while Dad ran down to the mud pit that had been our campground.

"He should have stayed here with us," Mom said, blame and worry thickening her voice.

I frowned even as I stared uphill. *Come on, Quattro, where are you?* "He's helping everyone else," I told her.

"But he should be here. With us now." She repeated the words stubbornly like they were a talk track on an infinite loop. One that had played in her head since the diagnosis. Since their

135

wedding. Since they met. He should be here with her, protecting her always.

I peered down into the drizzling gloom. Made out Dad sprinting heedlessly toward the tent Grace and Stesha shared, racing into the avalanche of mud, rocks, tree limbs sliding down the mountain, cascading toward our campsite.

Our tent was gone. Swept away. So was Grace and Stesha's tent, which had been next to ours.

Grace. Stesha.

Where was the woman I was supposed to watch over? Reb's grandmother? The Gamers? Ruben and our porters? And Quattro? I yelled for them now, screamed their names, prayed they were safe. Where was everybody? I spotted Dad darting around the perimeter of our campsite. Another round of yelling.

"Here, here," Stesha panted, surrounded by the crew of porters, who set her and Grace on this safe ground. All of them fully dressed, ready for an early start. Grace even had her backpack, which one of the porters had been carrying and now dropped at her feet.

Grace said dazedly, "We were just having our morning tea...." Then she threw her arms around the men. "*Gracias, gracias.* Damn, how do you say 'hero' in Spanish?" There was no time for more; the men were already returning to the destruction.

"Has anyone seen Ruben?" Mom asked, looking frantically down at the campsite. "Or Helen and Hank?"

Even as she said those names, a woman screamed, high pitched and frantic: "Help!"

At the edge of the mudslide, I spotted a half-swamped tent,

sited for maximum viewing. Helen was pinned inside, waving desperately. I started down the slope despite Mom's screams for me to stop. "Shana! No!"

A witch's grip, nails digging into my arm. Mom must have flown after me. My answering yell—"Let go!"—was swallowed by the noise of another part of the cliff shearing off. I scanned the mountain. Quattro! Where was he?

And then there he was, dashing downhill with his dad, both of them racing straight at the screaming woman below. With headlamps on their foreheads and wearing their back-packs, they looked like a search-and-rescue team, prepared for this disaster. Quattro's dad—this skinny ghost of a man—waded through the mud and yanked Helen out of the tent. Quattro and one of our porters now threw their powerful arms around her. Two of our porters pointed in our direction. I could almost see the sagging relief in Quattro's body when he spotted me. They carried Helen to us.

"There's Ruben!" Mom called, spying him as he circum-navigated the far edge of the mudslide, helping other trekkers out of the danger zone. "Nine o'clock."

Stesha scanned the campsite, a captain unwilling to leave her ship until everyone was accounted for. "Where's Hank?" She caught my eye. "Do you see Hank?"

"You're bleeding," I told her, and patted my pants for the handkerchief Mom insisted I carry with me at all times, only to remember that I was in my fleece leggings, clutching my rain gear like a security blanket.

Not that it mattered, since Stesha shrugged off all concern.

Helen wrenched her arms free from Quattro and the porter and staggered toward us, demanding hysterically, "Where's Hank? He was with me in the tent. But then"—she waved—"he was gone...."

"Gone?" Mom asked her, frowning.

"I don't know where he went." Helen bit her lower lip. Tears streaked down her face.

And then I didn't hear another word because Quattro was wrapping his arms around me, hugging me tight. My arms encircled his waist. When had this boy become my pillar of strength?

"I thought you were down there," he said into my hair. "I thought that was you shouting."

"I was worried about you!" Only then did my body begin trembling as the enormity of the mudslide hit me. We had been so close to dying. Dying!

Quattro held me even closer. "We're okay."

I was so glad that he didn't ask if I was okay, just assured me that we were. What words could possibly express how I felt after my first near-death experience? Any of us could have been killed. Helen, for one. I pulled back far enough to study Quattro and his melty-warm eyes and the mud speckling his chin and the side of his nose. "You looked for me."

"Well, yeah."

I couldn't formulate a response because Quattro was staring at me intently, staring as though he had spent hours thinking about me, spent the last few minutes worrying about me in spite of himself. The silence stretched out long, the moment growing hot. Neither of us moved. We may not have been clenched close to each other anymore, but my body tingled where he had pressed against me, and my lips throbbed. And still we stared. And still the moment lengthened. My lips parted. He exhaled.

From far off, I heard his father shouting for him. "Quattro! Bring your backpack!"

I heard his sigh, felt his arms releasing me, and then his hand squeezing mine. He was as reluctant to let go as I was. Quattro nodded over at his dad. To me, he said gruffly, "You should photograph this."

My cameras! They were lost in the mudslide. I shook my head. "I don't have a—"

He pulled a basic point-and-shoot out of the front pocket of his backpack and offered it to me. "Will this work?"

It felt like a homecoming, holding a camera again. To be honest, creating a photo essay of this destruction hadn't even occurred to me until now. In all my photographs, I had tried to prettify the world. Crouch down and the angle would obscure a man's beer belly. Wait for the right light, and the acne scar on a girl's face would fade, a middle-aged woman would look more youthful, a boy's beak of a nose would shorten. Tears threatened again.

"You need to document this," he said before he ran toward his dad.

I lifted the camera. I would start telling the truth now.

"Quattro," I called.

He turned to look directly at me, and even when he saw the camera aimed his way, he didn't avert his face but allowed himself to be shot in his full glory—sweaty, mud-stained, smelling like coffee and old gym bag. His eyes shone at me. I had no more doubts that I wanted him. Not a single one.

"I've got to go," he said, then paused. "I'll find you."

And let me tell you, that single promise couldn't have been more thrilling.

—m—

A terrible burial site lay below us: trees ripped from the path of the mud; their upturned trunks and branches had become a jagged landscape. I lifted the camera, and even as I made my shot, I knew I couldn't just photograph the destruction.

"We've got to help," I told Mom, who nodded. Together, we picked our way down, weathering Dad's "What the hell are you doing?" before he gave up. We probed around the edges of the mudslide. Helped another group search for their missing guide. Consoled a curly-haired woman who was beside herself, bleating, "My sister! My sister!"

"Hank!" Helen yelled, not more than ten feet from us. Her voice may have been hoarse, but her relief was absolutely clear.

I spun around to find Hank near a pile of mud-flattened tents, carefully picking his way toward Helen even as she stumbled over the debris to reach him. Hank hiked the backpack he was holding in one hand over his shoulder so he could widen his arms for her.

"Helen! You're okay," he said.

"I thought you were dead!" she cried before collapsing against him. "I was looking and looking for you."

No matter how softly Mom spoke the words to me, I heard the condemnation in them: "Looks like he saved himself."

I was about to ask what she meant when I noticed that Hank was wearing his trekking pants, an undershirt, hiking boots, no jacket. His fedora was in place. It looked as if he had bolted out of his tent the moment the mud poured off the mountain, grabbing his hat and backpack, everything but his fiancée. But he couldn't possibly have left Helen behind to fend for herself, could he?

"Mom, you don't know that." Even as I said it, I wondered where Hank had been, why no one had seen him, and why he was half-dressed.

"No, but I do know this: It takes a crisis for you to know a person's true character," said Mom firmly. "And trust me, you want to be with a man who'll wear himself out looking for you." Her eyes sought out my father, who was wading knee-deep in muck with Quattro, his dad, our porters, all of them splattered with mud, all of them still helping where help was needed.

Chapter Thirteen

Two hours later, all the trekking groups at the campsite had accounted for their parties. Luckily, not one person had been buried under the mud or been badly injured. We were just bruised and scared. At the sight of Quattro's group, now inching down the mountain with all their gear, the tenor of our morning grew even more somber as we tallied our loss: every tent, every sleeping bag, most of the backpacks except for three: Ruben's, Hank's, and Grace's. That meant almost all our supplies were gone.

"Where are we going to sleep?" I overheard Mom ask Dad. My instincts pricked, and I maneuvered for a better angle. If ever I hoped for a decisive moment to shoot, this was it. I could feel it. I waited.

"We'll figure it out," Dad assured her. For the first time in days, he pulled Mom close and tucked her head under his chin.

Through the lens, I could see the tension releasing from Mom's body as she sank into Dad in homecoming. Their eyes closed. And there it was, the moment I so wanted, even more than as a photographer: the first glimmer of hope that my parents would actually survive Dad's blindness.

Another bunch of tired trekkers spilled into our ruined campsite, telling everyone that they had come from a kilometer away. Worse, their guide and porters had abandoned them. I snapped a quick photo of Quattro, who was standing with his dad and trekking group, listening attentively to their guide.

Whatever Stesha and Ruben were talking about, it couldn't have been good, judging from their grim expressions. Nervous, I focused my camera on Grace and Dad providing medical attention to every trekker who needed bandaging with the supplies from Christopher's small but well-stocked first aid kit. As I continued to shoot the scenes unfolding around us, Mom stuck close to me, worried that I'd be swept away by a second wave of mud. I was glad for her company; I kept glancing uphill, suspicious of the mountain. That unease disrupted the usual Zen I found while photographing. Correction: that, plus the fact that Quattro met my eyes but turned away to help his dad dig out a backpack covered in muck. He hadn't even acknowledged me, as if he didn't want to talk to me.

My cheeks flamed. More than hurt, I was confused. Part of me wanted to crawl behind a boulder to hide, rescue myself, no different from Hank. What was wrong with Quattro anyway? I could not possibly have misjudged another guy again, could I? But there was no way I could have misread that earlier tenderness. I knew I hadn't imagined our almost-kiss.

Whatever was going on with him, I forced myself to focus on my work. I crouched down to frame the mud-buried tents. As I did, Hank's voice carried over to me as he spoke with Helen: "If you see an extra pair of socks, let me know. I'm starting to get a blister."

"Wait, where are yours?" she asked, frowning as if only now taking into account Hank's pristine fedora, his clean backpack, which he had somehow miraculously rescued, his undershirt, his bare feet in tied-up hiking boots.

"I . . . I—" he stammered.

"Hank, why aren't you wearing socks?" Then her own flood of disbelief unleashed on him. "Where were you this morning? Didn't you hear me calling from the tent? I thought I was going to die. And I looked for you." Finally, the damning question: "Did you leave me?"

The flush on Hank's face was the one emotion I never thought I'd see him wear: shame.

"I'm sorry! I wasn't thinking, but it doesn't mean anything." He reached for her, but Helen shook her head, first slowly, then furiously. "I came back to look for you."

"Don't touch me!" she cried, backing away so suddenly she stumbled but regained her balance. Her face crumpled, and she wound her arms around herself. Grace hastened to Helen, and I followed to flank Helen on her other side, the way my friends would have if I had only told them about Dom. Change the environment, replace the guy, and that could have been me, alone at a restaurant table, set for two.

—ᗰ—

After I'd apologized at least five times by text for my critique of Dom's website, then didn't hear from him for days, he had finally responded. Relieved that he suggested getting together for dinner, I nervously chatted through the appetizer and main course, barely eating more than a bite. As soon as I told him I'd spent the morning taking the senior portraits for two of the guys on the varsity soccer team, he was on my case. I tried hard to understand why he was angry about it when I'd told him way back on our first date that portraiture was how I was helping to pay for college. I was so focused on deciphering his terse words, I hadn't even noticed the young couple sitting next to us until they were leaving.

The woman with a lion's mane of blonde hair and a birthmark on her face stood up, glanced swiftly at Dom, and told her boyfriend, "I'm glad you don't have a problem with what I do."

The man's coffee-brown eyes dropped on me before he smiled crookedly at her. A faint scar scored his upper lip. Placing his hand on the small of her back, he said, "I'd be a complete idiot if I did."

Fuming, Dom pushed back from the table and strode outside, leaving me with our unpaid-for, half-finished dinner. I was positive he was coming back once he'd cooled down in the fresh air. For ten minutes, the waiters walked by our table, alternately curious and pitying as they checked in on me: Was I finished? Did I want dessert? Coffee? The check? But I had no credit card, only a ten-dollar bill, which didn't cover the cost of our appetizer. After twenty minutes, Dom finally returned, but not before one of the waitresses had asked if she could call me a taxi.

"You can come back tomorrow with the money," she had offered.

"He'll be back," I had assured her.

The waitress had studied me briefly before she attended to the new set of diners at the table next to mine. "Honey, you'd be lucky if he didn't."

—⚬—

The waitress was beyond right. So was Grace. I was better off without a guy who'd punish me for not fawning over his website and had an issue with my job. I glanced over my shoulder at Helen, sitting like a pariah on her rock. I knew how she felt. But Hank was staring down at his hiking boots, looking so lost that I felt sorry for him, too. Every minute or so, he'd glance over at Helen, confirm that she was still ignoring him, then stare again at the strips of bare skin between his boots and his rain pants.

A few yards away, Stesha motioned for everyone to gather around her while she relayed our new game plan.

"I'll be fine," Helen whispered to me. "Go."

So Grace and I left her side in time to hear Stesha: "Ruben and I have decided that we're going to push on to Machu Picchu. From there, buses run regularly down to the town, and then we'll be able to take the train back to Cusco."

For a long moment, we stood in awkward silence. No one wanted to stay in this death trap of mud, but no one wanted to leave either. What if worse lay ahead of us? Yet there was zero assurance that backtracking would be any safer. This was supposed to be a once-in-a-lifetime expedition, not the only expedition in our lifetimes. All I wanted was to be safe at home in our little cottage.

"We'll ask that group without a guide if they want to join us," Stesha said, nodding toward the leaderless trekkers who were milling around aimlessly.

"We're slow enough as it is on our own," Hank countered as he cast about for support. He looked pleadingly over at Helen as though trying to redeem himself. "A couple of us could make it to town tonight if we pushed hard. Get some provisions, be back with help."

"We need to stick together," Stesha said.

"But we could do it." Hank's eyes glowed passionately as he turned the full firepower of his charm on Dad, the same charisma that I had admired earlier. But charisma meant nothing in the middle of a crisis. Hank told Dad, "The two of us could get to town fast, make sure we've got tickets for the train. Buy food for everyone. Divide and conquer."

Dad replied firmly, "I'm not leaving anybody behind."

At that, Mom eyed Dad with the same fierce pride she always wore when she talked about him, reminding me of her recurring dream: Dad flying overhead as if he were some kind of superhero. I caught the envious look Helen shot at my parents—the same one I'm sure I wore when I first met her and Hank at the airport in Cusco. My parents—not Hank and Helen, not me and Dom, and clearly not me and Quattro—were the It Couple.

"No one is being left behind," Stesha said. She pulled herself up to her full five feet. "Right now, everyone's safety is my concern. There's a hostel a couple of hours before the Sun Gate. We can take shelter there tonight."

"But what if it's already full? We don't have tents," Hank persisted. "What about the porters and Ruben? What's our contract with them?"

"I'm staying with Stesha," said Ruben, and he added a question in Quechua to the porters, who all nodded. Addressing our entire group, he said, "None of us are leaving you."

So the decision was made: push on toward the hostel together. At that, Stesha and Ruben went to invite the other groups to join forces with us. Not getting the answer he wanted from our group, Hank stalked over to Christopher. I trudged behind, camera in hand. I could tell myself I was fulfilling my duty as the trip photojournalist, but I knew the truth: I wanted a chance to talk to Quattro.

The sonic boom of Hank's voice could have unleashed another mudslide as he confronted Christopher: "Your group's going all the way to Machu Picchu today, right?"

"Not all of the group," Christopher corrected, pointing his thumb at their porters, who were unloading their backpacks, reallocating the supplies. "David and Jorje have little kids at home, and Salvador's mom is sick. So our porters are going straight back to Cusco."

I gripped the camera in my hand, feeling guilty. I hadn't exchanged many words with our porters except for a dozen *gracias*, *por favors*, and smiles, lots of wordless smiles.

"But you need them," Hank said.

"We'll be fine without them," Christopher said confidently, chin raised as he stared Hank down. Without hesitating, I took my shot, knowing that I was seeing the real Christopher, the man he had been before Quattro's mom died. There was no muting him now.

"Hey."

Quattro. At his voice, I felt an impossible spurt of happiness. Our campsite and plans were in disarray, but here it was. Joy. He had come looking for me after all, just as he'd promised. But then I read his shuttered face.

"How're you holding up?" he asked, sounding more clinical than concerned.

I sighed, shrugged, shook my head. How could I explain how I was feeling? Still reeling that we'd survived a mudslide. Whiplashed by his behavior. The whisperings of boyfriends past filled my head. How many guys had called me out on my flirt-and-run habit? Now that I was experiencing it firsthand, I had to say: I felt more unwanted than a speck of dust.

"Are you avoiding me?" I asked him point-blank.

He flushed. "I've been helping out...." When his shoulders slumped tiredly, I softened. There was no question about it: He'd been pushing himself hard.

"We were lucky that you and your dad came when you did."

"Hardly."

"A minute more, and Helen might not be here." My eyes welled up with tears at the close call. The mudslide had scraped me raw; my emotions were bouncing all over the place. "If we had stayed in our tent for another couple of minutes...If Dad didn't pull us out..."

He closed his eyes tight, balled his fists. "I just can't."

"Quattro."

At once, he averted his face, but not before I saw his expression ruined with more than grief, but anguish.

"I have to go," he said, as if he had made a fatal mistake by caring for me.

"Quattro! Wait!"

He was gone.

—⚏—

According to relationship roulette, I was the last person to comfort Helen. I mean, who was I to give advice when I had fallen for Dom, who had existed in a haze of romance that had been all in my head? I didn't even want to begin to think about Quattro, who was as love damaged and afraid as I was. But Helen was still sitting on the rock while everybody was making final preparations to leave—not that there was much to do, since most of our belongings were under sludge.

"Helen," I said, and paused, then continued clumsily, "you know, my mom thinks that everybody has a *sine qua non*."

"A what?" She may not have understood Latin, but her cheeks flushed as though she knew I was suggesting that Hank wasn't good enough for her.

I blushed, too. Why would she listen to me any more than I'd listened to my brother Max, who had tried to warn me off

Dom? Besides, what did I know? I'd wasted almost a year, boycotting Max's every effort to repair our relationship when I owed him thanks.

"Oh, nothing, I'm just rambling, but you should ask her," I said hastily. "So do you want to walk with Grace and me?"

I mistakenly thought we were alone, but Hank had been hovering close behind us, back to being Mr. Caring. "I'll walk with Helen," he declared. But at his offer, she shoved away from the rock and marched over to Grace.

I could hear Grace's every lilting word: "Mind? Helen, I've been waiting to walk with you!"

Grace tucked her hand in the crook of Helen's arm and led her to the others, who were inventorying the three backpacks left between us. The last I heard before they started for the trail was Grace asking, "Have I told you about the Wednesday Walkers?"

Chapter Fourteen

B ack on the trail, I was aware of my every footstep, where I planted my feet, where I shifted my weight. Every minute, I half-expected a second avalanche of mud and trees, boulders and debris to sweep us away. So I didn't protest when my parents insisted on taking the rear position, no doubt to guard me with the same eagle-eyed attentiveness I paid to Grace, who was sandwiched safely between Helen and me.

Our first rest break only ratcheted up my anxiety. By the time we reached the porters, Ruben and Hank had gone ahead, scouting the next section of the trail. Before I sat, I made an effort to talk to our porters, stitching together my broken Spanish and hoping my smile would fill in the grammatical gaps: *"Gracias para tu ayuda."* Why had I been too embarrassed about sounding stupid to talk to them? Their answering grins and pats on my back communicated their relief that all of us were okay.

Afterward, I peered up the mountain. No sign of Quattro, which was unsurprising. All along, his group had trekked faster than we did, taking side trips and still managing to establish their campsite before us. Every time I thought about Quattro, my heart felt like it was tripping. I hadn't known how scared I would be to trust my heart to another boy. Or how much it would hurt to be rejected again.

At our next break, Stesha kept casting worried glances at Grace, as though wondering whether she would make it through the next day and a half. From our meager supplies, we divided three PowerBars among all of us for lunch, one sticky bite a person. Improbably, Grace smiled as she considered her puny segment. "Sort of makes you miss the round-the-clock quinoa diet we've been on, doesn't it?"

"Here," Mom said, holding out her piece to me.

"Mom." I shook my head and almost didn't hear her soft request: "Do you mind walking with your dad? He's all twitchy, like I might slip any second."

"Don't say that!" I protested, shivering. "But I suppose now you know how he feels with both of us hovering."

"Well, it's making me nervous! I'll walk with Grace, okay?"

Whatever Grace had said to Helen in the morning must have been encouraging. She lost the forlorn look of the recently widowed, and she didn't gaze at Hank with naïve puppy dog adoration anymore. Instead, she scrutinized him when he spoke, as though she were weighing his every word and action against some mental checklist. I got the feeling I needed to do a bit more of that in my own love life.

"Hey, Mom," I said before I joined Dad as she had begged, "ask Helen to walk with you guys, will you?"

After two days of trudging at Grace's pace and being weighed down by my heavy backpack, I felt like Dad and I were sprinting when we set off on the trail together. But I knew he wasn't going at his full race pace. Neither was I. Both of us wanted to play it safe.

"You seem unhappy," Dad called up to me. Even without looking at him, I could hear the concern in his voice. "Does it have anything to do with a certain boy?"

"Maybe," I admitted to my surprise.

"I liked how he came to find you."

"Me, too."

And that was the problem. The pause in our conversation had less to do with the altitude or the arduous climb and more with processing what both Dad and I had noticed: Quattro's first instinct was to ensure that I was safe. Just look at Hank and how he'd done in the same crisis: a big, fat selfish F.

I glanced back over my shoulder at Dad, who had his eyes trained on my feet, ready for the slightest hint that I was losing my footing. That's where I'd learned how to be vigilant for Grace. Dad had always been there for us, always putting us ahead of himself. He hadn't run to save his own life, but he'd reached back to save ours.

"Dad, you were amazing this morning," I told my father, wanting so badly for him to see himself clearly.

"I didn't do anything."

"Are you kidding?" I stopped on a wide stone step to face

him. "If you weren't with us this morning, Mom and I wouldn't be here."

"If I weren't going blind, we wouldn't be here in the first place."

"Dad."

"If I had made more money, we would have visited here earlier."

What I now knew for a fact was that money, ambition, and big plans mean nothing at all when you're staring down death. So I said, "You saved us this morning, Dad. You did."

As my words sank in, we tackled the next steep section of the mountain in silence. I couldn't get enough breath to continue a conversation with Dad anyway. All I could manage was a steady rhythm of five plodding steps, then a brief panting rest. If my breathing was labored, how was Grace doing behind us? Ruben, Hank, and the porters waited for us at the crest of this section. We reached them just in time to hear Hank's sarcastic assessment: "This is *exactly* the way I imagined the Inca Trail."

I actually understood that complaint. My parents had taken a healthy chunk out of their retirement savings to fund this expedition with me, and the two following trips, with my brothers. This was hardly the Inca Trail I had imagined or would ever wish upon anyone.

"Then my apologies," said Ruben smoothly. He gestured for the porters to push ahead. Somehow, drawing from a deep well of patience and good humor that I didn't have, Ruben continued, "Just because we're trying to make good time doesn't mean that we can't appreciate what we're seeing." He looked downhill to the other half of our group, still with one long set of stairs to climb before they caught up to us. "You know, this is one of the most beautiful cloud forests in the world."

Strange as it might sound, I had been so distracted by worry and hunger and burning hamstrings, I hadn't even noticed that we were surrounded by low clouds and wind-battered trees. While Ruben tried to satisfy Hank with a lecture on the function of moss in a cloud forest, Dad paused before a small orchid, an improbable, show-stopping pink flower that thrived without the benefit of direct sunlight.

"Your mom really wanted to see this . . . and a hundred other things. I just never made the time to take her," he said finally with a defeated sigh.

"Dad."

"You should check on your mom," he said gruffly. "Why don't you wait here until they catch up?"

I started to protest. After all, what the heck was the point of a family excursion if all we were doing was excusing ourselves from each other's presence? Without wasting another moment, though, Dad began plodding uphill like a travel-worn pilgrim who'd been walking for such a long time, he'd given up hope of seeing whatever he'd come to find. His resignation was way worse than his anger.

Laughter—rich, joyous, and just shy of hysterical—signaled that the women were nearing. It was almost unfathomable that just hours ago, a chunk of mountain had sheared off, and we'd been screaming in fear.

"Sexy to the end, girls!" Grace cackled. Spying me, she added, "Right, Shana?"

The rain fell harder. Even with the thick foliage that arched overhead, drops of rain penetrated the canopy. But not a drop seeped through my military-grade barrier of rain gear. That was no less a miracle than Mom's cheeks flushed as pink as the stubborn orchids blooming around us. No less a miracle than the women's laughter.

What could I do but laugh helplessly, too? Laugh at my ludicrous mud-spattered rain gear and agree, "Oh, yeah, we are sexy to the end."

Chapter Fifteen

All along the Inca Trail, we'd stood in awe at the stark beauty of ancient ruins. The barest suggestion of stone buildings could stop us. Yet it was the first sight of the sickly green Trekkers' Hostel that made me tear up, and not because the eyesore of modern architecture was long overdue for a date with a bulldozer. I wasn't the only one grateful for this last official campsite before Machu Picchu.

"Thank you, Lord!" cried Grace, so ecstatic I was a little worried she was going to kiss the building. But she only leaned her forehead against the concrete walls. "Thank you!"

The backpackers inside squeezed tighter to accommodate us. If they hadn't, we would have been stranded out in the rain, huddling and shivering through the night. Everyone insisted that Stesha and Grace take two of the beds. Dad muttered a single halfhearted warning about bedbugs, too worn out to do much more. (And yes, for the record, bedbugs can thrive at high altitude.)

I couldn't sleep. Every little sound made me think that we were being hit with another mudslide. Sick of feeling this claustrophobic panic, I crept around my sleeping parents to head outside, which made no sense at all. I was no safer out in the open. Plus, the ground was sopping wet, but at least it had stopped raining. The air smelled cleaner than anything I'd ever experienced, even while hiking in the Cascades back home.

A crunch of footsteps crept up behind me. Stupid, why had I ventured alone into the dark? I spun around to face Quattro, my cry strangled to a quiet gurgle.

"Sorry. Didn't mean to scare you," he said, holding out his hands to steady me.

At his touch, I felt scared for an entirely different reason: I was fighting the inevitable. Tell myself that all I wanted was to be focused on my photography. Tell myself that I wanted to be relationship-free. Tell myself that I was done with commitment and expectations and compromises. But here I was, wanting Quattro to want me right back. It was so hard not to know where I stood with him, firm ground or mudslide zone. But now I knew I had to know.

"I didn't know you were here," I said in a low voice. *Dude, do you like me, or what?*

"We had our tents. So we thought we'd let everybody else stay inside," he answered. "You couldn't sleep either?"

"No," I whispered, and told him sheepishly, "I keep imagining being buried under mud. Lame, huh?"

"Not even."

Moonlight bathed us through a parting of clouds. I was good at the chase, even better at the breakup. No depth required. And I knew how our story would go unless I made a decision: Boy ruins Girl's photo shoot. Boy chases Girl on the Inca Trail. Girl loses Boy because she's too much of a coward to ask him one question: How do you feel about me?

For crying out loud, this was a guy who'd searched for me when disaster struck. What was I waiting for? Just grab his hand. That'd be a start.

Naturally, this had to be the one moment on the entire trip when my palms went slick with cold sweat. Naturally. So much for my plan to go all bold. But it was Quattro who cocked his head over at the small grouping of tents. I nodded. I was more than a little relieved and nervous to spend time with him. We found a log to sit on. For a long minute, Quattro didn't say a word. I didn't either.

Finally, I asked, "What were you doing out here?"

"Thinking about my mom," he said simply. "I just haven't had any time with everything going on. In a weird way, she would have loved all this."

"What? The mudslide?"

"Well, not that, but the story she'd tell about it later. She always had a way of making our lives sound a lot more interesting." He paused, testing different words in his head. "No, more meaningful."

"What would she say about this?"

"You never know when it'll be your time. So live it all—

not live without regrets. She'd say that was stupid and selfish. But live so you never regret anything you do, any decision you make."

His face tightened as if he was remembering something painful. I knew I was. Funny how a single word can trigger memories better left for dead. Selfish. The zombie memory of my last conversation with Dom reanimated and staggered to its feet. I could hear Dom's chilly voice as if he towered over me, all righteous anger the night we broke up.

—m—

It was mid-August, and Dom had invited me to a party at his rental house, where beer flowed as easily as stories about summer travels and internships from hell. The night was hot, one of those rare heat spells in Seattle, and I was so relieved that our relationship was back on track. All was forgiven! I had taken special pains with my sexy and sophisticated older-woman disguise: delicately perfumed, hair styled in a messy topknot, the designer sunglasses from Dom perched on top of my head, white skirt with towering wedge heels. And I was drunk, just one sloppy kiss away from saying, "Fine, Dom, tonight." Why not give in? What the hell was I saving myself for when I knew I was in love with him?

"Half the guys here are staring at you," Dom said with a smile that verged on smug. He changed out my beer for a glass of red wine, leaning in close to tell me, "You'll like this. A Montepulciano. When we go to Italy..." It didn't matter how he finished that thought, not with that self-assured "You'll like this," not with that exotic "Montepulciano," and definitely not with the delicious clincher: "When we go to Italy." What more proof did I need that Dom thought of us as the It Couple? And even better, the kind of couple who lived my kind of future: adventure and travel. Just as I leaned into him, just as I tilted my head up at him and pursed my lips in the way that drove him crazy, he was wrenched out of my arms.

My brother Max loomed in my vision. Unlike everyone else at this business school party, he had completed his MBA and was about to relocate to San Francisco. That's why I didn't expect him to show up. He started shoving Dom, not caring that the party had gone graveyard silent or that everyone was staring at him, at us. I didn't realize then that it would be the last time I could ever consider Dom and me an "us."

"Do you even know how old she is?" Max demanded, his face right up in Dom's.

"Stop," I protested, not knowing whether I was begging Max to keep from hitting Dom or from revealing my secret.

"She's a sophomore." Shove. "In high school."

Dom's accusatory expression landed on me. More than pointless, I knew my words would only make things worse, but still I corrected Max softly: "Junior."

Dom glanced around the living room, his face flushed bright red with embarrassment. A minute or two later, I was running after him to the street. His shame became rage. His face twisted as he yelled at me, "You could have ruined my life!"

"I'm sorry!"

"Don't you think you should have told me you were underage?"

"Dom, I'm sorry."

"Sorry?" Dom glared at me with poison and contempt and regret. He spat, "Selfish. That's exactly what you are! God, I wish I had never met you."

And then there was Max, leading me to his car. He didn't have to convince me to go with him.

"What were you thinking?" he demanded once we were locked inside. I scanned the street for Dom, but he'd already disappeared. "Shana, what the hell were you thinking?"

"You don't know him," I protested, still searching in the darkness for my dream guy.

"You don't either."

—⟋⟍—

"What?" Quattro asked me now, even as my pulse was jumping from the memory of that breakup. But there was something new—not anxiety, but relief. I was truly free from Dom.

Where could I even start? I shook my head. "You?"

Quattro shrugged, which made two of us hiding secrets from each other. The silence sprouted with a thousand questions. But as I studied him, the need for conversation vanished. Instead, there was just one question: What were we going to do? The moment stretched. I knew what I wanted to do. I drew nearer to him. My lips parted in a sultry way that had slayed dozens of guys before him. Just as I knew he would, Quattro shifted toward me, cupped his hands gently around my face.

Here was the kiss that I had fantasized about for longer than I cared to admit.

Now. Yes. Finally.

And yet...

No red-alert sirens blared in my head. No early-warning system to assert my independence. No emergency ejection procedure to launch me on my toes and propel me back to the safety of the hostel.

All was quiet and still with the exception of a soft but emphatic no.

Gently but firmly, I pulled away.

Once upon a time, the hurt and baffled expression I saw on Quattro's face would have made me stop and sink into a kiss out of sheer guilt, but now...no.

I'd already blinded myself once to the cold truth that Dom hadn't returned my feelings, not really. I wasn't about to repeat that mistake again. And frankly, I wanted more than great banter and delicious kissing.

"We're both on moratoriums," I said, and scooted from him so I was out of temptation's way. There was no denying the thrumming desire to drag him over to me. On top of me...I cleared my throat. This time, I was going to be absolutely clear. "And I don't do hookups, I don't do booty calls, and I definitely am not a friend who provides benefits."

"Okay," he said slowly.

The fact was: If I didn't want our story to end the way all my so-called relationships had, I was going to have to tell him the truth. The whole truth about me.

"About a year ago, I went out with an older guy." My fingers entwined into a tight hard shell, the same way I had sheltered myself since Dom. "He was in business school." I sighed deeply. "I wasn't exactly up front that I was still in high school."

"That probably didn't go over well."

"That's an understatement." Even that revelation was an artificially sweetened version of the truth. If what Mom said was true about needing to see a person react in crisis, I needed to see Quattro in crisis, in my crisis. I needed to show him my most ugly shame. If he couldn't deal with the truth, if he thought less of me, I'd rather know now. "I was almost sixteen; he was twenty-two."

"Whoa."

"You know, I told myself that the age difference didn't matter. I mean, my mom's five years older than Dad. But in high school it makes all the difference. I didn't sleep with him," I said bluntly, "but if I had..."

"Statutory rape. Wow."

"Yeah. It really was naïve and selfish," I said flatly.

"Yeah, it was."

I wasn't prepared for how much the truth confirmed by someone else could sting. Even if Grace was right, and Dom had known, I had kept my age a secret because I knew deep down that we were wrong.

"But look," Quattro added more gently, "love makes a person crazy. I mean, look at my dad. He would have done anything, broken any law, if it meant keeping my mom alive. He's been like the living dead since she died." He actually looked disgusted, but it was hard to tell whether that revulsion was directed at me or his father. "But you're right. I can't do this. Not now."

"Why? Because you're on a moratorium? What's up with that anyway?"

"Actually, no, not because of that. Or not entirely," he said. "I don't know. But this isn't about you. I mean, you . . . your photography, the way you look at things." He shrugged, gazing at me with respect. "This is all me. The timing is all wrong, and I don't think I can—" He broke off whatever he was going to admit, then ended brusquely, "You should get some sleep."

I blinked at Quattro, stunned by the familiarity of these words. It was as if I were being visited by the ghosts of breakups past. All the guys I had let down with almost the same script, except now I was on the receiving end. Even though I wanted to run from him, I forced myself to nod—*okay, then*—and walk away slowly, head high. I forced myself not to glance back at Quattro and his ironclad secrets. I forced myself to stand for a second in the pearly moonlight and to imprint in my memory what it felt like to know that I had survived revealing the truth about me.

Chapter Sixteen

A few hours of sleep later, Stesha woke our group. Yesterday, we had agreed to salvage the last of our trek. At the very least we were going to see the first rays of sunlight illuminate Machu Picchu. Who cared that it meant we had to get up at three in the morning? Who cared that the chance of a break in the clouds was about one percent? Who cared how many tourist photos had already memorialized one of the most famous sunrise vistas? I planned to take exactly one of those photos myself, cliché or not, Ms. Associate Dean of Admissions at Cornish College. I patted my back pocket to make sure that Quattro's camera was still there.

Quattro.

I flushed at the memory of last night, squeamish about running into him this morning. Through the rain-speckled windows, I spied him helping his dad dismantle their tent. They obviously were on the same time line we were. As if he felt me, Quattro glanced my way. I ducked down, face flaming.

"What're you doing?" Mom asked, yawning widely.

Humiliation à la Quattro. It's my new specialty.

Dad sat up, grimaced. I could hear his spine crack when he stretched. "Man," he said, "I'm getting old. That other group might have the right idea." The leaderless tour group that had joined ours yesterday had made the executive decision last night to sleep in this morning, opting out of our early morning trek. I personally chalked it up to the aftershocks of being abandoned. After all, it didn't much matter if it was guide, fiancé, or boyfriend (past, present, or imagined) who took off; being the one left behind was exhausting.

As I tugged on my hiking boots, I wondered whether Quattro remembered our silly bet: to be the first at the Sun Gate. Then again, maybe he wouldn't so much as brush a single fingertip against that portal to Machu Picchu if he happened to reach it before me. Given last night's conversation, I wouldn't have been surprised if he sprinted right past it.

The memory of his "it's not you, it's me" words made me blush. But once we reached the town of Machu Picchu Pueblo and were safe on the train back to Cusco, I'd never see Quattro again. At least that's what I told myself, even as a faint and annoying strain of "It's a Small World" taunted me in my head.

"So," Mom said casually as we walked out the door together, "late last night, we found out that the rest of your friend's group decided to take their chances on the trail back to Cusco."

"My friend?" I asked, even as little warning bells started to chime in my mind. Alarmed, I stared at her, forgetting all about hiding from a certain boy. "What are you talking about?"

"Quattro and his dad are joining us the rest of the way. Wasn't it nice of him to give your dad his headlamp?"

"What?" My gaze landed on Quattro hefting his backpack on. Hastily, before we could make awkward eye contact, I whipped back around to Mom. "Why?"

"I just told you. The Andean Trekkers decided to head back to Cusco on the trail. They'd heard rumors that the train tracks have been flooded."

"When was all this decided?"

"You must have been in the bathroom," Stesha answered for Mom before I could protest further. She fluffed her hair. Those efforts literally fell flat. The spunk had gone out of her deflated curls. I knew how they felt. "And your boy's joining us."

I hissed at Stesha, hoping to shut down this conversation, "He's not my boy."

"You mean, not yet." Although Stesha lowered her voice, her eyes kept darting over to Quattro. Poor spy skills must have run in her family. She was no better at covert operations than Reb. "I think once he's done working through some big grief, he'll be begging to be your boy. Give him time. You're both worth the wait."

Five minutes later, our group was ready to go. Mom was so busy chatting with Grace about the Wednesday Walkers that she stepped in front of me to keep their conversation going. I didn't protest until I realized that Quattro had staked out the spot at the very back of our group.

Dude, really?

After being Mr. Fast and Furious of the Inca Trail, now, today, he suddenly decided to plod behind everyone? Really? With Quattro just feet behind me, I felt self-conscious, and not only because I was highly aware that he had an unobstructed view of my rain-gear-clad, shapeless glory. Hadn't the guy ever heard of giving a girl space after the Talk? Guiltily, I thought about all the Talks I'd delivered by text. How could I have been so blasé about breakups? I really had been the Genghis Khan of boys' hearts, and the knowledge of my callousness stung.

"Hey, Mom," I said to her urgently, "I should walk with Grace." Then I used those three special words that had the power to upend any photo safari with Dad and any family vacation in the past: "It's my job."

Fortunately, Mom nodded and traded places with me.

"Watch your footing," Stesha said up ahead of us, pointing to an especially saturated edge of the cliff. "This could go, too."

Our group had fallen into a meditative pace. Maybe it had something to do with no one wanting to chance another accident. Maybe the enormity of yesterday's mudslide was only now sinking in. All I know is that there was no more casual chatter, no more trading of harrowing stories about travel nightmares. No more Ruben telling us about the terrain, the region's history, the rich biodiversity. No more Stesha infusing us with doses of spirituality: What is your purpose here, today? My eyes remained on Grace's muddy boots ahead of me. Somehow, I felt better hearing Mom stomping behind me, one heavy footstep after another.

"I wish your dad were here with us." Mom sighed wearily. Only then did I turn around. I was careful to train my eyes on her and only her, not dipping anywhere close to Quattro. Her shoulders drooped, exhausted, as she caught her breath on the step.

Dad.

"We're fine," I assured Mom. But was Dad? I kept picturing him slipping on the mud, unable to see the trail's edge before plunging over the cliff. Frankly, Hank as a trekking partner was almost no better than Dad hiking alone. The image of Hank stoically watching Dad fall without moving a muscle to help was so troubling, I had to focus on the rhythm of my footsteps as we continued climbing. The weather worsened, now pelting us with icy rain. My hands were frozen; I could barely move my fingers.

"So how ya doing?" I called back to Mom, who couldn't have huddled more deeply into her gear.

"Cold, damp, and miserable," she said.

"Okay." Pause. "Top three words to describe the Inca Trail?"

Mom smiled wryly at me. "Cold, damp, and miserable."

That made both of us laugh before we continued up the endless trail.

"How about you? Glad we came?" Grace asked me from up ahead.

"I'll tell you after we're home." My answer reminded me of what Quattro had confided last night about his mother, how she could point out the silver lining in every cloudy condition. I wouldn't have blamed him if he saw me and my family as the poster children of gloom and doom. Was that the real reason why I didn't fit the bill as his girlfriend?

Over my shoulder, I asked, "How about you, Mom? Glad we came?"

"I think so." Then Mom, with her uncanny radar for boy on my brain, said, "I bet I know someone who's even more glad you came."

What was with Mom and Stesha and all their precarious conversations about Quattro? It'd be beyond mortifying if he overheard. I wanted to quicken my pace, but I was trapped behind Grace, who was plodding along slower than ever. Honestly, snails on hot asphalt crawled faster.

"All I'm saying," called Mom so loudly it would have been a miracle if a deaf person couldn't overhear her, "is that you two seem to share a *sine qua non*."

My curiosity warred with my embarrassment, and I almost, almost, almost asked, *Oh, really, and what sine qua non is that?* But I wasn't about to have this conversation with Quattro in earshot. There was no time to shush Mom, though, because a frightened yelp shocked me into stopping on the trail. Even worse, I heard the alarming sound of a hiking boot losing traction on gravel. For a terrible moment, I thought we were caught in another mudslide until I watched Grace fall with a hard thud. I flinched at the sickening crack of her head hitting one of the stone steps.

"Grace!" I called out in panic.

But it wasn't Grace who'd fallen.

It was Reb's sure-footed and confident grandmother who lay still on the path. Grace, wearing her unmistakable leprechaun-green raincoat, was already crouching at Stesha's side. Paralyzed on the mud-slick trail, I might as well have stared into the Gorgon's eye of disaster and been hardened into cold marble. Where was Dad? He always knew what to do in an emergency.

Instead, my nimble soccer-playing mother sprinted up four stairs to Stesha. Meanwhile, I didn't move. I couldn't. Quattro had to dart around me on the rock steps.

Mom said, "Stesha! Stesha! You okay?"

No answer.

Stesha remained motionless on the graveled trail. A thousand worries dashed through my head: Was she dead? Had she broken her neck? That could have so easily been my dad...

Finally, I forced myself to close the distance and reached everyone just as Stesha attempted to sit up.

"Slowly," Mom cautioned, helping her. Quattro knelt to prop Stesha up, cradling her against his chest and knee.

Blood spilled down Stesha's chin. Mom swallowed hard, looking vaguely green, and glanced away. Grace whipped out a red bandanna, which she pressed to Stesha's chin. She asked, "Are you hurt anywhere else? Your neck? Your back?"

"I'm fine," Stesha said weakly as she struggled to stand.

"Hold on. You took a big spill," said Quattro.

However unsteady Mom felt at the sight of blood, she focused on Stesha and held up three fingers. "How many?"

"I'm fine," Stesha protested. We all hovered around her as the rain continued to fall.

"How many?" Mom insisted.

"Three," Stesha said, shaking her head impatiently, then wincing at the movement. "My gosh, you are all such worry-warts. I'm fine."

Without thinking, I blurted out what was probably the last

thing you're supposed to say to a victim after an accident: "It's bleeding more."

Stesha blinked rapidly, seeking Mom as though she knew my mother would take care of her. "How bad is it?"

"I don't think it's bad at all," Mom said calmly. She placed a reassuring hand on Stesha's shoulder, but only now did I notice the betraying tremble. The sight of blood made her famously queasy. At home, my brothers and I all knew to find Dad if we cut ourselves. "We'll check after it's stopped bleeding. Keep the pressure on it." She sighed. "I wish we had Band-Aids."

Quattro removed a small plastic container from his backpack and said, "I not only have Band-Aids but antiseptic wipes and Neosporin."

"Look who's a Boy Scout," I teased before I thought better of it, and Quattro's eyes flashed to me. How could hazel eyes possibly be so caressing? And why did his smile hold so much promise? I could practically hear Reb and Ginny cackling over how hard I'd fallen for him.

After a few minutes of Quattro and me drawing Stesha into a conversation, asking about her favorite places to trek around the world, Grace gently pulled away the bandanna. Because the fabric was red, the bloodstains weren't obvious, which was a good thing because Mom paled. Stesha's chin was scored with an inch-long ragged gash. As we watched, a few droplets of blood collected at the torn edges of her skin and fell onto her rain jacket.

"I think we need to find a doctor," I whispered to Mom.

She nodded.

But where were we going to find a trailside doctor who

174

could stitch Stesha up? We still had at least an hour's hard walking to reach Machu Picchu, and then how long would it take to make it to town? However far, we were going to have to hurry.

Stesha forced a crooked smile. "I'm feeling fine. The only thing that's hurt is my pride."

"It was my fault," Grace said. "If I hadn't been so slow—"

"Nonsense," Stesha interrupted. "You didn't do anything. Accidents happen. And besides"—she waved at Mom—"we had ourselves a real hero."

"We did," I said, surprised, before eyeing Mom with pride. "Mom, you were awesome!"

Without thinking, I lifted the camera to catch the tail end of Mom's astonishment: the slight quirk in her lips, the new gleam in her eyes. Next, I bent down to photograph the uneven step, the culprit of Stesha's accident. No different from any of the hundreds of stones we had climbed over the last few days, this one was also smoothed from generations of footsteps. I framed the shot, included the droplet of blood. Maybe that's all we're supposed to do after we've taken a spill: brush ourselves off, get back on our feet. No fuss. No blame. Just soldier on.

"Stesha," I cajoled, raising the camera to her, "give us a picture here."

With a lift of her chin, patched with a bandage, she unfurled the bloody bandanna like it was a victory banner. As soon as I made my shot, she leaned over and threw up.

Quattro caught her before she tumbled a second time. He shot a swift glance at me as though I were his partner. "We got to get her to a doctor. Now."

Chapter Seventeen

N
othing about the Inca Trail could be described as easy. Beautiful, yes. Arduous, yes. Unexpected, hell yes. But never easy. Even so, I wasn't prepared for the final flight of near-vertical stairs up to the Sun Gate.

"You have got to be kidding," I muttered, and glared hate at the stones I had once admired. It was inconceivable that I had actually marveled at these steps, listened in awe to Ruben talk about the tenacity of the Incas who had hauled every last one of these stones up to this oxygen-poor height, carefully placing them on the trail. What had I thought would be waiting for us now? That the final approach to Machu Picchu would be an easy downhill stroll on a plush carpet of green grass, accompanied by the sweet notes of harpsichords? But how could I possibly complain when Quattro was carrying Stesha?

Remembering Stesha, ashen in his arms, was enough to

force my quaking thighs to take the next step, then the next. Every hesitation only delayed getting her medical help, which was why Quattro and I were hustling as fast as we could. We had left Mom and Grace far behind, but even so, I berated myself. I wasn't moving fast enough. If I was struggling, how on earth was Quattro powering up these same stairs, carrying a hundred extra pounds behind me? The thought was humbling.

As I neared the top, I began yelling, which was more like rasping since my breath was so ragged and shallow: "Help! We need help!"

A more welcome cavalry, I don't think I'd ever seen: Ruben thundering down the steps toward us, Hank and Dad bringing up the rear. In a matter of moments, Ruben was reaching out to take Stesha from Quattro.

"What happened?" Ruben demanded.

"She fell, then threw up," I said between pants. "She needs a doctor."

Ruben nodded. He looked at Quattro, whose legs were trembling from pushing so hard, then at me. "You both did great," he said. Then he wrenched around and began racing back up the route to the Sun Gate, cradling Stesha tenderly in his arms. Dad and Hank followed close behind while Quattro collapsed on the stairs, hands on his knees, bent over. He tried to catch his breath and wheezed instead.

"You okay?" I asked.

He nodded, unable to get a word out.

"You were amazing. Really amazing."

It no longer mattered that boundaries had been reasserted

and reinforced the night before. I placed a hand on Quattro's shoulder and squeezed. The last thing I expected was for Quattro to reach across his chest and place his hand over mine. I shut my eyes; the undertow of emotions so strong. This wasn't about working hard to win Dom's respect. Or flirting with countless boys after Dom to prove that I was lovable. It wasn't sizzling-hot desire, wanting Quattro's body against mine. His fingers curled around my own. What this was, I was afraid to name, especially when I knew that Quattro didn't want anything to do with a relationship.

"Did they get her okay?" Grace demanded as soon as she and Mom reached us.

"They did," I said. I noticed that neither he nor I pulled our hands away from each other. "Thanks to Quattro."

He shook his head. "I should have been faster."

Quattro's father made his way down to us. Only then did Quattro lower his hand.

"You did good, son," Christopher said, eyes bright with pride.

From what I'd seen over the last few days, Christopher was a man whose few words mattered, but his rare compliment seemed to burn Quattro, who refused to make eye contact.

"I didn't do anything," he said in a low voice.

Christopher scratched his scruffy cheek, shifted his weight. As Mom shrugged off the backpack that she was carrying for Quattro, Christopher stretched his hand out to her, saying, "I'll take that."

Quattro flinched. "No."

What was his problem? All his dad was trying to do was lessen his load after Quattro had practically given himself a heart attack racing up this last mountain. As if he knew he had hurt his dad's feelings, Quattro softened his tone. "I can carry my own gear, Dad. I'm fine. Really."

Still, he held his hand out to Mom with such a firm expression that she finally returned the backpack to him. In the exchange, Quattro nearly dropped the heavy pack, his trembling arms pushed past exhaustion. Why did he have to insist on carrying his stupid load? I was so irritated, I could have whacked him on the head.

Grace and Christopher exchanged a meaningful look as Quattro took the lead without a backward glance at us. Sighing deeply, Grace stared up at the final stair climb. "Oh, dear Lord."

"We got this," I assured her, even though my legs protested otherwise. My gaze strayed to Quattro, who was making steady upward progress. "Just think about the Wednesday Walkers."

Calling on her friends was the right move. She rallied, straightened her shoulders, and said, "Okay, girls, up we go." Then, to me, she said, "And you, my girl, need to go at your own pace. I'm fine with your mom and Christopher. Really, go."

So I flew up those last stairs, wanting that first sight of Machu Picchu—and yes, wanting to catch up to Quattro. Breathing hard, I finally neared the imposing stone pillars of the Sun Gate, Intipunku. Quattro stood before the gateway. A small sliver of hope sprouted inside me. Had he remembered our bet? Was he waiting for me?

If he had been, he sure wasn't acting like it. After the first "Hey!" Quattro looked like he regretted the betraying warmth in his voice. He stayed where he was, alone. Hurt, I pretended to fix the zipper on my jacket, then watched Hank urging Helen to join him on the other side of the Sun Gate: "Come on, Helen. Come on." He might as well have bent over and patted his thighs the way I called to Auggie: *Come on, girl. Come on!*

Hank jerked his head toward the trail leading down to Machu Picchu, and with a heroic puff of his chest, he said, "The other guys already left, but I waited for you."

"Hank," Helen said slowly, "they left to get Stesha help. Besides, we started as a group. I think we should finish as one." Her eyes rested on Christopher, who was walking patiently uphill behind Mom and Grace. "Why don't you catch up to Ruben and Gregor and see if they need help?"

"This isn't how the trip was supposed to end," Hank grumbled. The way his shoulders hunched miserably as he left made me pity him. We all like to think that we'd be heroes in a crisis, but look at me when Stesha fell. Besides, I had plenty of opportunities to tell Dom the truth about my age. But had I taken any of them? No.

Even though I wasn't looking at Quattro, I was fully aware of where he still stood at the top of the stairs, gazing down at his dad, Grace, and Mom. He hadn't been waiting for me; he'd been waiting for his father. Feeling stupid, I forced myself to continue making conversation with Helen. I confessed, "I get what Hank was talking about. This isn't how I imagined finishing the Inca Trail either."

"What'd you imagine?" she asked.

Sunrays were supposed to dance on the stone ruins, instead of this oppressive curtain of gray rain clouds. Quattro was supposed to be at my side as we each strained to be the first to touch the pillars. And my heart was supposed to remain safely intact. Unconsciously, I glanced at Quattro. A breeze ruffled his hair, making me jealous of the wind.

In case he could overhear, I answered, "Well, not blood."

"Or mudslides," Helen agreed. She peered at me. "What do you think Stesha would say?"

With a wry half smile, I channeled my best Stesha: "I've found that once you let go of your expectations, something better usually comes along."

Helen laughed lightly before she added her own Stesha-ism, complete with a tiny bounce on the balls of her feet: "Doesn't that always happen?"

Just then, Grace crested the hill with a victorious "Hallelujah!" She didn't spare the Sun Gate a glance, just focused on the trail beyond. Clasping her hands together, she threw her head up to the sky and yelled, "Blessed, blessed downhill!"

I burst into laughter. Quattro's brief answering grin almost undid me. We both looked away. Fast. Honestly, I didn't know whether I should laugh or cry because Stesha was right. Once I had let go of my fantasy of an older, wiser love of my life, someone unbelievably better had come along.

If only Quattro knew it.

Chapter Eighteen

Machu Picchu gleamed before us, a pale jewel pillowed on a lush green peak. Even shrouded in clouds, the ruins were more glorious than I could have imagined. No amount of careful study of photographs, no amount of compulsive reading—nothing had prepared me for the full impact of the sanctuary. I gasped, and Mom placed her arm around my shoulders. My feelings may have been smarting from Quattro's hot-and-cold relationship schizophrenia, but this—this—was rearranging.

Mom said, "We made it, baby."

Our appreciation of the ancient site was cut short when Ruben rushed back to the remains of our group, waving his cell phone.

"We have to hurry," he blurted, and held up his phone as if it were about to blare out wartime instructions. "I just heard that the officials are only running two more buses up here. They've closed Machu Picchu entirely."

"Wait," said Christopher, looking heartbroken, "so we won't be able to walk through Machu Picchu? At all?"

"I'm afraid not," Ruben answered regretfully. "We should head down to the parking lot as fast as possible to get on one of the buses."

"What about tomorrow?" Quattro asked, stepping closer to Ruben.

"We'll have to see," said our guide with another apologetic shrug.

There's nothing like a group of rapidly moving, .purpose-driven people to set off primal survival instincts. So when a fleet of highly fit Japanese tourists trotted past us while we lingered, I felt an electric shock of unease, especially when one of the trekkers shook her head at us as if we were making a fatal mistake by remaining in place.

"What do they know that we don't?" I heard Grace ask from behind me.

That's what I wondered. Ruben caught up with their guide, both men wearing the solemn expressions that my parents had perfected these last few weeks. As the other tourists barreled down the trail, Ruben returned to us.

Mom asked, "What did he say?"

"We need to catch the bus now," Ruben said. "The road to Machu Picchu Pueblo is starting to flood."

The meaning wasn't lost on any of us: We could be stranded.

Grace's face was taut with stress from walking faster than I had seen her move during this entire trip. Miraculously, we caught up with Eduardo, one of our porters, whose forehead was damp with sweat from the strain of carrying Stesha. Hank and Dad followed closely behind them.

"Let's take a two-minute break," Ruben said, gazing at Grace worriedly. She was bent over, huffing hard.

"Put me down," Stesha commanded, but once she was on her feet, she listed off balance. Dad immediately lifted her. When Mom started to protest, Dad said, "I can at least hold her while we're standing."

Mom nodded, which made two of us grateful that Dad wasn't under the illusion he could manage the trail with Stesha in his arms.

"I can walk on my own!" Stesha protested, but her feeble attempts to free herself from Dad must have exhausted her. She sighed, closed her eyes, and rested her head against his shoulder.

From behind me, I caught a fragment of an argument brewing between Quattro and his dad.

"We might never get this chance again," said Quattro as he began to unzip his backpack.

"No," said Christopher with a tone of finality I hadn't thought he was capable of producing. He placed his hand atop Quattro's to stop him. "Son, this isn't the right time."

So I wouldn't be tempted to eavesdrop, I took the camera out of my pocket and trained my lens not on Machu Picchu but on our group standing before it: banged up, heartbroken, and going blind. They were drinking in the ruins so thirstily, it was like they were desperate to find any bit of beauty in the rubble of this trip and our lives.

As hard as I tried to ignore Quattro, I shifted the lens to him. He was gazing at the ruins intently, as though it were his ancestral birthright to rule this place. But then, without a word to anyone, Quattro stomped down the trail with Christopher staring after him. Sighing, Christopher held his arms out to my dad, saying, "Here, I'll take Stesha for a bit."

Mom and I exchanged another look. Was Christopher even strong enough to carry Stesha? Maybe it was a trick of the light, but Quattro's dad looked like he had solidified. For the first time on the trip, his cheeks were ruddy instead of faded pale, and a new steeliness energized his gaze.

"I'm stronger than I look," Christopher said. He may have shrugged wryly, but even his shoulders looked wider. He was occupying space.

"I'd trust you," Helen said, tucking her hair behind her ear. Her vote of confidence reminded me that it was Christopher, after all, who had rescued Helen from drowning in mud. Ducking his head, Hank took off down the trail without a word.

Despite a bashed-up chin and what was probably a nasty concussion, Stesha swung back into tour guide mode and asked us triumphantly, "See? Didn't walking every single step here make this view so much more meaningful?"

No one answered. In the uncomfortable silence, Ruben reminded us that not a single person alive today knew for sure what Machu Picchu's true purpose had been: religious sanctuary or military citadel? As we continued down the trail, I kept my eyes lifted to the ruins. Maybe the what and the why of Machu Picchu didn't matter. Maybe all that mattered was that it was still standing.

—⚹—

Just as we reached the turnstiles guarding the entrance to the sanctuary, one lone bus pulled into the parking circle. The doors remained shut. I didn't blame the driver. The long line of dirty, tired, and impatient backpackers at the curb surged forward as though prepared to storm the bus.

As soon as we reached Hank and Quattro near the back of the line, the few tourists behind them grumbled in different languages, none that I spoke, but I'm pretty sure I interpreted correctly: No way in hell were all of us cutting in line. As it was, only a magician could have squeezed in every person angling to board the bus.

"We should have come down earlier to secure our spot in line," Hank said to no one in particular.

Dad said, "We can walk. I think I read that it's only about an hour on foot to town."

"Helicopters are coming today to fly people back to Cusco. That's what everyone's been saying," Hank said, shaking his head emphatically. "We've got to get down fast."

"I can walk," Grace agreed.

"I can walk, too," said Helen. Overhead, the sun broke free

186

from the clouds. She brushed her thick hair off her face, tilting her cheek up to the sunlight. The massive stone on her engagement ring no longer glittered; it was covered in mud, like all of us.

"People are saying that the train isn't running. The track's been flooded," Ruben informed us after checking in with another guide. His brow furrowed with concern. The helicopters are our only chance of getting out."

Stesha cleared her throat, but her voice was still strained. "First things first; the porters need to get home. There is no way the helicopters are going to fly them back to Cusco. The government is only going to evacuate tourists. We all know that." With trembling fingers, she handed a wad of cash to the porters, asking Ruben to translate. "Tell them thank you and that I'm giving them a huge bonus when I get back to Cusco." Her voice faded. "Let's give them as much food as we can."

The porters refused to leave, backing away from the money until Stesha threatened to do all the cooking on the next trip.

From the corner of my eye, I watched Quattro move away from our group like he was going to make a run for it with the porters. Christopher blinked then as though waking from a hundred-year sleep. First, he asked Quattro, "Can you scout out the trail?" Then to Ruben: "You need to get on that bus and get Stesha to a doctor and on the helicopter." When Ruben protested, Christopher explained, "You're the only one who can speak the language. The rest of us will be fine."

Both Christopher and I watched as Quattro scowled but readjusted his backpack before walking across the parking lot to the trail head. Only then did Christopher glance over first at

Grace, then at Hank. "You and Grace need to go ahead and make sure we have rooms."

"Grace?" Hank protested. "I can handle the hotel by myself."

"Yeah, Grace," Christopher answered, casting a quick glance at Helen, who nodded her approval. "She needs to get off her feet." As Hank began grumbling again, Christopher added, "And no one's going to complain about you getting on the bus if you're accompanying her."

That shut Hank up, but not Grace, who planted her hands on her hips. She demanded, "Don't I get a say in this?"

Mom rushed to answer: "Grace, you've walked the entire Inca Trail."

Even though I felt like a traitor, I nodded when Grace glanced at me, because Mom had a point: There was no reason for Grace to prove anything more, and we needed to hustle if we had any chance of snagging a spot on the rescue helicopters.

While we watched, Ruben pounded on the bus door until the driver cracked it open. Catching the gist of the conversation wasn't tough: Ruben kept waving over at Stesha, who was sitting on the curb with a bloodied bandage hanging off her chin. After a few minutes of negotiations, Ruben waved us over in triumph. People behind us began complaining loudly again as the reality of scarce seating sank in.

"I can walk with you," Grace protested once again.

"Grace, Stesha needs you." I pointed to Stesha, who was now seated on the bus, her head leaning against a window, her eyes scrunched shut like she was in pain.

"And Hank's going to need you to sweet-talk the hotel into giving us rooms," Mom added.

Grace nodded reluctantly before promising, "We'll see you there."

I felt like chasing after the bus as it departed the parking lot, not because it was transportation but because it was our link to half our team. As the bus disappeared around the corner, the porters reluctantly accepted the rest of our food supplies. I teared up at the sight of them leaving, too. No, this wasn't how our trek was supposed to end.

"We should go," Christopher told all of us now. I wondered if his urging was really meant for Quattro, who had returned with his report: "The trail looks fine." He was staring at the gates barricading the ruins like he wanted to vault over the turnstiles, scale the chain-link fence, and break into Machu Picchu.

Mom sighed, lifting her eyes to Dad, and murmured apologetically, "I'm sorry about this trip. You were right. We should have stayed home."

As we cut across the parking lot to the trailhead, a woman in a high ponytail and pink stilettos better suited for a beach resort picked her way between potholes and rocks back to the hotel, the only one sited next to the ruins. Her loud complaints to her husband echoed over to us: "There were nothing but rocks. For this, we're spending five hundred bucks a night at an overrated Holiday Inn?"

Dad scrutinized that woman and her dissatisfaction the way he would an especially nasty pest. For the first time since the mudslide, he reached for Mom's hand and told her, "At least we got to see Machu Picchu in person."

"You really think so?" Mom's smile was so brilliant, it made up for the sun's disappearing act.

"Yeah," Dad said, reminding me of who my father really was—not the bitter man who had grumbled through the past few weeks but the one who appreciated even the second-best things in life.

—⁂—

Our choices were to follow the longer asphalt road with steep switchbacks or to take our chances on the trail, which cut a sheer vertical path down the mountain to the town. Naturally, what remained of our group chose the mud chute of a trail, especially when Quattro reconfirmed that what he had seen looked fine. But where there weren't stairs, there was mud. Every gloppy footstep through the thick jungle felt like a prelude to a fall. My quads trembled on the steep, slick path.

"Be. Careful. Be. Careful," I chanted to myself, then gasped when my right foot slipped on a slick rock step. I fell hard on my tailbone.

In front of me, Dad's shoulders hunched in defeat as he grasped an overhead branch for balance. He yanked off the headlamp Quattro had given him earlier that morning. "I've got to walk on the road. It's so dark here, I can't see where I'm stepping."

That rare admission about his failing eyesight shocked me.

Mom edged around me on the narrow trail and asked him softly, "Is it getting worse?"

Dad flushed, shrugged, then conceded, "I don't know. Probably, yes." Finally, he admitted, "There's a black dot in my good eye now."

I wanted to scream at the unjustness. The ophthalmologist had warned us that Dad could begin to lose vision in his good eye during our trip, but the reality of Dad going blind was still hard to accept, especially when he was so stubbornly mobile.

"I'll walk with you," I told him.

"No, I'll just meet you guys down in town." He started rifling through his pockets.

"What're you doing?" Mom asked, annoyed.

"Getting the cash. You two might need it."

"That's ridiculous," Mom said at the same time that I protested, "We're sticking together, remember?"

By now, the rest of the group had stopped to check what was causing the delay. Dad explained, "I'm walking on the road."

"Shana's right," said Christopher firmly. "We'll stick together. I'm pretty sure this trail intersects with the road up ahead, and it might be faster and safer if we continue instead of backtracking. Quattro, take the lead."

While Quattro cast an annoyed look at his father, he did what he was told. Dad's jaw was equally tight, but he didn't protest either. In fact, no one spoke. A few more minutes of tough downhill, and we made it to the slick asphalt on the narrow, zigzagging road, just as Christopher had predicted. I couldn't imagine how two buses heading in opposite directions could pass each other safely. Backing up would be suicidal; the road was so steep and without any guardrails that I could see.

Almost two hours later, the road leveled out. The entire walk had been devoid of conversation. Our silence only accentuated the thunder of the whitecapped and muddy river running alongside the road now.

The river.

I'd never told anybody about the dream I had the night Dom broke up with me. I was inside a log cabin that smelled like the forest and wild growing things. Standing in front of a mirror, I stared, horrified, as sheets of skin peeled from my forehead, my cheeks, my lips. The roar of a river drew me away from my reflection and out to the ironwood deck. Water rose around the cabin, turning it into a houseboat. Or an island. All I knew was that I had to cross the churning waters. Had to reach Dom on the opposite shore. Scared, I started wading. The river was waist deep, unforgiving and cold. Thousands of silvery fish darted around me. I was convinced I was going to drown. And just as I finally, finally staggered onto the shore, Dom climbed into a pickup truck and drove off without me.

Nobody could survive this violent river, churning wild and angry, if they fell in. But I wasn't trapped in a dream, stranded and alone at a riverbank. Quattro stood next to me. Over the river's raging, he said loud enough so I could hear: "You were practically running back there. You okay?"

"I was just remembering a stupid nightmare."

"What about?"

"I thought I was going to drown in a river." Sheepishly, I admitted, "I'm a little freaked out."

"I won't let anything happen," Quattro said flatly.

No, I knew he wouldn't, whether he was boyfriend or friend. Wistfulness tightened my throat, as I thought about how much I wanted him to be my guy. The one who would think about me as constantly as I thought about him. Who would want to be with me. So much for my Boy Moratorium. That self-imposed no-boy diet didn't do a darn thing to stop me from falling for Quattro, much less stop me from feeling hurt.

Why did I have to fall for the one guy on a well-enforced Girl Moratorium? A guy who seemed pretty much impervious to me?

Why?

Anything was better than beating myself up with these thoughts. So as we approached the stone footbridge, I asked Quattro, "Everything okay with you and your dad?"

"Sometimes Dad can be so by the book. I mean, life is just going to pass him by if he doesn't watch out." Quattro took a deep breath. On his exhale, he gestured to the river and asked, "What's going to calm this down, do you think?"

It wasn't me who answered but his father, who had caught up to us: "Time."

Had Christopher overheard Quattro? His face, impassive as always, didn't show it.

"Time." The word came out as a derisive scoff from Quattro. He looked dangerously remote.

I understood. In all these months after Dom, I had retreated into my own fortress, refusing to let anyone get close to me, even my best friends. But now I wanted to echo Christopher and reassure Quattro: Time hadn't just dulled my heartache over Dom. It had allowed me to see clearly. I'd never had a real relationship with Dom: We flirted, I chased, he showed me off when it suited him. For the first time in weeks, months, I actually felt at peace.

As soon as my parents neared us at the river's edge, Christopher urged, "We better keep going." As if to second that motion, the river swelled over the banks, spraying our hiking boots. I took a quick step back. "Looks like once we get across, we'll have to follow the train tracks."

"But what if a train comes?" Mom asked, worried.

"The trains aren't running," Dad answered.

"According to the rumors," Mom said. "And there's a tunnel I read about in some woman's blog..."

The truth was, if the trains were running, we'd be roadkill, and we all knew it.

"We'll have to make a run for it then," said Helen. I saw her sidelong glance at Christopher, who nodded back at her confidently. He said, "We'll just have to have a little faith."

"Whoa, you sounded like Stesha there for a second," I teased him, hoping to ease Mom's anxiety.

"Yeah, I did," Christopher said, grinning, looking exactly like his son at his mischievous best. I missed that Quattro.

"You sure this is safe?" Mom asked suspiciously as she studied the bridge. Frankly, the bridge's stones and concrete looked fragile and insubstantial against the ruthless current.

"Nothing in life is ever a hundred percent safe," Christopher said softly, his gaze flickering to Quattro. Without another word, Christopher accompanied Helen across the bridge, holding out his arm for her to take as water spattered them. Dad followed them and held Mom's hand. He stopped to shoot a look at me. "Wait right there. I'll help you across."

"I got it," I told him confidently even though I had my doubts, reinforced when another wave swamped the bridge.

Give it time, and a wild thought just might sweep away the last pangs of falling for the wrong boy. I took Quattro's camera out and snapped a photo of this threatening river and whispered, "Good-bye, Dom." Quattro's eyes were trained on me when I lowered the camera.

The next best thing to having Quattro as a boyfriend was claiming him as a friend. So while my every girl instinct told me to flip my hair (which probably wouldn't have moved, given how greasy it was) and challenge him with a coy "Afraid?," I didn't.

Instead, I said, "Our turn." I held my hand out to him, waiting patiently as he hesitated before clasping mine in his.

Chapter Nineteen

At the end of our slog back to civilization, I was alarmed by the teeming crowds of bedraggled trekkers in Machu Picchu Pueblo. Every square inch in the town plaza had been turned into a homeless encampment and garbage dump. Whatever charm the square had was lost in the mess of tents, trash, and unwashed bodies. I stepped over a couple of discarded beer bottles on our way to the main street. A snaking line of frustrated people waited at an ATM, but after Christopher made an inquiry, we learned that all the cash had been withdrawn. What everyone was waiting for, I don't know. Even worse, tourist after tourist confirmed that every single train had been canceled. A state of emergency had been declared. There was no way out.

Mom said, "Maybe we should find Stesha now?"

"Let's try Ruben. Who's got a phone?" Christopher asked,

but Quattro didn't own a cell phone, and all of us except Helen had lost ours in the mudslide. Luckily, she had programmed Ruben's number, but there was no answer. Not from him or from Stesha, Grace, Hank, or our hotel.

"Maybe we should go straight to the hotel then? Make sure Hank got us our rooms?" Helen suggested, glancing around uneasily. Half the people near us looked drunk, messy drunk. "We may be here for a while."

Christopher studied the throngs and started going all militia on us. "I think we should buy as much water and food as we can carry first. Grab anything packaged."

Nobody argued with his logic. Most of our provisions had gone with the porters. So we fanned out in three groups, me teaming up with Quattro. Fifteen minutes was more than enough time. Five would have been fine. The stores had been mostly cleaned out, leaving us with few choices.

"Beef jerky?" Quattro asked me. Then with a vestige of his old self, he held up a package of Twinkies. "America at its finest."

"Hey," I said, "you know, if we can find maple syrup, we can make our own—"

"Do-it-yourself bacon maple bars?" he guessed. His eyes glittered as he laughed. "I knew you'd see the light."

I did.

Who would have known that his wide, easy grin could have hurt in the best and worst way? As thrilled as I was to see its reemergence, I wanted it to mean more than an inside joke between friends. *Get it together, Wilde Child.* So I wrinkled my nose. "I still think bacon and doughnuts are two food groups that should never be combined."

"See? I knew you secretly agreed."

"About what?"

"Bacon is its own food group."

As I sputtered, Quattro grabbed the bottles of water I was holding and brought them to the cashier.

—∭—

Between all of us, we had managed to assemble a small stockpile of water, crackers, and peanuts. Christopher asked for directions to our hotel from a backpacker wearing a Union Jack T-shirt. The reaction we received was one I didn't expect: total antagonism.

"Good luck with that," the backpacker said, mouth puckering like he was preparing to spit at us.

What had we done to him? We must have looked confused because, disgusted, the backpacker said, "Your embassy airlifted some people out yesterday. But they would only take *Americans*." With a last disdainful look, he turned his back on us, but not before one parting shot: "All the hotels have jacked up their prices."

Worriedly, Mom asked Dad, "What if our rooms have been given away?" Her hand fluttered toward the plaza. "I mean, look at all these people."

Dad had no solution, just more problems. He pointed out, "Just think about all the other groups who are still coming down from the trail."

At last, after a few wrong turns and a helpful shopkeeper, we reached the modest hotel where we were supposed to spend the night, only to discover that it was overbooked and no one at the front desk remembered seeing Hank or Grace. But then again, everything was a blur to them, considering the fifty tourists who'd dropped in that morning alone in hopes of finding available rooms.

"But we have reservations," Christopher protested firmly. The receptionist gave a helpless shrug, explaining that guests were refusing to vacate.

"Well, we can't exactly boot people out," Mom said, shaking her head. Still, she leaned forward as if she might hurdle over the reception desk and commandeer the computer. But the electricity had gone out. The computer was useless. "Are there any rooms in other hotels? What about the hostels?"

The receptionist shook her head regretfully. "Even the train seats are being used as beds. You can try Inkaterra."

Mom glanced at Dad. "That's the spendy one."

If the hotel had been expensive before the floods, I hated to guess how much a room would cost now that beds were hot commodities. An anxious expression calcified on Mom's face.

The sound of a chopper sent us scrambling outside, all of us craning our necks to spot where it would land. We followed the exodus of tourists to the makeshift helipad that some volunteers must have cleared earlier. People actually pushed and shoved each other to climb aboard until two soldiers disembarked, each gripping a machine gun. Did the Peruvian government really think automatic weapons were necessary?

Without thinking, I began photographing the scene, starting with the unlucky soldier who got the job of announcing that the first helicopter would evacuate only the elderly and infirm.

"This place looks like it's going to blow," said Quattro softly in my ear.

When had he moved to stand close to me like he'd appointed himself my personal bodyguard? Before I could spend more than a nanosecond processing that thought, Grace's distinct objection—"I am not elderly!"—cut through the crowd's mutterings. I scanned the area until I spotted her, then shot her with Hank, who was holding a visibly pale Stesha near the front of the line. Ruben was gesturing emphatically to one of the impassive soldiers, universal sign language for "She's getting evacuated. Now."

Grace hurried over, intercepting us as we walked toward them. "You made it!" she said, hugging me tightly. "I was so worried about you all."

"What'd the doctor say?" Mom asked, bending her head down to Grace as they walked side by side back to Stesha.

Grace shook her head. "No doctor. She's worse, but she's refusing to leave."

Overhearing Grace, Stesha cracked her eyes open and said, "I'm the captain, and I'm not leaving until you're all safe." That spot of defiance sapped her energy. Stesha sagged into Hank's arms.

"Come on, Stesha. You might have a concussion," said Quattro, glancing at me with a slight nod to tag-team with him.

So I added, "Reb's going to kill me if your chin gets infected. You've got to have that taken care of."

"It's just a little cut," Stesha protested feebly, but she didn't even bother opening her eyes this time. Yet with some kind of finely tuned internal radar for trouble, they opened just as a soldier approached her with Ruben trailing close behind.

"Traitor," she said softly to him.

"You have to go," I told her.

"I know." Still trying to take care of us, Stesha dug a last PowerBar from her pocket and pushed it on Ruben. "But I'm not leaving Cusco until you're all there." Even as she was led to the helicopter, we could hear her calling back to us, "I'm not leaving Cusco."

"Where's Grace?" Ruben asked, glancing around increasingly worried. There was no sign of her.

"Figures," said Dad, rubbing his temples.

What possible reason could compel Grace to remain in an overcrowded town with no promise of a bed, hot meal, or shower? I knew what would make me stay. My gaze shifted over to the remainder of our ragtag group, lingering on Quattro.

"At thirty-five people per helicopter," said Dad, now eyeing the growing crowd, "this evacuation is going to take an eternity."

"But you're lucky. You're going blind," said Hank, who then ducked his head, embarrassed. "I mean, you and your family can be evacuated now."

"I'm not an invalid," Dad answered, and he straightened himself to his full height. I was so glad to hear him say those words aloud, and wondered if he was listening to himself.

Twenty minutes later, my eyes filled with tears as the helicopter door slammed shut and the rotor whirred loud. Our group was fragmenting. None of us had been able to say a proper good-bye to Stesha. I hadn't even hugged her. Everything had happened so fast once she was trundled off with a soldier. The lump in my throat grew larger as the helicopter rose. Selfishly, I didn't want to see Stesha go. My eyes caught on Quattro, who nodded in understanding at me.

—⁀ℳ⁀—

As soon as we left the perimeter of the helipad, Grace magically reappeared, smiling innocently. I could feel Dad fuming, but any scene I was afraid he might cause was trumped by a more urgent problem.

"We don't have a room at our hotel," Helen told Hank, concern creasing her forehead.

"We'll figure it out," Hank said confidently, and with a homing instinct for the only five-star hotel in the town, he steered us to Inkaterra.

The boutique inn could be reached only by crossing a private wood bridge. On the other side, we found ourselves in a lush oasis that couldn't have been farther from the fear, filth, and garbage back in town. Elegant, understated casitas dripped with vibrant bougainvillea. The fountain in the central courtyard burbled sweetly, nothing like the bellow of the river. A discreet wood sign pointed to the spa, gift shop, and restaurants.

I could hear my parents murmuring as we approached the reception building, worrying about the cost of the rooms. Having to admit to everyone—including Quattro—that we couldn't afford this place was going to be sheer awkwardness.

Hank strode in as though he'd stayed in places this luxurious hundreds of times before. Of course, he had. The woman at the front desk had her hair pulled into a sleek updo, not a strand out of place, as if this sanctuary made her immune to the disaster beyond the bridge. After Hank inquired about a room, she informed us that there was, in fact, one ultradeluxe casita available, complete with its own plunge pool and private garden.

And then she named the price.

I'm not sure who gasped louder, me or Mom. I could have dressed myself for two years, maybe three, with the cost of a single night here; we'd never be able to afford this.

Dad cleared his throat. "We'll find other accommodations in town and meet up with you all later."

"Come on. It's what? Nineteen hundred square feet? We can all fit in," said Hank, plunking down his platinum card. When the receptionist mumbled something about an extra fee per guest, Hank waved her off. "No problem."

"We can pay—" started Christopher.

"This is on me," Hank said with finality, glancing at Helen. The way he still sought her approval was sad, especially when she just nodded once in agreement. His gushing fangirl was gone. Maybe it wasn't confidence that made him come off all brash and bold but insecurity. Who was I to talk? Hadn't I been all I-know-boys to Reb and Ginny when, really, I had been dumped by Dom?

Grace said, "Well, this is so kind of you, Hank, Helen. I know we all appreciate it."

At last, a real smile spread across Hank's face. "It's the least I could do," he said, no longer fighting to be heard or first or right.

If anyone had told me that a hotel casita could be larger than our home, I'd never have believed them. But here I was, standing in one. Handwoven rugs brightened the terra-cotta tile floor. A couch and two chairs were arranged before a fireplace in a snug sitting area. Another rich tapestry that Mom immediately inspected hung on a wall. If anyone thought I was weird for taking a picture of the king-size bed with blankets made from alpaca, they didn't mention it. I think we were all overwhelmed. One moment we were escaping tents collapsed in a mudslide, and the next we had stepped into a man-made paradise.

I geared myself up for Dad to jump into his usual bedbug-hunting mode, but he just lowered himself into one of the dining room chairs as though he'd given up. It was futile to fight anymore.

Chapter Twenty

Reacquainting myself with running water and flushing toilets—blessed, beautiful porcelain toilets—took no time at all. Which made me doubt whether photojournalism could ever truly be my calling. Four days without bathing was more than enough for this girl. I didn't mind sleeping on the rug in front of the fireplace that night, especially not when I luxuriated in a five-minute shower with lukewarm water the very next morning. Electricity was so spotty, I had three minutes to blow-dry my hair before the power disappeared. Who cared about a little dampness? My hair was clean.

My parents returned from their walk around town with a couple of browning bananas they had scavenged for our breakfast and news. First, Stesha had called sometime while everyone was out. So she had left a message at the front desk, assuring us that she was recuperating so well in a hospital she was ready to make a break for freedom. And second, rescue helicopters were arriving today. Even better, Mom's age-group had been called, which meant that families lucky enough to have someone fifty-five and older would be home-free in four or five hours.

So why was I reluctant to leave? Quattro's eyes and mine met across the sitting area in our casita as though he had the same thought, both of us looking away shyly.

With a dramatic flourish, Mom placed her hand on her chest as she eyed Dad and me. "O ye of little faith. Aren't you glad that I slept with our passports and extra cash in the waist wallet that you two made fun of me for buying?"

It was only now, as I listened to Mom gloat about safeguarding our passports, that I kicked myself for leaving the cameras in the mudslide. I knew I should concentrate on being grateful to be alive, but if I had only reached back into the tent and grabbed my backpack. One second and I would have rescued the cameras and all the photos I'd taken.

Gone.

Just like our departure.

Wouldn't you know it. After all our good-byes and hugs at the casita—even Quattro embraced me briefly but tightly—it started to drizzle on the way to the helipad, and Dad was back to ominous frowning. An hour before the helicopters were supposed to land, we were told that the rescue mission was back on hold due to rain. Nobody but Grace was in the casita when we returned, and that only because she had come back to collect her raincoat. Mom and Dad huddled together on the sofa, complaining about the disorganization of the Peruvian government.

206

Grace lasted all of a minute before she interrupted their ode to woe. "Then let's get out and do something."

"No, we should wait right here in case Stesha calls with more info," Dad said, jabbing his finger toward the handwoven rug. "Besides, it's not like any of us will be able to do anything to help much."

"It's better than sitting around."

"Yeah!" I agreed. When did my take-charge dad ever just wait for someone else to fix a problem and right a situation?

"And staying here when you could have left and straining our resources is better?" Dad asked.

"Gregor!" Mom protested as Grace's cheeks flushed. She said, "Grace, I'm sorry."

"Mollie, you're not the one who should be apologizing," Grace said as she thrust her arms into her raincoat. She left the casita without another word.

White-hot anger burned inside me. Where was my real father? What did Dad have to be bitter about, really—or any of us? There was no reason for my family to harden into lumps of black coal. As I shoved my feet into my hiking boots, Dad sniped about how selfish Grace was being by remaining here. It was as if he wanted to get rid of her. . . .

"No way," I muttered, straightening before I tied the laces. Horror-stricken, I looked at my father, who had successfully purged the room of Grace, no different than if she were some troublesome bug. With a shock, I realized that Dad had deployed one of his tried-and-true pest control techniques: Create a hostile environment so pests couldn't possibly want to stay. I caught a glimpse of myself in the mirror near the entry. Hadn't I done the same exact thing with every boy since Dom? Purge them from my life? Get rid of them before they could get too close and hurt me?

I groaned and backed away from my reflection in the mirror. "Whoa . . ."

"What?" Mom's eyebrows furrowed at my outburst.

I spun toward Dad. "Have you noticed that we use pest control techniques on people?"

"Your dad exterminates pests, not people," Mom said.

"Well, didn't you just do a hostile environment on Grace?" I asked him. He crossed his arms over his chest.

"What do you mean?" Mom asked, shaking her head.

"We froze her out," I said. "Classic relationship ender."

"Oh." Mom's mouth pursed as the truth hit her.

Dad said defensively, as he gestured to the daybed, "We gave her a bed last night. Your mom and I slept on the floor. We're not freezing her out."

These exact same denials could have spewed from my mouth whenever I justified my quick and efficient breakups with boys. Holding out the camera that I had borrowed from Quattro as if it were a divining rod, I searched for a vestige of my parents' former selves. I wedged between them on the sofa and commanded, "Look at this."

Dad squinted at the camera, moving it closer, then farther, which made me feel guilty, but not enough to back down.

"Perfect composition," he said about the photo of a bromeliad, pale green and ghostly in the cloud forest. A semblance of pride animated his face, an expression so familiar, I ached with homesickness. The deep, warm, unflappable man I loved existed somewhere inside that bristly shell of bitterness. But even as he handed the camera back to me, I watched his expression harden once more into resignation.

"And another of you two." I was rewarded with Mom's approving coo when I forwarded to the photo of them holding each other right after the mudslide. Each image, each sentence was part of the trail of crumbs leading my parents back to themselves. Advancing to another shot, I said, "Here we are, just yesterday, trekking through the mountains and cloud forests. A trip of a lifetime, right? But who knew when we started the trip that water and dirt could be so destructive?"

"That's life for you," Dad said.

That was the opening I had been waiting for: the exact moment when I could charge ahead and, with the right aim, hit the impossible target: *Dad, remember who you are.*

"You know something?" I stood up from the couch to face my parents, my eyes on Dad. *Please hear this. Please.* "This is life. Anything can happen. So we've got to deal with it and move on. I mean, look at where we're sitting right now after we almost died—died!"

The luxurious casita with its thousand-count bed linens and indigenous artwork and handcrafted textiles and plumbing and heating was perfectly quiet as my words rippled over them, but had they sunk in?

"That's so..." Dad started to say, but he stopped as though his positive attitude had withered and died these last weeks. Neither

Mom nor Dad closed the gap between themselves, choosing to remain separate peaks on the sofa.

"Hey!" Christopher called as he strode into the casita. The door banged shut behind him. His thick hair was damp from the rain. "What're you guys still doing here?"

"The evacuation was called off," Mom said, her eyes drilling in on Dad, who was staring down at his clasped hands.

"Maybe tomorrow then," Christopher said hopefully.

"Do you know where Quattro is?" I asked, unable to help myself. Luckily, Mom was so tuned in to Dad, she didn't pick up on my question.

"Oh, he's volunteering with the cleanup. I was just going to grab my gear and help." Christopher brushed his hand through his tousled hair, leaving it in even more disarray. The edges of his eyes crinkled warmly when he smiled. The dark circles under them had been erased. After he lifted his rain gear from the coatrack, he paused at the door just long enough to ask us, "Want to come?"

I waited for my parents to answer, hoped that they would say yes. But Dad shook his head with a rueful smile and said, "Maybe later."

"Dad, all those memoirs you read? About explorers? You've always said you wanted one big adventure." I gestured around us, no longer caring that Christopher was right here, witnessing our family drama. "Well, there's an adventure happening to you right now."

It was as if Mom were experiencing an epiphany. She stood up, gazing down at Dad alone on the couch. "It's true, Gregor.

No matter what, you'll always be my hero. I just wish you believed that."

Dad's jaw worked. Frustrated and unable to stay cooped up inside for another minute, I pocketed the camera and strode to the door, not caring that my shoelaces were still untied. "Wait, Christopher, I'll go with you."

What I didn't expect to hear was Mom's echo. "Me, too."

—๛—

Navigating the stone-paved Inca Trail, climbing thousands of uneven steps, traversing different ecological zones—those challenges were nothing compared to shoving our way through the frazzled crowd lined up at the train station. Apparently, the frustrated and scared tourists with their death grips on their luggage didn't get the memo that the trains weren't running and the tracks themselves were out of commission.

"Oh, there he is!" I said to Christopher, pointing down to Quattro on the train tracks, where he was clearing debris with a couple of other men and women.

"Where?" Christopher craned his neck.

"Two o'clock."

"Wow, you got good eyes."

More like a homing instinct where Quattro was concerned. I blushed when Mom nudged me meaningfully. But then Quattro himself glanced up and looked directly at us, as if his homing instinct for me was just as well developed.

"He's had a hard time of it, losing his mom and all,"

Christopher said to me with a sidelong glance while Quattro hopped over the embankment to make his way to us. As Quattro closed the distance, Christopher hurried to say in a lowered voice, "You're good for him."

What was I supposed to do with that revelatory piece of information? I had already let Quattro know my feelings, and if he wasn't biting, I wasn't baiting. I told myself again that I was content with being just friends with him. But then, a heavyset woman pushed me out of the way just as Quattro smiled at me, and I knew she wasn't the sole reason why I was thrown off balance. He reached out for me before I stumbled. I could have kissed the portly woman.

"I thought you left," he said, his hands still on my arms.

"The evacuation was canceled. So we came to help," I told him.

"Cool." Another grin, another flutter in my heart. I was such a goner for him. "Follow me," Quattro said as he parted the crowd for us. I envied the easy way he carried himself through the platform.

"Wow, this is worse than a concert," I said, glad to be free from the throng when we reached the edge of the tracks. I breathed in deeply.

"Worse than a mosh pit," Quattro countered before he leaped down to the tracks. He held his arms up for me and said, "Jump."

I had no doubt that Quattro would catch me, but I hadn't counted on the exhilaration of being caught in his strong arms. Swooning. I never understood that word until this very moment. But I didn't want to hope for something that would never be; I had spent way too much time doing that for Dom.

"Gotcha," he said.

In more ways than you know.

Christopher called down to him, "Hey, what about me?"

"You're on your own, Dad."

We joined the volunteers, all wearing daypacks, none toting luggage, as they gathered around a familiar short and stocky man: Ruben. His eyes lit up at the sight of us. "You all came."

"You're still here!" I said to him. "I thought you left yesterday."

"No, I told you I wasn't leaving until you were all safe," he answered.

Then Christopher explained, "Ruben stayed in our tent last night."

"You should have stayed with us," Mom protested now, as I said, "We had enough room!"

"I'm happier outside," he said simply, understated as always.

Really, I should have known that Ruben would be at the center of any kind of relief effort. Here was a man who'd shown us nothing but quiet steadiness since the start of the trip, never drawing attention to himself, never needing to be the hero. He just was, always doing more than what was required. I didn't have a single doubt that Ruben would stay until each and every one of us in his tour group had been safely evacuated, not because it was in his contract or because he had promised Stesha, but because it was the right thing to do.

"How can we help?" Christopher asked him.

Ruben blew out, his breath barely lifting the lank tendril of greasy hair that hung over his right eye. He was holding a lengthy to-do list jotted hastily in pencil. Just skimming the list of projects was overwhelming: removing the debris off the train tracks. Filling empty sacks with sand. Constructing make-shift walls. Half of the work seemed senseless in the face of the relentless river still churning so strongly that a five-foot chunk of concrete bobbed like a bathtub toy before the current hurtled it farther downriver. Dad was right. Even if we worked all night, would we make a dent of difference? Maybe if every single tour-ist behind us would help, we might be able to clear this small section of track. But how do you mobilize volunteers when des-peration is real and danger feels close?

Without thinking, I knelt down to take a photo of some of the workers, focusing first on a thin young man dragging a mas-sive tree limb that looked three times his weight. My lens found a familiar figure who should have been lounging in Cusco, sip-ping pisco sours, but was clearing the train tracks with vol-unteers a third her age. The same woman who'd lagged so far behind everyone on the Inca Trail that my father had accused her of jeopardizing the trip. The same woman who encouraged everyone—Mom, Helen, me—with her stories.

This was the photograph I knew I had to make: a woman who chose to build instead of tear down. I framed Grace just left of center and waited until the exact moment when she straight-ened, holding a bouquet of torn branches. I got my shot. Next, I zoomed in to a ponytailed woman in a Penn sweatshirt, who scowled at me. Complaining to her friend loudly, she said, "If everyone would stop playing tourist and actually help, we might get something done around here."

Chastened, I lowered the camera and tried to listen to what Ruben was saying to the group around him. He lifted his eyes off the to-do list and said, "We need a couple of people to play soccer with some kids."

"That's helping?" asked a balding man with a potbelly.

"Have you ever seen what kind of trouble bored kids can get into?" countered a stout woman whose wide-brimmed rain hat could have been an umbrella. She said, "I'd volunteer, but I blew out my knee gardening."

"I'll play," Mom offered. The last time she joined the Thursday night soccer league filled with cutthroat mothers, she had been given a red card for bodychecking an opponent. Those poor kids on the soccer field here in town. Even though I didn't inherit any of her killer instinct on the field, I was about to volunteer for soccer duty until Quattro placed a hand on my arm and drew me away from the crowd.

"No one in the press is covering what's happening here," he said in a low voice, gesturing to the disarray around us. "That's why there's no aid coming. No one knows, and no one cares. But you know. The right photograph can make all the difference."

But Dom had told me that only videos could make a difference these days. And that's what I said now: "A video would be better."

"I'm not so sure about that," Quattro said. "My mom used to do a ton of development work for nonprofits." The last time Quattro had talked about his mom, he had shut down on me.

I waited for a repeat performance. Instead, he continued, "She was all about the visuals helping with fund-raising. Video or photography, I'm not sure what's more important so long as you're telling a story. We've got to activate people into doing something about all this."

That rang true. How many times had I heard Mom talking about "visual narratives" when she prepped for meetings with her clients—telling executives that one iconic image could create a lasting impression. Could communicate information more effectively than even their words.

"Where'd I post it?" I asked.

"CNN."

"Please." I shook my head, calculating the minuscule chances of that ever happening.

"They show photographs from citizen journalists. That could be you. But it's your decision." With one last shrug, Quattro said, "I heard entire villages have been washed away. People have died."

The image of people trapped in their demolished homes dampened my objections until nothing but the truth was left: If a photograph might possibly help, I literally had to give it a shot.

"Oh, and that"—Quattro nodded at the camera—"shoots video, too, if you wanted to try something new?" Then Quattro lifted his chin at Ruben and raised his hand. "I'll play."

As Ruben gave the volunteer soccer team directions to the field, Quattro kicked the ball to my mom, who stopped it easily with one foot. The roar of the nearby river grew louder, and a breeze blew my hair back out of my face. Maybe I had approached my photography all wrong. It wasn't about beautifying people so they looked their best in senior portraits, erasing acne, thinning the girls, beefing up the guys. Maybe it wasn't even about documenting destruction. Maybe it was about telling stories, the ones that people were living and I was viewing. The ones that knocked my heart open.

I let my self-doubt go and left the volunteers and makeshift soccer team to scout around town and find stories to share.

Two dark-haired men digging through the debris on the swollen riverbanks. Planks of wood mingled with mud, the remains of their home. One pulls out a shard of a ruined plate and bursts into tears.

Muddy tendrils surging and swirling, ready to grasp and drown the unaware.

An iceberg of cement bashing against rocks.

A middle-aged mother, hair braided into a single plait, slumped in despair outside her home, a hovel of wood and recycled aluminum. Upon seeing a photographer, she stands and vanishes inside. In a moment, she returns with a feast of a bruised banana for the two to share.

A tourist filling a plastic bag with beer bottles and empty wrappers, tidying one corner of the town square.

A tour guide who could have trekked back to his own home and family like half the other guides. But instead, he stayed. And while he waited to get his group to safety, here he was, working to make conditions better for everyone, not for any money, not for any applause, just because it was the good and right thing to do.

A young man with strong features tucking two squealing kids under his arms and dashing down a soccer field. A young man who takes off his long-sleeved T-shirt and literally gives away the clothes on his back to a boy who's lost everything.

Afterward, the kids gathered around me as if I were a candy vendor when I bent down to show them the photos and videos. It didn't matter if some of the videos were shaky or if most of the photos would never make it anywhere near my portfolio, much less CNN. For me, nothing compared to this very moment, when the children laughed with pure delight as they saw themselves through my eyes.

Chapter Twenty-One

Not soon enough that evening, our group turned in, one by one, leaving my parents, Quattro, and me in the spacious lounge adjacent to the closed restaurant at our hotel. The stress of daily uncertainty was wearing on everyone. Mom yawned widely for the tenth time in the last fifteen minutes.

"I'm calling it a night," she said. "Boy, those kids could play soccer." At last, she stood up from the well-worn leather couch across from the potbellied stove and held her hand down to Dad to pull him to his feet. "You two going to stay up a little longer?"

Quattro and I glanced at each other. When he nodded slightly, my own tiredness vanished.

"Yeah," I said, and then flashed Mom the key card just as she asked me if I had mine. "Got it."

Dad warned us, "Don't go into town tonight."

"Dad," I said, barely refraining from clobbering him with the throw pillow. "It's not like anything's open."

"Just saying. People can turn into animals when they're scared. Be back in the casita in an hour."

I shot a silent plea at Mom. Understanding, she slipped her hand through the crook of Dad's arm and told him, "Okay, honey, I'm wiped out." With one final don't-mess-with-me look at Quattro, Dad paused at the door before telling us, "An hour."

I sighed. Loudly.

"Sorry about that," I said to Quattro with a wry smile as the door swung shut behind my parents. "They used to be so normal."

"Nah, now I've got a model for how I'll talk to all my sister's boyfriends." As if he only now heard the implication of those words, he flushed.

My heart actually thumped with excitement. More times than I could count, I had caught myself wanting Quattro to be my boyfriend, but did he subconsciously do the same? But no, what was I thinking? Since our moonlight conversation outside the hostel on the Inca Trail, we had barely even talked to each other until today. And even then, it was Quattro urging me to photograph, all friend, no hint of boyfriend.

Silence stretched between us. I hugged a throw pillow to my stomach.

"Hey, can I see the pictures you took today?" he asked.

"Sure." As I removed the camera from my pocket, he walked around the coffee table to sit beside me. I was aware of his closeness, aware of him reaching for the camera, aware of the brush of our fingers as I placed the camera on his palm. We were sitting so close, it'd be easy for me to lean into him, angle my head nearer to his, as I supposedly looked at my photos. . . .

A scuffle broke out in the walkway outside: shouted words, a few choice obscenities, pounding footsteps running back toward us. Then, my dad's voice, loud and authoritative: "Hey! Stop!"

Without hesitating, I leaped up and rushed out into the cobblestoned courtyard, Quattro at my side. Clearly, Dad had no problem with being a hypocrite, ignoring his own warning to stay safe inside.

"Hey!" Dad shouted again at two brawling men with stubbled faces and dirty clothes that reeked of days-old sweat. Dad stepped between them. There had been reports of fighting in town, especially with food running out and no further word on the helicopters returning. Fear clogged my throat, but as I tried to join Dad, Quattro placed a hand on my arm. On the opposite side of me stood Mom, her eyes watchful, but she looked calm, almost expectant.

"Let go," I hissed, trying to shrug Quattro off. What if they had knives and Dad couldn't see the weapons? What if—

Then a familiar confidence emanated from Dad, the calm that soothed countless people who were scared of their rat-infested attics and cockroach-filled kitchens. The authority he had to stop my twin brothers from bashing each other. With quiet assurance, Dad said, "It's time for you to leave."

The moment was taut, the same knot of tension I'd felt at the helipad and the train station. Dad stood firm. He wasn't giving off menacing vibes, just ones that said he meant business. Whatever the guys mumbled, they left docilely.

"Wow, your dad's good," said Quattro, nodding his head.

"He is."

—⟶⟿—

After a long moment, shivering out in the cold by ourselves, Quattro nudged me. "Head inside?"

I nodded even though I should have slipped back to the casita, safe and sound without any possibility of making a fool of myself with a boy who so obviously didn't know what he wanted. If this were Ginny, I'd have lectured that she deserved a Chef Boy who knew with a thousand percent certainty that he never wanted to cook in anyone else's kitchen.

But did I leave? No, I walked back to the deserted lounge with its dim lights and fire banked low. A room couldn't have sparked with more romance. We sat at opposite ends of the couch, where he'd left his backpack.

"So," Quattro said from his side of Siberia, "your photos?"

I'm not sure what I loved more: how he had tracked our conversation, remembering exactly where we had left off, or how he actually wanted to see my work. I fished out the camera and cued it to the photos I'd shot today. Our hands brushed each other, and I could have sworn that Quattro swallowed hard at the touch. I know I did.

"These are awesome," he said after a while, his voice deep and gruff. If I closed my eyes, I could easily imagine him sounding exactly that way after hours of kissing. What was I thinking? Luckily, he just cycled through the photos without noticing my discomfort. Finally, he reached the series I'd taken of the soccer game. "You really captured...I don't know, real moments."

Pleased, I smiled at him. "That's what I was hoping to do."

He handed the camera back to me. "Like this one. Those kids had moves."

"The best thing is," I said, then cleared my throat to shake out its huskiness. I tried again. "The best thing is, none of them are letting the flood bring them down."

"You aren't either."

"You must be going deaf." I thought guiltily of my grumbling earlier that night about having to down yet another PowerBar for dinner.

"You're still having an adventure."

Was I? I'd preached at the pulpit of girl power with the best of them, bragging to my friends that I was going to travel the world, enjoy an amazing career or two of my own, and never settle down until I was thirty. I'd reminded Dad that he'd always wanted a shake-your-soul kind of adventure. But I had let one bad breakup scare me off relationships and allowed a bad attitude to drag me down here in Peru, when, really, Quattro was right: I was in the middle of an adventure.

"We are," I said slowly, then grinned at him.

"So did you fulfill your purpose on this trip?" Quattro asked, smiling sheepishly at his question. "You know, Stesha's tours and all that?" He shrugged and ducked his head. "She told me that people always come on them with a purpose."

Back on the morning I'd encountered Quattro slipping out of the cathedral in Cusco, Stesha had told me as much: *Figure out why you yourself are here.*

"Did you?" I countered, because it was easier to hear his answer than to be aware of the silence in my own. "Fulfill your purpose?"

"Not yet, but I will," he said, nodding his head firmly as though making a pact with himself. He angled a cautious look at me. "I'm going back to Machu Picchu."

"But it's closed."

"I know."

"Isn't it dangerous? I mean, the trail looked like it was going to be washed out."

"But it hasn't been."

"You'll be arrested for trespassing!"

"Unlikely."

"Your dad's cool with this?" I asked. The wood in the fireplace crackled.

"He doesn't know. Besides, he's the one backing out when he promised..." Quattro's expression shut off then. Just when I thought the conversation was over because I had trespassed into no-woman's territory, he confessed in a low voice, "My mom told Dad that she wanted her ashes scattered somewhere beautiful and remote."

"So what better place than here?"

"And this"—he gestured to the mountain somewhere behind us, lost in darkness—"this was supposed to be our way of saying good-bye to Mom."

Quattro now removed a metal canister from the backpack at his feet, cradling it tenderly in his big hands.

"That's her?" I asked, raising my eyes to his as he entrusted me with the real reason for his pilgrimage to Machu Picchu with his father.

"I carried her almost every step of the way."

The tiny container looked too insubstantial to contain a woman's life. My eyes watered, and I wiped away the tears. Quattro shot me a rueful look and said, "My parents never had a Fifty by Fifty. They had a One. My mom—all she ever wanted to see was Machu Picchu. Since I was a kid, she had a postcard of Machu Picchu on our fridge and would tell us, 'We're going there one day.' But she wanted me and Kylie to be old enough to walk the entire trail and to remember it all. So we waited until Kylie was twelve."

And then it was too late.

Or was it?

"You're going?" I asked. "Tomorrow?"

He shrugged.

"By yourself?" Why did I ask when I already knew his answer as much as I knew what mine should have been: Let's go. Together.

But I hesitated too long as every objection formed in my mind—it was dangerous, my parents would ground me forever. So instead, it was Quattro who said those words: "We should go." And he placed the canister carefully in his backpack, rising from the sofa as if he had revealed way too much.

Chapter Twenty-Two

Well, my dears, I am being ousted," Grace announced dramatically the next morning as she returned to the casita, all banging doors and clomping feet. I yawned, tired from waking myself up at four on the off chance that Quattro might sneak out. I wasn't sure what I would have done. But as it turned out, Christopher had suspected Quattro's plans and hidden his hiking boots. I hadn't seen Quattro since he grabbed his boots from his dad and stormed out about an hour earlier, with Christopher following close behind.

"What's going on?" Dad asked, setting down a travel memoir that he had found in the lounge this morning. He was making notes on hotel stationery.

Without breaking her stride, Grace walked directly toward her bedroom and began tossing her few remaining possessions onto the bed. "Orders of the military. Can you believe it? I knew

I should have hidden, but one of the armed rascals actually cornered me when I was loading the final sandbag. This...this is ageism! You know, if we were in the States, I might hire a lawyer."

"But we aren't," Mom said in a placating tone. "So what exactly happened?"

"Another helicopter is flying in this afternoon, and apparently the Peruvian government doesn't want an international crisis on their hands with any old people keeling over. So they're insisting that every single elderly person be evacuated. Elderly!" She threw up her gnarled hands, looking like Yoda, a character not exactly known for his youthfulness. "I'm not like one of those senior citizens who take the train to Machu Picchu. I'm sorry, but did I or did I not complete the Inca Trail on my own?"

My mom exchanged a look with me, both of us smiling slightly. Right then and there, I promised myself that I'd be this spry and spunky at Grace's age.

"Since there are so many gray-haired wonders walking around town, your age-group's been delayed. Lucky you," said Grace to Mom, with a wistful sigh. "Well, put on your best clothes. I'm taking everyone out to lunch."

"I wouldn't trust anything being served at a restaurant," Dad said, grimacing.

On the third day post-flood, the restaurant scene in Machu Picchu Pueblo had become one giant gastrointestinal health hazard. Intermittent electricity shut the town down for hours at a time. No one with a working brain cell was about to touch a morsel of food that wasn't prepackaged in plastic, not to mention the fact that the few sketchy restaurants that remained open for business had quadrupled their prices. Besides all that, there was no such thing as "best" clothes—only dingy clothes that were gray and grayer from being washed with hand soap, then dried stiff overnight.

Who was I to complain? I'd grown oddly attached to my rain gear. It did the job, keeping me warm and dry. Who'd have known that I'd choose survival over style? But now I wondered why great rain gear couldn't be chic and shapely. Maybe I should try my hand at designing a line. Why not? There was nothing and no one to say that I couldn't.

"Don't worry about food. I got it covered," said Grace as she sashayed to the bathroom with an impish expression. Over her shoulder, she added, "Bring your camera, Shana. Hotel restaurant. Eleven thirty." She flashed a pirate's grin: huge, smug, and slightly dangerous. I vowed to practice in the mirror until I perfected the same.

—⚏—

Only Grace could have sweet-talked the surly and over-worked hotel manager into allowing her to use the kitchen. What she intended to prepare was beyond my imagination, since we had scavenged only precooked food-like substances.

The dining room may have been filled with chatter from the other tourist groups, but our long, communal table felt life-less without Stesha and our porters. Despite showers and sleep, the Gamers looked travel worn. There was no bounce left in Helen's hair, and I noticed that she hadn't bothered to clean her engagement ring. No one had seen Quattro or his dad since they'd left this morning. Maybe they had gone back to Machu Picchu together. I couldn't wait to find out.

The door opened, and I swiveled to see if it was Quattro. No, just Ruben. We greeted him with a standing ovation, not minding that we were being stereotypically loud American tourists. Who cared if a few other tables stared disapprovingly at us for causing a scene? Ruben hadn't just gotten us up and down the Inca Trail safely. He was a hero for helping the town itself.

From the kitchen, Grace strolled out holding a tray with tiny bowls of steaming noodles. "Top Ramen à la Grace." Then she asked Ruben, "Now, admit it. Aren't you glad I had these in my backpack all this time?"

The mere notion of hot noodle soup was almost enough to make me lose all semblance of manners, swipe a bowl from the tray, and chug it down, noodles, salty broth, rehydrated vegetables, and all. Mom poured Grace a glass of beer and raised her own in a toast: "To our chef!"

But Grace had her own agenda. First, she corrected Mom, "To our guide!"

After we applauded again, Grace waved her hands to shush us as she stood behind her chair. I assumed she was going to make a speech about Ruben or our group, the Wednesday Walkers or Stesha. But Grace surprised us by clambering onto the chair, then stepping carefully into the middle of the table between the dishes.

"Grace? What are you doing?" Mom said, jumping to her feet with her arms outstretched, ready to catch Grace in case she took a swan dive. I scrambled to the opposite side of the table.

"I think you should get down," Hank said as he stood, too.

"Well, I think it's long past risk-taking time, bucko," Grace retorted as she untucked her floral-embroidered T-shirt. She glanced around for a safe place to set her glass but ended up handing it to me.

"Grace, what're you doing?" I asked, genuinely confused, staring up at her as she unbuttoned her hiking pants. "Um...Grace?"

Dad cleared his throat uncomfortably but didn't say a word.

She unzipped her pants.

"Grace?" Helen asked. "Do you think this is a good idea?"

I hissed up at her. "I mean, we aren't exactly the Wednesday Walkers."

"Now that's the truth" was Grace's tart reply.

"And you've got an audience," I continued, my eyes darting around the dining room.

"The more, the merrier."

"No offense, but I'm not sure this is the last image I want to have," Dad said, looking down at his lap.

For the record, Grace was in remarkable shape for a septuagenarian. How she'd managed the mountains without succumbing to the altitude or the trail's steep angle, I have no idea. However.

She let go of her waistband.

"Grace," groaned Mom, as she shook out one of the linen napkins and held it behind Grace. That did little to conceal or camouflage her tight compression shorts. Seventy-year-old buttocks are seventy-year-old buttocks, whether in grandma underwear, in the buff, or tucked into tight spandex. The expressions on the other diners' faces morphed into dismay. I didn't blame them.

Dad covered his eyes.

"You're going blind. What are *you* hiding for?" Grace demanded as she wriggled her hips.

With a final swivel, her pants pooled at her ankles.

Her *ankle*.

There, standing before us as proud as any perfectly proportioned Aphrodite fresh on the clamshell, was Grace, glorious in her hiking boots that sheathed one foot...and one prosthetic leg attached at her knee.

Glancing around the table at one shocked person after another, Grace's eyes finally rested on my father. She said, "I promised the Wednesday Walkers that I would complete the Inca Trail sooner or later. And a promise is a promise." She considered Dad hard before her gaze bore into Helen. "My husband was there for me during my first bout with cancer. We never imagined that the second would lop off my leg."

Dad was still dumbstruck in his front-row seat before this miracle. Grace smiled kindly at him and said, "You look like you need another round."

"You walked the entire Inca Trail," Dad said, slow to comprehend.

"Every step of the way." She beamed at me. "I had good company."

"You're sexy to the end!" I called, raising my bottle of water. That seemed like the only appropriate toast.

We all cheered. At that moment, Quattro strode into the restaurant with his dad, both of them looking bleak and angry until they did a double take at Grace, half-naked on the table. The sight of their shock made us all laugh again.

"Now you may take a photo," Grace told me after hiking up her pants and buttoning them. She posed on the table, hands in the air, an impish grin lighting her face.

—m—

After Grace's big reveal, everyone demanded to know how she'd managed the trek. Casting a glance around to make sure no one was eavesdropping, I asked Quattro my own burning question: "Did you go . . . ?" But he shook his head, lips thinning as he glowered at his dad, then ate his ramen noodles in stoic silence. The conversation turned to the clear skies and whether they would hold long enough for the helicopters to land. That brought us right up to the four thousand tourists packed into this tiny town, each of them vying for a spot on the helicopters. The dank smell of tension permeated the streets.

Mom joked, "That's the scent of the unwashed."

We all knew better. My own sense of uneasiness only increased at the end of lunch, when Helen piped up to say that her dad had worked in a bunch of different emergencies, and that there was a tipping point when fear and desperation led to riots and worse. As we all accompanied Grace to the helipad, I could feel the entire town teetering on that sharp tipping point.

A crowd of gray-haired senior citizens was already waiting, most clinging to their luggage even though the orders had been to leave behind all nonessential items to maximize the number of people who could be squeezed onto the helicopter. One push on the flimsy gate that separated the impatient crowd from the path to the helipad, and the barrier would topple. And then all these elderly people who the Peruvian government wanted to protect would be trampled.

"You should grab the first helicopter that you can tomorrow morning," Grace urged us. I shot a quick glance at Quattro. The days were dwindling, if he wanted to honor his mother.

Now an armed Peruvian soldier, menacing in his military fatigues, pointed at Grace. As though we were planning on sneaking aboard the helicopter, he snapped, "Only her."

I lifted the camera to capture this farewell and framed Dad enfolding Grace in his arms, telling her in a tear-clogged voice, "I'm so sorry."

No one, least of all Grace, had to ask him what he was apologizing for.

"It feels like this place is going to implode." Grace's frown deepened. "You should go back to the casita now."

Mom smiled patiently at her. "We're your groupies, haven't you figured that out yet?"

"Yeah, and we're demanding an encore performance," I said, giving Grace a last hug.

"Don't tempt her!" Dad said; his old teasing tone was back. A glimmer of a smile danced on his lips before he handed Grace over to the soldier. On the basis of that expression alone, I felt like my family had already been airlifted to safety. But when I saw the forlorn look on Quattro's face, I made up my mind: I was going with him to Machu Picchu.

Chapter Twenty-Three

Other girls sneak out late at night to party or fool around with their boyfriends. But I was preparing to sneak out before dawn to hike to ancient ruins with a friend who was on a mission.

From the thick rug where I lay swaddled in comforters, I could trace the barest hint of pink lightening the sky through the window slats. Only a few clouds blocked the stars. If Quattro didn't attempt to break into Machu Picchu this morning, he might never get another chance.

Just as I was debating about whether to wake him, the door to the walk-in closet where he had been sleeping opened slowly. Quattro padded out to the living room in socks, holding his hiking boots. He must have slept with them so his dad couldn't hide them again. Last night, I had noticed that he'd stashed his backpack and rain gear behind the couch. He collected them now, as I rose from my nest of comforters and tip-toed after him.

"You can't come," he said in a low voice after I shut the front door softly behind us.

"Excuse me, free country," I reminded him as I laced up my hiking boots.

"No, this could be dangerous."

"Rule number one in hiking: Always go with a buddy."

He continued to shake his head.

Unstoppable now that I had committed to this, I continued, "Or no, because you want privacy? If it's that, I'll walk with you up to the point where you want to"—I paused, uncertain how to phrase it—"be with your mom." Then more firmly, I said, "I'm going with you."

He finally relented with a grudging "Fine."

We set off across the bridge that connected the hotel with the rest of the pueblo, skirting the barrier that blocked the road to the heritage site I thought I'd never see again. It was a good twenty-minute walk along a dirt road next to the river before we got to the trailhead. Time had done nothing to tame the seething river, and I was glad we'd be leaving it behind before long for the steep uphill climb. I stopped in front of the foot-bridge we had crossed three days earlier, still under assault. My pulse raced. If either of us slipped and fell into that deadly whirlpool, there was even less of a chance of survival. We only had each other.

Not far from the bridge, Mother Nature had provided her own barricade in the form of a fallen tree. This was as close to real photojournalism as I had ever come—encountering obstacles, flinging myself into the unknown. I was going to say as much to Quattro, but he was lost in his own thoughts. We barely exchanged any words on our rapid walk other than instructions: Watch out for that rock, careful over that slime. He needed solitude; I understood that. It wasn't every day that you laid your mother's ashes to rest.

For the next few minutes, I had to concentrate on my footing. We'd decided earlier that the trail through the jungle was the fastest way up to Machu Picchu, but littered as it was with wind-torn branches, our progress was slow. Quattro sighed, frustrated.

"We'll get there," I assured him.

His only answer was to push a low-hanging branch out of my way. I wished I had my old camera to zoom in on Quattro, staring at the trail ahead of us, ready to tackle any challenge handed to him: tough and resourceful, protective and well meaning. And irritating. Very irritating. He glanced at me after I clicked the shutter of his point-and-shoot. Even before I lowered the camera, I knew that I had captured something special.

"You want to turn back?" Quattro asked me, his first real words in half an hour, as he leaned his hand against a mossy tree trunk.

"Do you?" I asked.

He vaulted over another log that lay across the trail.

"Show-off," I said as I hoisted myself up on the fallen tree and swung both legs over. Not graceful, but it would do the trick.

"What does that make you?" he asked.

A hundred responses formulated in my head, few of them

G-rated. While I might not have said a word, I couldn't quite conceal the curve of my smile: challenging with just a hint of suggestiveness. I couldn't help it, really. As Quattro held my gaze, he shook his head at me with an expression I was still deciphering when he said in a low voice, "I give up."

He gave up? On me? On this mission? I frowned, confused.

"You're impossible to forget," he said. His tone was almost accusatory, but he stepped closer to me.

Ohhhhh. I breathed out. My lips softened into a smile. "That makes two of us."

Before my toes could even graze the trail, he caught me in his arms, held me so tight our bodies were imprinted on each other, and kissed me as if every bit of pent-up passion was unleashed in that moment. He pressed me back against the tree, his hands protecting me from the rough bark, and deepened the kiss. And then just as suddenly, he lifted his lips, both of us breathing hard, as we stared at each other.

"What happened to starting college without any ties?" I asked. I had to know.

"Ancient history."

"Prehistoric?"

"Mesozoic."

I smiled, pleased. He grinned, even more pleased.

The rushing in my head when he kissed me a second time, then a third, had little to do with altitude. Not that I would ever tell him. Boys, bravado, egos, and all that.

—ᴍ—

Our ascent to Machu Picchu was going to end up being much slower than the descent a few days before, and not just because we were plowing straight uphill. We kept stopping every couple of feet to kiss each other: the hollow at my throat, the side of his neck, our lips. Our lips. Our lips.

When we reached the first intersection between the trail and the road, we found the asphalt was even more treacherous, covered with mossy slime.

"You okay?" Quattro asked, reaching over for my hand to lead us across the road.

"Never better," I said softly. Even so, I gripped his hand tighter for the sheer pleasure of it.

"You know, most people wouldn't do this."

"I'm not most people."

"Definitely not." The sexy look he shot me could fill an entire bookshelf of romance novels.

A few minutes later, the evidence of another small mudslide lay before us once we'd crossed to the other side. More ragged branches torn from trees jutted out of a thick layer of mud. More ankle-twisting rocks. How many more slides were up ahead? How many more were waiting to unleash from these precarious slopes? What if we got trapped?

I shivered at the memory of our flattened tent. We would have been buried alive. I wondered what my parents were thinking this very moment, wondered about myself always plunging into things without full consideration. . . .

Far below us, the sound of the river had eased from enraged roar to warning growl. I ventured forward, fighting my fear, hiding my trembling by hugging my arms around myself. I refused to let Quattro know just how scared I was.

We started to hike, the mocking river filling the grooves of our silence. My foot slipped. The echo of my surprised cry reverberated around us.

I fell.

Chapter Twenty-Four

E ven Quattro with his lightning-fast reflexes couldn't arrest me as I skidded along the muddy asphalt. I slid fast. The sky became a blur of eye-poking branches and cheek-scratching bramble. I knew what waited for me below: a ravine with a straight shot down the steep slope. Drop over the cliff and some jungle plant would probably spear me. Adrenaline spiked as I grasped anything, clawed at everything to stop my flight. My torso torqued one way, my right leg the other. A painful jolt traveled the length of my left leg. Quattro grabbed my shoulders, jerking me to a stop before I sailed feet-first over the ledge.

Sharp pain. Everywhere.

I was too afraid to open my eyes, too afraid to assess the damage, too afraid to feel the pain.

"You're okay," Quattro said reassuringly, his hands gentle

on my shoulders now, his legs around me. He must have flung himself downhill to rescue me. More firmly, willing it to be true, he repeated, "You're okay."

My eyes dared to crack open. He wasn't on the other side of the river, abandoning me. He was hovering right over me, here, now.

"What hurts?" he asked, steady gaze fixed on me.

What didn't? Pain radiated from everywhere. Dull throbbing from landing hard on my tailbone. Sharp pangs at the back of my head from bouncing on the dirt. Knife stabs at my ankle.

"My pride," I answered, and flushed, hearing myself echo Stesha after her fall.

"Can you stand up?"

"I think so." But when Quattro placed his hands under my armpits, my ankle still gave out. Even with his arm wrapped around my waist, mine around his shoulders, I couldn't place much weight on my left leg. I gasped. My eyes watered. He tightened his hold. "My parents are going to kill me."

"Only after they're through with me," Quattro said, "and that might take them a while."

As lightly as I laughed at that, the movement jarred my body. I winced. "I think I need to rest for a second."

Leaning on Quattro, I hopped on my right foot, gingerly using my left big toe for balance. After a moment of that nonstarter, Quattro swept me up into his arms, glanced around briefly for a resting spot, and lowered me onto a boulder.

"We need to elevate your ankle," he said, gently propping my leg on the rock. After dropping his backpack to the ground,

Quattro crouched down to unzip it, rummaged inside, and pulled out a first aid kit, then handed me an Advil and a water bottle. As I swallowed the pill, he probed my ankle. As hard as I tried not to flinch, I failed.

"Sorry," Quattro said, kneeling next to me. He met my eyes. "It's starting to swell. We need to get a brace on this. It might hurt."

"I'm fine," I assured him.

Only then did he unroll an Ace bandage and begin loosening my hiking boot. Quickly, he wrapped my ankle, then replaced the boot. I winced as it slipped over my heel; he grimaced.

"I'm fine," I told him again.

Without another word, Quattro stood with his back to me, head bowed, back hunched. He could have been mistaken for praying except his arms were crossed over his chest, and his fingers were clenched in punishing grips around his sleeves, as though he were the one in pain. I'd have traded ten times more pain, a hundred times, to not be the one responsible for derailing his plans.

"You should go on," I told him. "You *have* to go on. I'll wait here for you."

What was I saying? It wasn't safe for him to set off alone. The trail was even darker up ahead. How was he going to see? Hadn't I just reminded Quattro earlier about the cardinal rule of hiking: Honor the buddy system. His own father had nearly dwindled away after one loss. What would Christopher do if anything happened to Quattro? What would I do?

"I'm not leaving you," Quattro said finally, turning back to me. His face was tired, defeated.

242

I teared up at that. "I'm so sorry."

He fell silent and angled away from me. I didn't blame him for that. What words could have exonerated me from this crushing guilt?

"God, I'm such an idiot," I blathered, needing to fill the silence between us. Needing him to know how terrible I felt. Softly, I said, "I know how important this was for you."

No response.

"I'm really sorry," I whispered.

More silence. I had ruined everything for him. It was a long time before Quattro managed to eke out "It was an accident." He shoved the backpack away and leaned against a rock across the narrow trail from me. Then he dropped his forehead on his knees.

In the private fantasyland in my head, I had pictured the two of us, the Bonnie and Clyde of World Heritage Sites, breaking and entering into Machu Picchu. I had constructed this whole image of us ducking under the turnstiles, hopping the fence, running into the sanctuary. But Quattro had lost so much more than an adventure; he'd lost his entire purpose in flying thousands of miles and trekking up narrow trails on rocky peaks.

"All I do is screw up, you know that?" he said, his eyes hot. "Why didn't I just force Dad to do this when we were right up there at the Sun Gate? We just thought we'd have another chance. A better day and more time and fewer people..."

And still, Quattro had allowed me to join him in what was an intensely private moment. I sniffled at that thought.

"This," I said, gesturing to my throbbing ankle, not that he could see, his head hanging low, "isn't your fault."

"I should have known this would fall apart. Everything does."

This Eeyore attitude reminded me of my father, who had been the farthest thing from a pessimist until his diagnosis. I frowned. "How could you have known that the road would have been washed out like this? You had nothing to do with me falling. I was the idiot who couldn't stay on my feet, not you. You just saved me from falling over the edge."

"But why did you have to fall *now*?" Immediately, he shook his head, frowning. "Sorry, I didn't mean that."

"No, you're right," I said, pausing. "The timing sucks."

Then it hit me, sitting here at the foot of Machu Picchu, which itself was a mystery. No one could tell Dad why he was suffering from a disease that typically struck men half his age. Or why I had to fall now. There was no explanation: It just happened.

After a moment of waffling, I scrambled for the camera in my jacket pocket, hesitating another second before pulling up the panoramic view of Machu Picchu on the morning we'd stepped through the Sun Gate.

"How'd the Incas make this?" I asked, leaning forward to hand him the camera. Huge rocks had been hauled up the mountain, then hand hewn into interlocking rectangles that fit so tightly against each other a knife blade couldn't slide through the joints. "I mean, these people didn't even have the wheel! If we can't answer that, how can we possibly know the real purpose they had for Machu Picchu?" Quattro's silence had grown icier with my every word, but I forged stubbornly ahead, want-

244

ing so badly for him to see the truth. "So maybe there's a reason why you can't leave your mom's ashes here right now, and we just don't know it yet."

"You don't get it," he said quietly, too quietly.

I gulped, wishing that I could reel back time. I had over-stepped. And what did I know anyway?

"You know how my mom died?" he asked, his jaw jutting out.

"You said it was a car accident."

His snort was derisive and self-punishing. He wrapped his arms around his bent legs, hands grasping each other so tightly his knuckles went white. I wanted to tell him to stop; he was hurting himself, but this time, I knew to be quiet. To listen.

"We had had an argument that morning. Door-slamming, I-hate-you kind of fight. You know, she had texted me. Apologized to me. Apologized. And I responded." He lifted his head to look me in the eye as though I were the judge and executioner. "You know what I said?"

I shook my head.

"Fuck off." His voice was pure anguish, but he forced himself to continue: "And she was answering my text when the truck slammed into her. She was telling me she loved me...."

"Quattro."

"I'm the reason she died."

What words could possibly console him? Not any of mine. When I reached out for Quattro, his answer was to stand abruptly. In a voice gone flat, devoid of emotion, he told me, "We should head down if you're ready."

Anybody eavesdropping on us would have thought I was a stranger, not the woman he had kissed just minutes ago as if his future depended on me being in it.

I managed a fighting smile, gritted my teeth, and told him, "I'll hop all the way back to town if I have to."

"That's my girl," he said before his face stiffened at those inadvertent words, regretting them. And me.

Chapter Twenty-Five

D ad may have been going blind, but his hearing worked just fine. Then again, mountaineers on Everest, miles above sea level, could have heard Mom's sharp cry when she spotted me hobbling toward the hotel's bridge: "Shana!"

Fury thundered in Dad's every step toward us. "Where the hell have you been?"

But Mom elbowed Dad aside; her angry frown had already transformed into an expression of fierce concern. She raced to me, inspecting me from head to toe first with her eyes, then with her hands.

"Mom!" I protested.

But did she back off? Still probing my scalp to determine whether I had sustained a head wound, Mom demanded, "What happened?"

"I just twisted my ankle. It's nothing," I said, pulling away as she lowered to a squat. Oh, dear Lord. Now what? I hopped back. She followed. "Mom. Mom. I'm okay." I sighed as she went all Red Cross on me, now poking at the swollen skin that covered what used to be my bony ankle. "Ow."

Satisfied, Mom said, "We should get some ice on this, but surprise, surprise, there isn't any." She sighed, frustrated. "Where *were* you? The helicopters have been flying all morning, and you weren't here."

An excuse! How had I totally and completely forgotten to craft the perfect, reasonable, and plausible excuse for sneaking out to Machu Picchu this morning? Quattro and I had had hours to coordinate our story, but our return trip couldn't have been more awkward, me limping with his arm around my waist, both of us sweating, neither saying a single thing. I was too busy trying not to cry, apologize, wince, or groan to come up with anything.

It was Quattro's father who answered for us: "They went to Machu Picchu."

"You could have been killed!" Mom's voice teetered on the fine line between anger and fear.

"What were you thinking?" Dad demanded before he turned to Quattro, his curt words damning: "You put her at risk."

Quattro hung his head, ashamed.

"It was my fault," I said, unable to stand his defeated expression, especially when I knew he already held himself responsible for my accident, and worse.

248

"No," Quattro said, straightening as he looked at my parents. "You're right. It was my fault."

"I volunteered to go with him," I said.

Dad held up his hand to stop any more words, studying me with disappointment. I couldn't meet his eyes, so I lowered mine. "We don't have time for excuses. We'll be lucky if we get on the helicopter now." As hard as his tone was, Dad placed his arm around me gently, taking over from Quattro as my human crutch.

"Quattro." Christopher sighed, the lines around his mouth deepening. "This was a total breakdown in judgment. I'm not sure what you were thinking when I told you no, but—" There was a pause. "I understand."

The barest sigh escaped Quattro. Maybe those two words were his own private Machu Picchu, which he had been trekking toward all this time. When I glanced over my shoulder back at Quattro, he had already disappeared, leaving his father alone on the bridge.

—⚏—

At least five hundred people were gathered in front of the flimsy gate at the makeshift helipad. No wonder my parents were so upset that I hadn't been around earlier. My ears were filled with competing needs: "My son! I need to be with him!" and "I've got a heart condition!" And those were just the sentences I could pick out in English from the torrent of languages. However tough the few soldiers looked, outfitted in their

249

uniforms and armed with their machine guns, they didn't seem prepared for the animal panic that swept through the crowd.

A helicopter lifted from the ground, the wind from its twin blades blowing my hair loose from my ponytail. The sight of the departing helicopter caused people to jostle more vigorously. Mom nearly lost her balance. She grabbed Dad's arm just as he tugged her tight. He glanced quickly over his shoulder to make sure I was close. I was—but only because Christopher acted as my battering ram. Where Quattro was right now, I didn't know, but I kept scanning the crowds for him. Nothing.

My eardrums throbbed from the chopper, so much louder than I had imagined. I watched it fly away. I just wanted to stay, unready to leave despite my injured ankle. Hazel eyes so similar to Quattro's focused on me now as Christopher said, "Thank you."

"For what? Being stupid?"

"For being his friend."

I highly doubted that Christopher knew about the real guilt weighing down his son. But it didn't seem like my place to share that confidence, especially when I couldn't say for sure that Quattro even considered me a friend, not the way he had rushed off without saying good-bye. Not when he was so point-edly absent now.

"I'm sorry you weren't able to get to Machu Picchu for your wife," I told Christopher, grasping his waist even tighter as the crowd around us shifted.

"Lisa herself would have said this was a sign that it wasn't meant to be. Kylie's not here. And I wasn't with you two this morning."

At these absolving words, I burst into tears. I had said as much to Quattro, but hearing it from someone else lifted a burden from me.

"Don't cry," he said, sounding so much like Quattro that I ached, literally ached for him.

I sniffled and cleared my throat. "Do you think you'll try again?"

"I'm not sure. Maybe we're supposed to wait and see."

"You know what Stesha would say? That once you let go of your plan, you might find something better."

"That's wise." Christopher looked at me closely. "You might want to remember that yourself."

From a distance came the unmistakable sound of the second helicopter arriving, its blades slicing through the air. The crowd surged forward. I would have been trampled if it weren't for Christopher holding me upright. The scene felt so familiar. I knew why. How many news reports had I watched with this exact setup? Frightened people, scarce resources, armed military. What would it take for one of the soldiers to open fire if the crowd's panic tipped into pandemonium?

Even so, I wondered whether I was supposed to stay. Maybe my purpose on the trip hadn't been fulfilled. But Christopher led me forward to keep in step with my parents. The weary official guarding the gateway scrutinized our faces, then glowered down at our passports. While he did, I murmured to my parents, "Maybe we should stay?"

Irritated, the man frowned, his skin pleating. He all but yelled, "If you're staying, get out of the line."

"We're going," Mom said firmly. "She is hurt. I am fifty-five, and my husband is going blind. We are leaving now."

I blinked at Mom as if I had never seen her before. So did Dad as Mom glared at everyone in a full three-sixty, challenging anyone stupid enough to deny us. Now, this was a woman who could coauthor a Fifty by Fifty Manifesto that spanned every continent and all adventures from dogsledding to surfing. This was the mother who'd threatened to shave my head if I got married before thirty.

"Welcome back, Mom," I told her.

She frowned, not understanding. "What?"

I just shook my head and nodded at the official, who was at last opening the gate. Everything moved in double time then. Christopher let go of me, and I would have toppled if it weren't for the changing of the guard. Dad grabbed me, holding Mom with one hand, me tucked under his other arm.

Almost with a mind of their own, words flew out of my mouth as I glanced back at Christopher: "Ask Quattro about what really happened between him and his mom."

I didn't have a chance to check whether he heard my parting words, much less thank him properly for his help. In a wild rush, the crowd became a vengeful river, roiling and surging. Dad yanked me through the opening in the gate. In her haste, Mom dropped some cash. She didn't notice. Everyone behind us was in such a panic to reach the descending helicopter that no one bothered to scoop up the fallen bills. I tripped. Dad righted me and tugged me along. I protested and scanned the crowd desperately for one last look for Quattro.

"Wait!" I cried.

Dad didn't listen, just lunged ahead.

The deafening whir of the helicopter was upon us. A group of soldiers motioned to us to crouch down and creep forward as though we were ambushing the aircraft. Creep? I could only crawl. My ankle throbbed. I could feel it swelling but ignored the pain. Once we neared the helicopter, the soldiers helped my parents to pile in, only to scowl at me when I lost my balance. I blushed. Two of them manhandled me into the cabin.

I thought I spotted Quattro, standing apart from the crowd in his unmistakable orange fleece. Prisoner orange.

But the helicopter lifted, and the crowd blurred. And Machu Picchu was just a memory, left behind.

Part Three

At some point in life the world's beauty becomes
enough. You don't need to photograph, paint or
even remember it. It is enough.

—Toni Morrison

Chapter Twenty-Six

Two days later, I was headed home, loaded down with a bleak novel Mom had pushed on me that I'd never read no matter how good for me it was supposed to be, a PowerBar I felt nauseous just thinking about, and a camera that wasn't mine. On our drive back to the airport in Cusco, the last sight of the cathedral had made me want to grab a return flight on a rescue helicopter to Machu Picchu Pueblo, track Quattro down, and order him to stop blaming himself for accidents.

But the official plan was for me to fly with Stesha back to Seattle after I saw my parents off on their flight to Belize. Ash would meet them tonight at their hotel. Barring any further disasters, natural or man-made, by tomorrow midmorning, the three of them would be knocking off one more of my parents' Fifty by Fifty adventures: scuba diving with manta rays.

"I still don't know about this," Mom said, frowning at my crutches while we waited for them to board.

"Mom, it's just a small sprain." I shifted my weight to my good foot and lifted the crutches like wings. "See? I'm totally fine."

"Ack! Stop! You're not in the Cirque du Soleil. And you sound scarily like Stesha."

I smiled, knowing that I did. Earlier in the same hotel lobby where we'd started our trip, Stesha had brushed off everyone's concerns about her getting on an airplane, huffing over our protests, "It was just a small concussion." Then more emphatically, "Not a single line of research suggests that flying after a concussion is dangerous."

Dad now returned from the airport gift shop, holding a plastic bag.

"What'd you buy?" Mom asked.

"Just a few things," he said evasively. Then to Mom he said, "You might want to use the bathroom before they call our flight. You know how you love the toilets on planes. . . ."

At that apt reminder, Mom hustled off to the restroom, and Dad thrust his bouquet of olive branches on me: a couple of fashion and gossip magazines in Spanish and a bar of dark chocolate.

"Hurry," he said, gesturing for my bag, "give me the book and the PowerBar."

I laughed as we traded. How well Dad knew me. Over the last day, we had reached a détente of sorts. He'd relented after I explained why Quattro and I had tried to make a mad dash up to Machu Picchu, not for cheap thrills but on a serious mission.

Still, Dad carried a fatherly grudge. "What really bothers me

258

is that he put his needs before your safety," he had said last night during dinner at the closest restaurant to our hotel. Then, he spat out one name—"Hank"—as if that were shorthand for selfishness and cowardice. "You can be friends with him, all right? Nothing more."

"That's not fair. Quattro's not a Hank," I had protested. "And Hank isn't so bad. He let us stay in his casita, remember?"

"She has a point," Mom had agreed, spearing two pieces of chicken on her fork as if she couldn't shovel in the food fast enough. I don't think any of us had ever been so ravenous for a hot meal.

Dad had started harrumphing, but I'd interrupted. "Dad, if Mom told you that she wanted to commemorate Grandma up on Everest, you would figure out a way to make it happen. And you'd go with her. I know you would."

Mom had leaned her shoulder against his, nodding over her wineglass as she angled a loving look at him. "She's right, you know."

As I dropped Dad's peace offerings into my tote bag, I felt myself softening. Our family had made a pact not to spend a single unnecessary penny or sol while on this trip. And here was Dad, trying to take care of me and smooth things over between us. I didn't want us to leave angry or awkward with each other either, not when I now knew how life could blindside us, a life-changing diagnosis here, a dream-ending mudslide there. From overhead speakers, a woman's deep voice called their flight. All around us, travelers sprang from their seats, ready to leave this flood-damaged region.

Mom returned from the bathroom, smelling of antiseptic soap. She hugged me tight, pulled back, and scowled at my wrapped ankle. "It still doesn't seem right to send you home alone. And damaged!"

"Mom. I'm not damaged. And I'll be with Stesha."

"And here we are," she continued, "off to have fun when all these poor people lost everything in the flood..."

"We'll figure out a way to help, but I think we're supposed to keep on living," Dad said, placing a kiss on the top of Mom's head.

"Now you sound like Stesha," she teased lightly, and beamed at him.

Dad swept me into one final rib-crushing embrace before he draped his arm easily around Mom's shoulder. That's when my photographer radar went into high alert. The moment was coming, and I discreetly pulled out the camera I kept tucked in my front pocket.

"Thank you," Dad told Mom. His eyes were full of her. "You made this trip happen."

"No, *we* did." Mom teared up. I did, too.

"All of us did," Dad agreed.

They smiled like they were seeing each other for the first time, back in their twenties again, newly in love. But strands of gray streaked their hair, and as youthful as they looked, their faces were yielding to time. Fine lines radiated from the corners of their eyes and bracketed their lips. Their love wasn't shiny and new, but one that had been tested and toughened. It would last. As Dad passed through the door first, I captured them in the exact moment when his hand reached back for hers.

Well-heeled Japanese tourists, the men in crisp linen shirts and the women wearing dainty sandals and pulling matching luggage sets, made me feel like an ungainly slob in my beat-up hiking boots. I hobbled on my crutches toward my gate and was struck again by the airport bustling with bathed people, the air pungent with aromas from restaurants. Machu Picchu Pueblo—and the stranded, homeless, unwashed tourists—seemed an entire planet and lifetime away. Quattro . . . Was he safe? Did he make it out? Why hadn't he contacted me?

Dressed in eye-popping teal and purple, Stesha was impossible to miss at the gate. The way she'd managed to pull together a colorful outfit for less than fifteen dollars in her one hour of power shopping yesterday was impressive. Even more impressive, she actually looked stylish sitting there in her hiking boots, woven skirt, and patched-up chin. I photographed her, my new muse for TurnStyle. That is, she would be my muse if I decided to maintain the site. After the mudslide and the photos I'd shot in its aftermath, I knew I couldn't focus solely on fashion anymore. What my new oeuvre was, I hadn't decided, and I was cool with not knowing.

Nearing Stesha, I noticed her deep frown as she read a message on her phone, one she had insisted on purchasing en route to the hospital in Cusco. According to Grace, she had refused to step foot in any hospital ward until she had a way to make arrangements for us.

"What's wrong?" I asked Stesha as I settled on the free seat across from her.

261

Her thumbs jabbed the keyboard as if that would make her message clearer. As she typed, she said, "Well, the good news is that everyone else is being evacuated today."

"Quattro? And his dad?"

"And Helen and Hank. Ruben's leaving today to trek back."

I breathed out, feeling twenty pounds lighter. They were all safe. Stesha set down her phone within easy reach. Her eyes lit up just the way intrigue could make Reb's glow: boy talk! Lucky me, we were going to have hours—hours!—together aboard the flight, first to Houston, then to Seattle, to dissect my feelings.

"You know," Stesha said, nodding approvingly, "Quattro's one of the good guys."

I shrugged. "Maybe, but he's not relationship ready."

"Interesting how he keeps showing up in your life, though. You met him in Seattle. You ran into him in Cusco. He looked for you after the mudslide. In my book, that means one thing: Pay attention."

"Yeah, well, I'm paying attention to the fact that he's going to college in a couple of months." Not to mention our walk in silence back to town, topped off with our non-good-bye.

"There are seasons for everything." Stesha laughed wryly at herself, reaching down to adjust her phone so she could see it better. And people think that kids my age have a problem being tethered to our devices. Right. "I sound like a fortune cookie!"

I grinned. "A little bit."

"I guess what I'm trying to say is that you never know what could happen."

"Wait a minute. I thought you could prophesy everything?"

262

"No, not at all. But I've got a good instinct when it comes to people."

"If anything, whatever Quattro and I—" I motioned helplessly in the air because I had no idea how to even define what we had.

"Shared?" Stesha prompted.

I nodded. "Whatever we shared had more to do with being here. I mean, the Inca Trail! Isn't it kind of like all the celebrities falling in love on movie sets? And we all know how long those relationships last." According to the tabloids that Dad had bought for me, Hollywood breakups transcend language, culture, and country. I tapped the cover photo of two unhappy-looking superstars underneath a bold headline—ACABO DE ROMPER—as proof. "See?"

"Not really. No," said Stesha, shaking her head once, then more emphatically so that her curls bounced around her cheeks. "How could you go on a journey with someone and face a disaster without getting to know them? Really getting to know them?"

"That's what Grace says."

"She's right. What you two went through—the trekking. The mudslides. His mother. And this"—she pointed at my ankle wrapped in a bandage—"I mean, this entire trip was nothing but a character test. And that boy passed with flying colors. He keeps showing up. Do you know how rare that is?"

Before I could answer, Stesha's phone lit up with a new text. "Oh, it's from Grace. Do you mind?"

"Tell her I miss her," I said, glad for some time to think. I replayed how Quattro had raced to me after the mudslide. He had looked for me. He had carried Stesha in air so thin, drawing a deep breath was hard work. He had literally given the shirt off his back to a kid. He had kissed me. . . .

Unable to dwell in those memories without feeling heartsick, I returned to people watching while Stesha texted a few messages in reply. Here in this heated airport, where a few women tottered around in five-inch heels and businesspeople were stuck to their phones, trekking on a half-millennium-old trail seemed as far-fetched as hoping that things would work out with Quattro. I didn't even know what working out meant where it concerned him.

"Grace wanted you to know that she was thinking of you," Stesha said as she placed the phone in her lap. A divot of concern lay between her eyebrows again.

"What's wrong? Is she okay?" We had met Grace last night for dessert, all of us sighing over the dense chocolate cake. "Her leg, is it okay after all that walking?"

"No, no, she's fine. Well, actually, she's upset. Have you been following the news?"

"Not closely, no."

"Well, you're not missing much. No one's talking about the flood in Peru, not here. And according to Grace, not in the States. She did a little digging, and none of the big three relief agencies have collected much in the way of donations."

"That's exactly what Quattro said would happen." I flushed as Stesha's eyebrows lifted. Quattro again. Hastily, I asked, "What's that about?"

"Yesterday, it was a mudslide in Peru. Tomorrow, it's an

earthquake in Bali. Or a hurricane in Louisiana." She pursed her lips. "People are fatigued."

"But all these villagers that we just left... they lost *everything*."

"Well, what can anyone do?" Stesha asked, more curious than philosophical.

The exact question echoed in my mind. What good could any of my photographs do if they only stayed on the SD card? If I was the only one who viewed them? "If you want to make a difference," Dom had lectured me, sounding like he'd come straight out of one of his MBA classes, "you need to make a video. With all the magazines folding and the ubiquity of camera phones, anyone can be a photographer these days. There's nothing special about what you do."

But he was wrong. I had spent a lifetime literally framing my view of the world on photo safaris, first with Dad, then on my own. I had watched my mom create visual narratives for countless executives. And in my hand, I held a camera loaded with still photos and video footage of the mudslide.

Make a video.

Slowly, I said, "I think I might have an idea."

"I thought you would."

"What if we produced a video about the mudslide?" I asked, mulling out loud. In my mind, I could already envision the opening sequence: a black screen. The ominous sound of the river. "Short, maybe two minutes, and we put it on your website? And distributed it to all of your clients? And we can put it on my blog. It's such a puny effort, but—"

"But that's how you start a revolution," Stesha said, already

265

jotting notes in the notebook she'd bought yesterday. "I like it. How much work is this going to take?"

"I don't know. I've never made one. . . . Well, other than a couple of little movies for physics and history," I said, already doubting myself. What was I offering? I knew less about making a video than I did about chemistry. "I'm just a photographer, and not even that, really. I take pictures of street fashion."

Stesha snapped her notebook closed. "The so-called man who told you that was threatened by you."

My breath caught. Protest all she wanted about her divination skills, but of course, Stesha would know the truth. And more surprisingly, I actually heard it ring pitch-perfect inside me. She was right. For whatever reason, Dom was threatened by me: that I had told him no, I wasn't going to sleep with him on our first date or our seventh, words he may never have heard from any woman. That I had exciting plans for my own life that didn't revolve around his. That I had opinions of my own that didn't center on flattering him. That I showed promise and talent. And that I thrummed with passion for life and adventure.

The way Stesha tightened her lips and rapped the phone with an agitated fingertip, I knew she was fighting hard not to say anything she might regret. Finally, she asked, "Did it ever occur to you that he was diminishing you as a way to control you?"

I shook my head, even as strobe lights were lighting my brain. "But he was so successful."

"I'm sure he was."

"I thought he knew what he was talking about. He had awesome ideas about building my senior portrait business."

266

"I'm sure he did." Stesha continued, "But, honey, of course, you don't know how to make a video. You'll learn on the job the way all of us do. I don't think we're supposed to spring out of the womb fully formed like Athena with every bit of knowledge embedded in us."

"Right." A huge balloon of self-doubt popped inside me. "You're right!"

"Good. So between Grace and me, we can reach out to the relief agencies. I have friends at the Red Cross. And Grace has contacts at World Vision." Stesha reopened her notebook and scribbled a nearly indecipherable sentence. "Who knows? They may want to add this to their own efforts." Even as she wrote, Stesha's lips curled into a smile. "And just where did this brilliant inspiration for a video come from, Ms. Shana Wilde?"

The impossibility of this truth made me rumble with a deep belly laugh. "Out of one guy's doubt."

"Well, I've always found that one person's dead end is another person's on-ramp."

"On-ramp," I repeated, staring down at the camera I was holding, already poised to shoot whatever I wanted, "I would have that tattooed on the inside of my arm, but I don't think I'll ever forget it."

Chapter Twenty-Seven

Bowing to my heated protests that I didn't need a babysitter, Mom had reluctantly arranged for Stesha to simply drop me off at home. Soon after we cleared customs at the Sea-Tac Airport, Stesha launched herself at a grizzled man in a plaid shirt and worn-out jeans, waiting for her at the top of the escalator with a steaming traveler's mug that smelled of coconut and tea.

"How did you know this was just what I needed?" she squealed at George, her former husband and current boyfriend.

The answer was in George's tender expression, which softened the ridgelines of his craggy face: *Because I know you.*

Suddenly, I felt a pang of loneliness because no one had been counting the minutes, anxious for my return. No one had been waiting for me with my favorite hot drink in his hand. No one had carved out time to drive to the airport, eager to bring me home. That feeling was slightly muted when Stesha's phone rang and she handed it to me. My parents with their lifeline of love. As much as I assured them that I had reached Seattle in one piece, I was lying. How could I be whole when a big huge part of me was lost in the mountains of Peru? Where Quattro was and how he was doing was a mystery. Even if he had a cell, I wasn't convinced he'd pick up if I called.

I had barely hugged Stesha and George good-bye at the front door to our cottage when I caught the scent of freshly baked biscuits. Without needing to turn the porch light on, I knew Mrs. Harris was near. She trudged up the steps with a large wicker basket on her arm.

"You're alive!" Mrs. Harris cried as though we were across the yard from each other instead of separated by a few feet. "Oh, my! I was so worried about you when you didn't come home on time. And just look at you! Skin and bones. Don't those Peruvians know how to cook?" She thrust a hot biscuit at me. "Here. Eat. You're two-dimensional."

"Mrs. Harris! You didn't need to do this," I protested, but I bit hungrily into sweet, buttery paradise. I groaned. "This is life changing."

Only then did Mrs. Harris notice my crutches, which launched another series of questions and exclamations, punctuated by an "I knew that trip was going to be dangerous!" Finally, she waved me into my own home. I was slightly annoyed when she followed me in until her lips quivered and she wailed, "I just missed you and your parents so much! And Auggie!"

269

"Mrs. Harris..."

"Then I heard about the mudslides. But after that first report on the news, there wasn't any information. My goodness, I was so worried! You have no idea!"

Here it was, another nudge to create a video of the wreckage. I almost raised my eyes heavenward and cried out, *Girls! Okay, okay, I'm paying attention! I'll start the video tomorrow.*

With an *oomph*, Mrs. Harris set the heavy basket down on the kitchen table and mopped the sweat from her forehead, looking exhausted. I could imagine why: She handled stress the same way Ginny did. They both baked. We're not talking about slinging a dozen chocolate chip cookies into the oven. No, that's amateur hour. We're talking about marathon baking by the batches, multiple batches.

I asked, "Mrs. Harris, what did you do?"

With a small self-conscious smile, she lifted the pink-checkered kitchen towel draped over the basket to reveal a treasure trove of bite-size brownies, biscuits, and an assortment of containers. The last of my annoyance melted away at the sight of all this food. Every last stir and spoonful was for me.

"Blame it on that Anderson Cooper," Mrs. Harris continued, shoving another biscuit at me before unloading the basket. "When even he didn't say so much as a peep—not a single peep, I tell you—on CNN about the mudslides, I just about turned into a Keebler elf."

"You think?"

We both laughed. Now that the basket had been emptied, Mrs. Harris looked around uncertainly, lost without a purpose, and I thought guiltily about how rarely we had invited her over for a meal.

"Well," she said, patting my hand, "you must be so tired with all that to-ing and fro-ing. I'll just say good night."

For Mrs. Harris, the pathway between her cottage and ours might as well have been the Inca Trail. Her life had shrunk pin-prick small since her husband's death, and I had done nothing but grumble whenever she beckoned me to her porch, always with a kind word and a homemade treat. If there was anyone who needed to rejoin the world, it was Mrs. Harris. And if there was anyone who ought to invite her, it was me.

"There's way too much food in here for one person," I said, pointing at the bounty on the table. "You should stay and eat with me."

"You're too tired."

"Come on, Mrs. Harris. Stay."

"Maybe for a little bit." She grinned at me, almost giddy, and I wondered just how lonely she was. Her children rarely visited. She had no one but our cottage community for company.

All through my hobbling around the kitchen to set the table, then through the entire meal itself, I found myself fielding her rapid-fire questions about the trip. Finally, when we had devoured two cookies apiece, I reached the part when Grace revealed her prosthetic leg, miming her striptease as much as I could on my one good leg.

"Whoa, this sprain makes me really appreciate what she did," I said, lowering myself back onto the chair.

"I think that woman would scare me," Mrs. Harris said, brushing the crumbs off her lap. It was strange not to hear the scuffling of Auggie's paws as she scrambled to lick the floor clean, but Aunt Margie was supposed to drop her off tomorrow after work. I couldn't wait.

"Well, maybe a little bit, but you'd love her," I said. Between the helicopter and the plane and the pueblo and Cusco and now this conversation, I had lost track of time. I straightened in my chair and exclaimed, "You know what we're going to do tomorrow?"

"What?" Mrs. Harris asked, cocking her head to the side.

"We're going on a walk. After school."

"You're on crutches."

"Trust me, a little thing like that wouldn't stop Grace. So it's definitely not going to stop me." And I hoped Mrs. Harris heard my unspoken words: It definitely shouldn't be stopping you. After demolishing two heaping plates of food, I leaned back in my chair, feeling bloated and ready for bed.

But then Mrs. Harris said the magic words: "Let's see your pictures."

I wanted to review them myself, only privately. Automatically, I said, "Oh, not yet. There are hundreds, and you don't want to look at them all."

"I do," said Mrs. Harris staunchly.

"Half of them might be terrible. And all the photos from the early part of the trip were taken by someone else. I was just borrowing this camera."

"Enough with the caveats!" said Mrs. Harris, her words softened with a smile. "I really would love to know what you saw."

How could I deny that request when I might hear the very same plea from Dad one day? So I gestured for her to follow me to the living room, where I retrieved Quattro's camera from the tote bag, then slid the SD card into the computer I had left down-stairs before the trip. I held the laptop between us on the couch and started at the beginning with the photos Quattro had shot: me, photographing the Goliath-size boulders in the ruins outside of Cusco. Me, admiring beautiful orchids, tenacious for life. Me, laughing with Grace as she yelled, "Sexy to the end!" Sharing a look of concern with Mom. Listening intently to a story that Ruben was telling.

"Whose camera did you borrow?" Mrs. Harris asked, leaning back into the plush pillows.

I stared at the image of me, taken from up high on the trail, as I gazed out at the fog-covered mountains, my profile dreamy and soft. Quietly, I said, "Just a guy."

"Well, you're obviously not just a girl to him."

"No, it's nothing like that. I don't think we're even friends, not really."

"Shana, let me tell you something." Mrs. Harris gently covered my hand. "No man ever takes this many pictures of someone he doesn't care about. Maybe you need to let him know how you feel about him."

—m—

Later, after Mrs. Harris called it a night and I locked the door behind her, the house was quiet. Too quiet. The familiar whiff of cedar and pinecones may have smelled like home, but it didn't feel like home without Mom warbling off tune, Auggie pattering from one set of cold feet to another, Dad prepping for the next morning's running, biking, or hiking adventure.

Holding my crutches in one hand and the handrail with the other, I hobbled up to my bedroom, feeling fortunate to call this space mine. In fact, our small cottage now seemed palatial compared to our tent. Tired, I set Quattro's camera down on my desk. A moment later, my cell phone, which I had left charging at my bedside, rang. All feelings of weariness disappeared. I lunged for it, hoping, hoping, hoping. But it was my brother Max, his smile beaming back at me from a photo I had shot of him long ago.

After spending the last year avoiding Max, I was a little worried about this conversation. I needn't have been. His first "Shana!" was so enthusiastic, he might have been throwing his arms around me. As usual, he spoke at warp speed, squeezing a billion thoughts into a minute: *How's your ankle? Bloated up like a sausage? Can you believe you were in a mudslide? So were you doing early training for the Tough Mudder, or what? What do you mean, you don't know about the Tough Mudder? It's this obstacle course race designed by the British Special Forces. There's an event where you crawl through mud under barbed wire. One wrong move, and BAM! You get literally nailed. Blood streaming from your head. So you wanna do it with me?*

The barrage suddenly stopped. Silence is never golden when it comes to Max. It's molten with burning questions. I braced myself by picking up the camera, switching it back on.

Max didn't disappoint, saying bluntly, "I've been meaning to apologize about being a dick."

I grimaced and moved to the comfort of my bed. "Do we have to do this now?"

"We should have done this months ago! Look, I shouldn't have barged into your life like that."

"Yeah, it was humiliating."

But Max's so-called betrayal was nothing more than him being overprotective, no different from Dad's response to my sprained ankle. And no different from why I had wanted to barge in on Helen's life and ask her what the heck she was doing with a narcissist like Hank. He may have had some redeeming characteristics, but he was still so self-absorbed, there was no room in a relationship for more than him and his ego.

"I was an asshole," Max said.

"Nah, I know you pest-controlled him because you cared."

"Pest-controlled?" Startled into laughter, he asked, "What are you talking about?"

"Scare tactics. You know how we use vibrations to scare off moles? Well, you yelling at Dom pretty much did that."

"Whoa, pest controlling."

"Yeah, in front of half the business school."

He groaned. "I thought you were going to die on the spot."

"I would have if the party had been in a frat. I would never have lived that down. You know how many kids from our school go to UW, right? People would have talked about that until I was eighty." Mortifying almost a year ago, humorous now. Max's boom of laughter reminded me of all the times he had tossed keys, balls, and my own stuffed animals at me to "train" my reflexes. All the hours he'd spent with me at parks, teaching me the art of throwing the perfect spiraling football. He was the real reason why I was so comfortable with guys, able to joke around with them, hold my own.

I told Max in a soft voice, "To be honest, I'm glad you did what you did."

"What the hell was I thinking?"

"It was love," I said, remembering what Quattro had told me. "Love makes everyone a little crazy."

Max cleared his throat, uncomfortable with the love talk. "Well, you better tell your new guy—"

"There is no new guy!"

"Not according to Mom. So if the new guy does anything to hurt you, I'm kicking his butt."

"You taught me to kick butt on my own."

"That's because you're one Tough Mudder."

"I am."

"Great, I'll send you the training schedule. Not sure how we'll train for the Arctic Enema. Or the Electroshock Therapy. But we'll figure it out."

"The what? Wait, I'm not signing up—"

"Awesome. See you after Guatemala." I heard a last evil cackle before the dial tone buzzed in my ear. I grinned. My brother was back.

—ౡ—

Jet lag, a full belly, and a long day of travel should have left me catatonic, but the conversation with Max had pumped me up too much to sleep. Possibly the image of plunging into a floating iceberg abyss in the Tough Mudder and hauling myself out before I went hypothermic had something to do with my insomnia. So I braved the stairs—not the easiest task on a sprained ankle— and retrieved the computer I had left downstairs. Hopping one-legged back up the steps with the laptop under my arm, I felt like I was already training for the obstacle race.

Safe on my bed, I opened the computer. While I may have skipped through the photos Quattro had taken of me, I was snagged on Mrs. Harris's pronouncement: I wasn't just a girl to him. But what if she was wrong? The thought made me so sad that I scrolled through the photos, picking a random one to open. Stesha, standing next to a gnarled tree wearing the same soul-seeking expression when she asked me what I was supposed to learn in Peru: What's your purpose for being here?

I leaned back against my pillows, as answers rushed at me. Maybe I needed to witness my dad pest-controlling Grace. Maybe that was the only way I could see the effect of all my boy control techniques on guys. Maybe I was meant to fall for Quattro, a guy on a strict no-girl diet, just so I'd know how it felt to be pest-controlled myself. Who knew?

What I did know for sure was that I had let Quattro go because I was afraid to fight for him.

What was the purpose of living in a safe, secluded, impenetrable bubble of one?

Girls! I could easily imagine Grace tipping her head to yell up at the sky. Girls! That doesn't sound like living.

No, it didn't.

Neither Stesha nor Grace would ever have allowed real love to fall through the cracks. I wouldn't either.

Chapter
Twenty-Eight

Some people might call it stalking, others sleuthing. I had the sneaking suspicion that Grace and Stesha would have named it search and rescue. But for me, I was seeking. Forty-five minutes after looking for Quattro, I finally remembered that I had blocked his e-mail, which meant I'd had his address all this time. Before I could chicken out, I composed a message, which I rewrote. Then rewrote again. It's amazing how much time it took to choose fifty-six words.

> Hey, Quattro,
> Did you and your dad get home OK? I hope so, but let me know. Plus, I've got your camera and need to get it back to you. I think

I owe you at least a dozen bacon maple bars. Maybe two. Let me know when you want to collect. I miss you.

xome

Hitting Send only led to an endless cycle of second-guessing: *The "xo" might have been okay by itself, but why did I have to add the "I miss you"?* I studied the shadows on my ceiling, kicking myself for tipping my hand too much. I should have kept it to a casual, hey-buddy "Miss ya!" But I knew I wanted to signal that I girlfriend-cared about him, not friend-cared.

Finally, I gave up on trying to sleep and spent two hours sketching the storyboard for the video and drafting what I wanted to say in only ninety seconds. By the time I finished with that, it was almost one, and I should have gone to sleep. Call me compulsive, but I thought I might as well drop in the images and footage that I had shot. At three, I yawned and finally pressed Save.

At last, I slid the computer off to the side on my bed, too tired to place it on my nightstand or set it on the floor. Even after I switched off the light, images played in my mind, not the ones I'd used in the video—the shots of the stark ruins and pristine mountains before the mudslide, the footage of the river bearing mammoth shards of concrete. But the ones of the people I'd traveled with, come to love, wanted to keep in my life.

Heart speeding, I pawed for the light switch even though no light could compete with my dawning epiphany. I finally understood what the admissions director at Cornish had asked me after viewing my portfolio: *What knocks your heart open?*

All around me, pinned to my bedroom walls, were my favorite photos of street fashion—all the crazy, unexpected, and truly bizarre outfits people assembled: sweater-vest coupled with skinny chinos and combat boots. But my photos had never been about fashion. They'd been about the personal statements people were making through fashion: *Take it or leave it, but welcome to Me.*

Forget sleep, I needed to look at the Truth of my journey to Machu Picchu, stripped of camouflage. I needed to look at the photos of what I had seen on the Inca Trail: Quattro, a guy who used humor to hide his broken heart as he waited for me on the trail. Christopher, a quiet man whose actions spoke loudly as he led Helen across the slippery bridge to safety. Stesha, who may have dressed like a lighthearted pixie but was more serious about life than anyone I'd ever met. Mom, who was a hopeless romantic but worked overtime at true love as she reached for Dad over and over again despite being rebuffed. And Dad, who was going blind but looked as if he had finally learned to see as he gazed down at Mom, boarding the flight to Belize.

And there was Grace, an old woman we had all written off as too feeble for the trip. Grace praying, head bowed in the cathedral. Grace lagging behind on the Inca Trail. Grace standing at the edge of the mud field. Grace kneeling beside a fallen Stesha. Grace helping to clear the railroad tracks. Grace standing triumphant atop a communal dining table, prosthetic leg finally revealed.

Maybe that was the heartbeat of my video, the one I wanted to make, not the one others thought I should. Maybe I didn't want to document the tragedy of the mudslide but wanted to profile the triumph of Grace at every step.

That knocked my heart open.

—m—

Missing five days of school the way we had originally planned would have been bad enough, but a nine-day absence made me question whether catching up was even possible. In one class after another, I sat catatonic, staring blindly at the whiteboards and listening to teachers who might as well have been speaking in Quechua for all that I understood. Somewhere along the day, I'd crossed over from feeling stupefied with jet lag to feeling just plain stupid. Thankfully, word about the mudslide had traveled far and fast, which won me sympathy points with the teachers, and I got extensions in every class and promises for private tutoring sessions.

Even with all the homework I needed to do, I collected Mrs. Harris after school for our inaugural Friday Walkers, West Coast edition. A stroll around the block might as well have been a treacherous marathon when done on crutches and with an out-of-shape neighbor who had rarely left home for the past few years. I wasn't sure which of us was breathing harder or sweating more, but both of us were grateful when we returned home. As we reached the lawn, Auggie bounded out of Aunt Margie's station wagon and nearly flattened me. Her joyous bark had the strength of a porcine opera diva behind it.

"Okay, Auggie!" I laughed as I wiped my cheeks dry of her slobbery kisses.

"Well, I'll leave you to it," said Mrs. Harris, mopping her forehead before she lumbered to her cottage. "I'm exhausted!"

Just a few weeks ago, I had been irritated that my mornings were given over to leading Auggie through her training exercises. This afternoon I was overflowing with appreciation that our brilliant bedbug sniffer didn't bark when I brought her inside, which meant that Auggie didn't detect so much as a single bedbug hitchhiker from Peru. That was hallelujah relief.

Above her wide grin, the circles under Aunt Margie's eyes were so deep and dark, she could have been the one caught in a mudslide with no rescue helicopter in sight. She flopped onto the couch as if her bones had liquefied, then kicked off her wide orthopedic shoes and wiggled her freed toes. "Wow, talk about exhausted! Try running the business and taking care of Auggie."

At forty, Aunt Margie was the baby of the family. Handling Auggie on top of her regular routine was a shock to her highly regimented, never-married, no-kids system. I grabbed one of Auggie's favorite toys—a once-plush hedgehog, its pelt chewed into rawhide—and lowered myself carefully onto the rug to play tug-of-war. Despite my waving the stuffed animal like a tantalizing matador's cape, Auggie had no interest. Zero. Instead, she circled around me as though I were a lost sheep that needed herding.

"Don't worry, I'm staying," I soothed her. She rested her head on my thigh to anchor that promise. I shot a grateful smile up at Aunt Margie. "Thanks for taking care of Auggie."

"Your dad needs to send me to a spa." Her eyes fluttered closed, as though keeping them open required too much energy.

I literally couldn't recall Dad ever asking any of his siblings for anything while he ran the family business year after year. In fact, I couldn't remember a single time when Dad even complained about giving up college while his brothers and Aunt Margie got their degrees.

"To be honest," I said, stroking Auggie's head, "Dad's worried about what he's going to do now to take care of Mom and us."

"Well, you kids will be fine on your own, so he doesn't have to worry about you. I mean, the twins are already so successful," said Aunt Margie. With a careless wave of her hand, she brushed off that concern like it was a pesky little aphid. "And your mom works."

"It's not like he can hunt for bugs if he can't see them."

"He can handle the office work. We'll just have to figure out some new systems." Her face brightened. "And he can learn braille."

"But, Aunt Margie," I said gently and firmly, "he never wanted to go into pest control in the first place."

She shoved her swollen feet back into her shoes, averted her eyes with the same painful, plastic expression that strangers wore whenever Dad mentioned Paradise, like it was some kind of rancid odor. Yet all of our family—myself included—had been eager enough to accept whatever profits Dad had shared with them.

No one other than Aunt Margie and a cousin or two over summer break ever pitched in to support the so-called family business. Though I had never sensed any pressure from my parents, there'd always been the unspoken expectation from Dad's family that my brothers or I would run Paradise one day. It was family heritage, after all.

Before I could say another word, Aunt Margie bustled out the door, citing errands upon errands to run before the stores closed. I'd never really looked at Paradise through Dad's eyes, and clearly none of his siblings had either. Somehow, I had to let the entire family know that everyone was going to have to step up if they wanted to keep Paradise going. It wasn't Dad's responsibility to bear alone. But how did I plan a military coup within my own family? My eyes landed on the computer I had brought downstairs this morning.

Another story awaited. This time, my father's as seen through my eyes.

Chapter Twenty-Nine

As if my parents had a radar for stealth projects in their own home, they called at the precise moment I removed their Fifty by Fifty napkin manifesto from the kitchen wall to scan for Dad's video homage. The normal "Hellos" and "How are yous" were so quickly dispensed with that I had barely mumbled a "My ankle's getting better" when Dad began describing every single tropical fish they'd seen over the previous four days.

"The colors were so bright, it'd have been impossible for even me to miss seeing them. And nurse sharks! Gorgeous," Dad said, his voice incredulous. It had been a long time since I'd heard him so invigorated. "I'm really kicking myself that you and Max aren't here. I should have sold the truck."

There it was, Dad's sacrificial generosity again, putting everyone before himself. I limped over to the couch to get more comfortable. "I got to see Machu Picchu, and Max gets to go to Guatemala with you. This is Ash's trip with you."

"I know, but still . . ." He cleared his throat. "So, kiddo, we looked at your video."

"You did?" I asked. That morning before school, I had e-mailed them the link to the rough cut. "Already?"

"Your mom forced the hotel manager here to let us onto her personal computer. Then she made all of us watch the video at least five times."

"Just twice!" I heard Mom protest off in the distance before she commandeered the phone from him. She told me, "It's ready to roll."

"Not yet." I propped my leg onto a throw pillow, my ankle swollen from the lap around the block earlier. "The transitions are choppy. And I need you to edit it. And Dad to do the voice-over. This was all placeholder."

"Post it."

"It's not ready!"

"You mean you're not ready. Spending five more hours on this, let alone another fifty, isn't going to change its emotional impact," said Mom before I heard a scuffle on the line. "Wait, Dad wants to tell you something."

There was a little static before I heard Dad say, "Besides, too much time has passed between the mudslides and now. You've got to post it."

"But it's not about the mudslides," I protested, running my fingers through the tassels on the throw pillow.

"It's better that way. I mean, how many videos asking for

286

donations after tsunamis and earthquakes have focused on doom and gloom?" asked Mom, sniffing. "After a while, it's almost like you've seen one, you've seen them all. And I don't mean to be callous, but from a viewer's point of view, there's only so much suffering you can witness before it all looks too hopeless."

Another truth. When Stesha had called to check in on me this afternoon, she told me that donations for the relief effort in Peru had slowed from a sickly trickle to mere droplets. So who knew how long reconstruction work would take because of the lack of funding?

"You know," Dad said thoughtfully, "the story you told isn't about destruction at all." He paused. "It's about the human spirit."

I moved the computer back onto my lap and studied the final still, two kids playing in front of a destroyed home that even in its best days had been little more than a hovel. Mom sniffled.

"Mom," I said, "you aren't crying, are you?"

"Honey, a girl may have started the Inca Trail, but a woman finished it," she said.

That made me sniffle. Whatever people sought from Stesha's tours—a pilgrimage to a spiritual mecca or closure to a difficult relationship—I couldn't argue with Mom: Not only had the trip knitted my parents back together but I had changed in ways I didn't know, maybe hadn't even considered, and hoped I would one day discover.

Dad must have grabbed the phone from Mom, because his voice boomed in my ear: "You're both going to make me cry if we don't get off the phone. Adios, sweetheart."

"My parents," I told Auggie as I tossed the phone onto the sofa, "are the best, but boy, are they weird."

Her tail thumped. I interpreted that as agreement.

—w—

The simple act of releasing my video was a lot harder than I thought. At least with TurnStyle, I knew that because new posts constantly refreshed the site, no one scrutinized any single photo for long. Plus, I knew how much I needed to learn about video production. But Mom always said about her own Power-Point work, no matter how many people review and rework a presentation, somehow a mistake always slips through. That's being human for you.

"Ready?" I asked Auggie before moving the computer off the coffee table and onto my lap. "It's time to send our baby out into the world."

Holding my breath, I posted the video for public consumption. That one action opened me to criticism in cyberspace from cynics who couldn't understand the need to help people half a world away. But hopefully, hopefully, the story and images would reach the right people, touch the ones who cared, inspire even one person to give. And maybe the one guy who'd trekked his way into my heart would find the Easter egg hidden inside and know how much I cared.

Chapter Thirty

Trust Mom to look out for me even when she was almost three thousand miles from home. Before we ventured off to Peru, she had arranged a special surprise: Reb. On a two-day reprieve from her treehouse restaurant project, my best friend showed up at our door early that evening, sleeping bag in one hand, bag of treats in the other, and a big squealing "Surprise!"

First thing, Reb reared back in horror—no pretense ever with her—when her shocked gaze locked in on my bare feet, bracketed by crutches: "Whoa...those are just wrong." She gagged. "Bleh. Ballerina feet."

"You mean old man feet," I said, wiggling my toes, banged up with blisters and topped with chipped nail polish that had once been angry purple. My feet were best hidden in socks, but I had better traction with bare feet on the slippery hardwood floors. I shrugged. "It was all those downhill miles in hiking boots."

"Good thing I'm such a great friend." Reb jabbed a finger in the direction of my offending feet. "I'll lead the SOS mission. Just remind me to thank Mom for telling me to bring supplies."

An hour later, my poor, trek-battered feet were soft from a long, pampering soak in Hawaiian bath salts—"My grandpa wants to know whether these would be good amenities for his inn. What's your vote?" (Two thumbs up.) Then she handed me a lava pumice stone—"He's testing these, too. What do you think?" (Only for guests into masochism.) And finally after vigorous scrubbing, we both lavished Notice Me Red on our toenails. While Reb waddled to the kitchen on the backs of her heels, doing an unintentional penguin impression, I surreptitiously checked my phone. Still no answering text or e-mail from Quattro. What did I expect when he didn't even own a cell phone?

"Quick, where's my phone?" asked Reb, scanning the kitchen counters frantically. "I know it's got to be around here somewhere."

"Why?"

"I need a picture for proof. The official end of your boycott."

"What are you talking about?"

"Ummm...that's like the fifteenth time you checked your phone. Does bending your own No Boy rule have anything to do with that rather spectacular guy I met? The rather spectacular guy that Grandma Stesha can't stop talking about?"

"Hey! Isn't there some kind of confidential tour guide—

client privilege?" I demanded as Reb rummaged in the grocery bag that she had brought with her. She held up a bag of fresh kettle corn triumphantly.

"Why would you want to keep Quattro a secret?" Reb asked me, dodging out of danger's way when Auggie bounded into the kitchen. Smart dog, she knows when food is about to be consumed. Reb's voice may have softened, yet her tone was insistent: "Why would you want to keep *anyone* a secret?"

Good question.

I sighed as Reb stopped Auggie from lunging at a stray piece of popcorn that had fallen to the floor after she ripped the bag open. "I guess you know about Dom."

"Well...yeah. It wasn't just that you never talked about him with me and Ginny after mentioning him once or twice but that you totally changed how you dealt with boys afterward."

"I think I didn't say anything—I *know* I didn't say anything—because deep down I knew he was all wrong. I mean, what kind of guy asks you not to tell anyone that you're dating unless he's embarrassed by you?"

"Or...maybe he was embarrassed by himself? I mean, isn't it a little creepy for a business school student to date a high school junior?"

"When you put it that way..."

Reb brought the popcorn bowl over to me, and we each grabbed a handful.

I continued. "I'm such a hypocrite. I gave you a hard time about staying with Jackson. What did I say again?"

"What are you guys going to talk about when you're in

college and he's still in high school? Prom?" Reb quoted with near-verbatim accuracy as she delicately plucked one piece of popcorn from the bowl and dropped it into her mouth.

"Ouch." I grimaced. "Sorry. How can you stand me?"

"You were just telling me the truth, Shana. I mean, any guy other than Jackson would have been a disaster. A total disaster. Plus, you're usually right about guys half the time."

"Only half?" It felt so good to be able to laugh about myself and not to have to be perfect. "So Quattro. I think I really like him. No, I know I do. But he's on his way to college. And"—now I smiled sardonically, repeating the very words I had thrown at Reb once upon a time—"what are we going to talk about when he's in college and I'm still in high school? Prom?"

"You're not just any girl, Shana. And"—she held up a finger to prevent an interruption—"I have it from a very good source—you—that prom is fun."

"But what if our time on the Inca Trail was all we had in common?"

"This, I've got to hear. The Love Guru speaketh. So you're saying..."

"Vacation is fake! Anyone can do a vacation! You'd have to be a total Eeyore not to be happy on a vacation! But in my real world, the one way, way off the Inca Trail, there's Dad's blindness and college applications and pest control"—I scrambled for another example—"and prom!"

"Aren't you being a little...dramatic?"

"Well, he hasn't exactly called me."

"Okay, I know this is going to be a shock to your system,

but in the real world, where we of the normal looks live, not all of us are chased nonstop by boys." She patted me gently on the hand as though I were senile. "It's hard to believe, but true."

"Reb!"

"So here's a wild idea." She who calls herself my friend now widened her green eyes. "Maybe you should call him? I know, crazy, right?"

"He doesn't have a phone."

"What?" Reb sounded the same disbelief I had felt before I knew Quattro's reason. "Why?"

That was private information I didn't want to share, not because I was afraid of what Reb would think but because Quattro blaming himself for his mother's death was his story and his alone to share.

"I've tried e-mailing him, but it's like he's a CIA operative or something. He's gone dark." I shivered at those words. What if something had happened to Quattro and his dad on their way home?

"Well, who knows why? Maybe he's not in a place where he can check e-mail? Or he's lost your phone number? A billion things could have happened. You never know." Reb shrugged. "It doesn't mean he doesn't like you."

Reasonable enough. I needed to move to safer topics: her treehouse building, weekend plans with Jackson, her kid brother. Luckily, Reb agreed that I was so behind in school, another night off wasn't going to hurt my grades more. So she insisted on helping me with Dad's surprise present. As we reviewed the storyboard I'd sketched on paper, Reb said, "If you don't mind me plagiarizing the idea, I'm so going to make one for my grandparents. I think Grandpa is going to pop the question soon. On the anniversary of the first time he proposed to Grandma Stesha."

"That's so romantic!" I said.

Our heads were bowed over Mom's computer as we clicked through folders. Photo after photo showed my parents not just living together through the years but loving together. In more than half of the pictures, my parents were laughing or hugging or just holding hands. The recent divorce of Reb's parents had come as a nasty surprise to everyone except her father, and I didn't want images of a happy couple to hurt her now.

I asked Reb, "You okay looking at these?"

"Yeah," she said, nodding firmly. Even though her smile was bittersweet, I could see she was telling the truth. "It's nice to see couples who've made it."

"Well, it hasn't exactly been all peaches and sunshine these last couple of weeks." I told her about how cranky Dad had been, first sullen and silent, then lashing out.

"Tough," said Reb sympathetically.

And then I replayed how Mom had treated him like an invalid before becoming all helpless woman in distress. "Oh, my gosh, she kept asking him if he was doing okay—like he was on his last legs."

"Ouch. Your dad's Mr. Climb Every Mountain Because It's There and all. He must have hated that."

"I know! Can you say 'total irritation at Mom'?" My breath caught. "You know what? Even when Dad was all cranky, he was the enforcer of thou-shalt-not-touch-my-daughter with Quattro. I swear, Dad could be my number one pest control technique. He totally intimidates guys."

"You have pest control techniques?"

"Had." I flushed when Reb burst out laughing. "Okay, so I had a couple of boy control techniques. But I didn't even realize it."

"Oh, my gosh, my mom always says that in her landscaping business, all she hears is rich-people problems: *Wherever shall I site my bronze statue? I'm just so weary of looking at those peonies.* But, Shana, do you have any idea how many girls would hate you for having pretty-girl problems?"

I blushed. Maybe Brian's mother wasn't terribly wrong about calling my streak of heartbreaking a pathology—a sickness. Discarding boys coldly wasn't fair, no matter how afraid of being hurt I was. Just because I had the power to win hearts didn't give me the right to break them.

In a small voice, I admitted, "I feel bad."

"Yeah, you should," Reb agreed simply, without any heat or judgment.

"Should I apologize to them all?"

"No!" Reb looked horrified. "I'm sure they all want your rejection to be a tiny little insignificant footnote in their lives. I wouldn't go ripping off their scabs now."

"I don't know...."

"Grandma Stesha would say, just be careful with people's feelings starting right now. And then maybe—maybe!—at your ten-year reunion, you can say something to them. Oh, like"—her voice went all soft and sultry as she fluttered her eyelashes—"Hey, baby! I hope you've recovered from pest control technique number five."

Laughing hard, I understood what Grace meant about her Wednesday Walkers. I told Reb about them now: trusted friends who had journeyed through marriages and divorces together, loyal friends who'd sat by one another's bedsides during childbirth and cancer treatments, beloved friends who'd kept secrets and poured honesty into each other's souls.

"Just like us," she said.

Reb and Ginny might not live in Seattle full-time anymore and they might be moving on in their own lives, but they were my own SOS squad and love-you-forever crew.

"Just like us," I agreed.

Chapter Thirty-One

Y ou would have thought I was training for the Indy 500 the way I raced home in Dad's immaculate truck from school two weeks later. My parents were supposed to return early that evening. "Supposed to" were the operative words. The last time we talked, they had sounded so excited after climbing yet another Mayan pyramid that it wouldn't have shocked me if they extended their stay. Budget hadn't even been mentioned once.

Halfway home, I checked the clock on the dashboard and accelerated. An emergency Chemistry tutoring session, encouraged strongly by my teacher, had whittled my three-hour party prep window down to one. I cast a glance over my shoulder before moving into the fast lane. I couldn't get myself worked up over the C+ on my latest Chem quiz. That was a small price to pay for experiencing Peru with my parents, meeting Grace, and getting to know Quattro.

If I wanted to execute all my plans, though, I'd have to pick up my pace. Think reunion mixed with surprise birthday party. For four exhausting hours after school yesterday, I had prepped the Peruvian-inspired meal with Ginny coaching me from her dorm room in the Hudson Valley. Ceviche. Arroz con pollo. And my own concoction: quinoa salad à la porter. While Peruvians might consume 65 million guinea pigs a year, we decided some culinary boundaries should never be crossed.

Although there was no pressing need to check my in-box, I did right after parking the truck in the garage. Messages from Stesha and Grace. Dad's family confirming their attendance. Ginny and Reb telling me how sorry they were to miss the party. It seemed like I'd heard from everyone but one guy with a soft spot for the color orange.

Even though I was on track to break my personal best record for getting home from school, I was worried. Worn out last night, I had fallen asleep before creating a playlist heavy on Andean mountain songs, not to mention I had all the dishes that needed last-minute assembling. But vaulting out of the truck now had more to do with outdistancing the sad truth that I found myself in yet another unrequited love situation.

I was so focused on Quattro's continued silence that I nearly missed the surprise waiting for me on the porch: Ginny. Good thing my crutches were planted firmly on the pathway, otherwise I would have fallen from shock. "What are you doing here?"

"What do you think? I was worried you'd mess up my recipes," Ginny said, throwing her arms around me. "No, actually, it's spring break. And Mom totally surprised me with this trip."

It'd been over three months since Ginny visited for Christmas. New red streaks wove through her golden-brown hair, cut so that it shattered against her creamy cheeks. No amount of texting could compare with being together in person, and I balanced on my good leg to hug her again.

"What's all that?" I asked, pointing at the platters and Tupperware containers in large cardboard boxes lining the porch.

"Reinforcements," Ginny said, already hefting one box in her arms. "Okay, hurry up and open the door! We've got work to do!" A few minutes later, she was slinging mounds of cookie dough onto the baking sheets, making me wonder whether she meant to say that we had a workout to do.

Concerned, I turned away from checking the oven's temperature and asked, "So everything okay in Ginny-land?"

"Boys are stupidheads," she said flatly, dropping a ball of half-frozen dough so hard, it almost bounced. "And I'm not sure I want to even try understanding them anymore."

"I totally get that."

"Okay, so you know Josh?"

"Chef Boy?" From her scowl, I had guessed correctly. "What's going on there?"

"Nothing, that's the problem. He's all simmer, no boil."

I laughed. Ginny did not. Still, a hint of a smile softened her expression as she slid the cookie sheet into the oven. She said, "I'm serious. He's all, 'Hey, I love your crust. Can you teach me how to make it for finals?'"

"Wow, great pickup line."

"I know, right?" She nodded, missing my sarcasm, as she peered at a tray of miniature pies, then frowned critically at one that was nicked. "So I go over to his apartment, right? And all we did was cook."

"Horrors!"

She placed the tray near the oven, turning the light on to check on the cookies. It was like watching a ballet, the way she flitted gracefully from one workstation to another in the kitchen. "So then I'm all, 'If you like mine, there's this new restaurant in town with supposedly crazy good pie. I've wanted to visit it.'"

I guessed, "And he didn't pick up that totally obvious cue for him to ask you out to taste-test the pie?"

"No! I mean, all those land-a-man books say that means he's blowing me off. But is he just clueless? I mean, for one of the top chefs who knows his way around a kitchen, he seems a little lost around women," Ginny said, glowering at me. "So come on. What do you think? You're the idiot savant of boys."

"Apparently, just an idiot." I hobbled behind her to grab a stack of paper plates from the pantry. "Trust me, I'm the last one you should ask for boy advice." So finally, I told her about Dom without concealing anything. It was like conducting a grand tour of my private diary: Here's where my heart was dinged; here's where my soul was damaged. "And that last time we saw each other, he yelled at me. Like top-of-his-lungs yelled. His veins were popping out, and I swear, the whole street shook."

Ginny's eyes were on me the entire time; she was no longer readying new trays or primping the cookies on platters. I

300

reached out for a broken cookie, but she pushed a whole one onto me instead. "Whoa. You know, it sounds like you totally dodged the bullet with him. I mean, what if he ended up being like the Yeller who was with his sister?"

"I never thought of that. Oh, my gosh, he sounded just like the Yeller."

"Who knows what was going on in Dom's family? Maybe his dad's a yeller. But whatever. Mom would say you're so blessed."

So blessed. "That's true."

"You don't need that in your life."

"I don't!" I nibbled the cookie, letting the sweetness spread in my mouth. "Ginny... maybe you don't want Mr. Top Chef if it means you have to be his sous-chef. I mean, what was with him asking you for your secret recipe?"

"That's so true!"

"And who wants to be with the kind of guys where we have to convince them we're good enough? I mean, Ginny! He should be so lucky to be with you. You're..." I grasped for a way to tell Ginny how precious she was, and my eyes dropped to a plate of gold-dusted truffles. "You're gold leaf!"

"I am! Whoa, I actually feel better now."

"Me, too." This time, I took a big bite and tasted the hint of smoked sea salt that I had missed before. "But then again, it could be the magical healing properties of your cookies."

She shoved her hand into an oven mitt to check her babies. "Probably."

—⁂—

"Shana! Where's my girl?" Dad bellowed before he was drowned out with a resounding cheer from thirty of our closest friends, my brothers, and the rest of our family, who had crammed into our home: "Surprise!"

They were so loud, Auggie cowered behind me. Mom pushed her way around Dad and bustled through the crowd. Nothing—not even a surprise party—was going to interrupt her single-minded mission to love on me. Her hug was choking, not that I minded. I dropped my crutches and hugged her even tighter. Over her shoulder, I grinned at Dad. Just as I had hoped, his attention was caught on the TV screen frozen on the first still of his video: *Fifty by Fifty Wilde Adventures*.

"What's that?" Dad asked, stepping closer.

Premiering this video to a roomful of friends and family was even more frightening than releasing one on the Web. There was a real risk that someone I loved could diminish my work with a condescending *Good effort*. And that would be so much more hurtful than criticism from a random hater.

But I hadn't created this homage to Dad for my private viewing any more than I photographed street fashion for myself. With no spoken word, just love screaming in my heart, I pressed Play and let this slide-show love note speak for itself.

WILDE ADVENTURE #1: CRADLE ROBBING

There was Mom, a chubby-cheeked five-year-old holding a crayon drawing: tiny house with five figures in descending height order and a dog that looked suspiciously like a guinea pig. And Dad, nine months old, toddling purposefully toward a toy camera. Both of them already knew what they wanted.

WILDE ADVENTURE #5: THE ORIGINAL PEST TEST

The maître d' at the waterfront restaurant must have swooned, and not in a good way, at the fashion faux pas couple before his eyes: Mom in a mustard-colored blazer with shoulder pads so enormous she could have single-handedly leveled an entire football team. And Dad in his original Paradise Pest Control uniform, all polyester. Dad supposedly hadn't had time to go home, shower, and change after an emergency concerning an infestation of slugs inside a client's house.

Supposedly.

After wiping tears from laughing so hard at the picture of the two of them, Mom wondered aloud, "So, Shana, based on your experience exterminating boys, do you think your dad was conducting his own pest control technique on me? See if I would pass inspection?"

I shrugged innocently.

WILDE ADVENTURE #25: BOBSLEDDING

Dad and his youngest brother, our uncle Bob, had transformed themselves into human sleds. Bobsledding went terribly wrong, ending with both of them in the ER with matching broken arms.

"Hmm, what do I always say about needing to see some-one in crisis to really know them?" Mom asked me, both of us snorting at the implications of that.

"But then," I said, "we wouldn't be here."

"Good thing your mom is so understanding," said Dad before he kissed her.

WILDE ADVENTURE #35: BEDBUGS, BEWARE

Dad with Auggie, fresh from the pound, on their first train-ing mission. Halfway through, Auggie had her Helen Keller moment, where understanding illuminated everything. Water for Helen, bedbug for Auggie. It wasn't clear who was happier: Dad because of our dog, or Auggie because of her chicken-liver treat.

WILDE ADVENTURE #45: LOVE IS BLIND

My parents at the kitchen table on the day they told me about Dad's eyesight, heads bowed with the weight of that life-upending news. The best photograph captures the truth, unspoken and unseen. What I saw now was the love knot of my parents' intertwined hands.

The following three photographs were taken after the mudslide on the Inca Trail, in the tourmaline waters of Belize, and atop the pyramid of Tikal. Luckily, my brothers had come through and e-mailed me those shots. No photographs could have made it clearer that my parents loved life. That was their true *sine qua non*. Their smiles were the same in the pictures taken of them at home and with their friends as in the shots of their adventures on their once-in-a-lifetime trips with us.

WILDE ADVENTURE #50: FIELD OF VISION

Frame after frame, fifty in all, in quick succession: a parade of Dad's favorite photographs shot over thirty years, the sum of his photo safaris, his life's work.

The slide show ended on a final image of our front door, half-opened to a fiery sunrise, a photo Dad had taken the morning after we moved into the cottage. Like a guardian of dreams, that photograph still hangs in the entry. *Get outside*, it says. *Go have an adventure*, it encourages. *Live*, it urges.

This was the moment; I could feel it in my fingertips. Yet again I mourned my camera, lost somewhere under mud on the Inca Trail. But I had Quattro's camera, which I would have to return somehow, someday. But not yet, not today.

Dad slung his arm over Mom's shoulder, an affectionate gesture I'd seen countless times before. They gazed at each other as though living and reliving thousands of conversations, spoken and unspoken.

And there it was: the decisive moment.

Dad's eyes glittered with tears as he stared, stared, stared down at Mom as if committing her to the deepest, most powerful part of his memory, one that no concussion could confuse or old age could erase. As I pressed down on the shutter, I knew without a doubt that Mom's face—not Machu Picchu or parrot fish or pyramids, but Mom's face—would be the very last image Dad would want to see.

Chapter Thirty-Two

I t took Mom a full ten minutes before her tears stopped rolling down her cheeks and she calmed down enough to say, "That was remarkable, truly remarkable. Beyond remarkable." Mom being Mom gazed at me as proudly as if I had snagged a Pulitzer. My brothers, Mom's best friends, the Paradise Pest Control employees, our neighbors—they bombarded me with a hundred compliments and a half-dozen requests for video valentines of their own. I noticed that the only people who remained silent were Dad's siblings, who looked ashamed and uncomfortable, as if for once they saw the sacrifices he'd made.

Throughout the ensuing hubbub, my father didn't say a word to me.

Not one.

Maybe I'd made the wrong choice. Maybe these images only magnified what would soon be his loss. Finally, Dad backed away from the screen, held me close, and simply whispered, "Good work," into my hair. When we drew apart, Dad smiled the same proud smile that had been the hallmark of every one of our photo safaris from the start. "Very good work."

I blushed under his broad grin, which could hold up the earth, and Mom's, which could give birth to any dream, the crazier, the better.

When Dad insisted on watching the slide show again, sitting close to the screen so that he wouldn't miss a single pixel, no one protested.

—⁓—

"Well, well, well. I think dessert just arrived," Ginny told me, eyes gleaming with mischief. I followed her gaze to the door, where I expected to see Reb but instead found Quattro bearing down on me in the kitchen, not with a dozen apology roses but with a pink pastry box. Just like that, my eyes teared up.

A few feet away, he said, "Bacon maple bar?"

"You're here."

"You invited us."

I flushed, only now noticing Christopher and a young girl with the same up-tilted hazel eyes as his and Quattro's. I flew over to give Christopher a hug, introduce myself to Kylie, and then finally sink into Quattro's arms.

"Technically, I invited your dad," I sniffled, my words muffled in his shoulder.

"Sooo," said Ginny, scrutinizing Quattro when we finally pulled away from each other. She was literally eyeing him up and down. "You're—"

Worried about what she would say, I cut in, "The one anthropologists should study. And the CIA. You don't exist online."

"But he's here right now," Ginny said smoothly, blinking at me expectantly for an introduction.

"Quattro," he introduced himself.

"Oh, yes, you are," Ginny said.

In spite of myself, my pulse quickened when Dad spied Quattro in the kitchen. I hadn't realized how worried I was about his reaction to Quattro. While he didn't throw his arms around Quattro, he didn't frown either. Instead, he held out his hand in what must have been a man's-man acceptance, then drew Christopher to the fridge for a cold beer and said, "So I hear we might be neighbors."

Standing awkwardly in the corner, Kylie played with the edge of her slouchy gold sweater.

"That is so blog worthy," I told her.

Her grin glowed brighter than the sweater. "You think so? I thought maybe I should have gone with brown wedges."

My eyes dropped to her white jeans. "Not even. Those Japanese sneakers are inspired."

"Winter meets spring," she said shyly before ducking her head.

My mind whirled. Had I just possibly found a managing editor to take over *TurnStyle*? Before I could even broach it with

Kylie, Ginny asked if she wanted to check out my closet to get a sneak peek at what would be hot a year from now.

"Are you kidding?" Kylie squealed, and the two of them dashed upstairs.

That left me alone with Quattro in the kitchen. I placed my weight on one crutch and swiveled around to face him. "What are you doing here? I mean, really, why?"

"You've got a right to be annoyed at me."

"Try hurt. And mad." It went counter to every single snag-a-guy self-help book Ginny devoured on a regular basis, but I let my emotions loose: "Why didn't you call me? I was worried about you. And weren't you worried about me?"

"More than you know. We called Stesha almost every day."

"You called her?"

"I didn't think you'd want to talk to me." He raised his hand, palm out. "I know. Lame. But I wasn't sure if I had totally messed up with you. And anyway, I wanted to tell you in person."

"What?"

"We were able to scatter Mom's ashes over Machu Picchu after all."

That revelation was a lightning bolt strike to the long three weeks of silence, a direct hit that burned my hurt clean. I forgot the pain of being ignored and let go of all my fretting that I had blown it with him by messing up his plans. A few of Dad's employees spilled into the kitchen, so I grabbed my jacket hanging on a hook in the mudroom and led Quattro out to our tiny backyard patio.

"How?" I asked him as I leaned my crutches against the

bench before maneuvering to take a seat. I noticed that Quattro stood nearby until I was safely sitting.

"The helicopter pilot," he said, dropping down next to me. "He totally got into it when I showed him Mom's ashes and told him what we had wanted to do. He flew us right over Machu Picchu. A woman said a prayer in Spanish. And then the clouds parted and the sun came through." His eyes were bright with unshed tears. "It was way better than what Dad and I had planned. You were right. There was a reason." His voice dropped an octave. "I wish you had been there."

"Me, too." There, I'd said it. Words that revealed my true feelings. Words that were practically "I do" for a commitment-phobe, reformed pest control guru girl like me. Words that propelled Quattro to tug me close, his arms ringing around me. I didn't protest.

His eyes were unwavering, as though he would never look away until I really heard him. "After my mom died, I started taking care of Kylie and making sure Dad ate. I paid the bills and went grocery shopping. And shopping for Kylie. And then you fell."

"I thought you blamed me."

"No! Myself for letting you get hurt. But I couldn't deal with feeling responsible for one more person when I'd already messed up with Mom."

"I don't need you to take care of me."

"I know, but I did. And I do. Sorry, I'm just wired that way."

I bit my lip, the echo of every single one of my frothing declarations of independence to Reb and Ginny ringing in my ears until it pealed with one truth: I liked feeling protected and cared for and nourished.

"After we were done with Mom's ashes, I had this feeling up in the helicopter. I know, weird, but I just knew Mom wouldn't want me to blame myself for the rest of my life." He drew a cell phone from his jacket pocket, so brand-new the burnished silver glinted in the outdoor light.

"You got a phone?" I asked, stunned.

That action was practically "I do" for a guy who had been determined to remain a devout and devoted single on his way to college. "And in case you still said no, I brought this." And now he placed a plastic bag in my hand. From it, I withdrew a napkin wrapped around the tiny SD card from my lost camera, more precious than any diamond.

"I forgot you had it," I whispered.

"I didn't." He unfolded the napkin and said, "Look."

From Voodoo Doughnut, the napkin had just one item written on it: "1. Inca Trail."

Blinking back tears, I found myself staring blurrily through the kitchen window at the original napkin, my parents' adventure manifesto of the fifty trips they wanted to take before they were fifty. For years, the napkin had presided over the kitchen table, but it was now framed in a shadow box that I had bought for my parents and commemorated in the video I'd created.

Quattro held the napkin, signposting this decisive moment that I didn't need to photograph to remember. It would be etched in my mind forever.

Reach for this napkin and I'd be committing to end my

history of flirt-and-run. Holding hands at a movie, casting a sultry look over dinner at an Italian restaurant—that was easy. Holding each other through fear, standing at the other's side through the worst bad news, that was tough. Maybe that's why Mom's romance novels only asked the will-they-or-won't-they-get-together question. The much harder challenge is will they or won't they stay together.

"What's next?" he asked softly.

From what I'd seen on the Inca Trail, the difference between romance and relationship is the courage to meet every *What's next?* with one answer: *Who knows . . . but I'll be there with you.*

Maybe it was finally time to dare a real relationship of my own.

So I closed the gap between us on the bench. And I lifted my face to his. And before his lips touched mine, I whispered, "Adventure number two. Us."

Chapter Thirty-Three

Of course, Mom insisted on showing the video appeal I'd made for donations to help Peruvians. That was just a notch less mortifying than her foisting my naked baby pictures on this captive audience. I wondered if Quattro had even seen the video, and if he had, whether he had noticed the message I had hidden in the credits. I could hardly stand still at the back of the living room, antsy up to the very end, when the production company name scrolled on-screen: GumWall Studio. The logo featured a neon-orange bicycle leaning against multicolored dots.

Quattro pulled me close and whispered in my ear. "Does my bike get a modeling fee, too?"

"You wish."

"But seriously, maybe you should think about going into film."

"Maybe," I said. Why not be open to new ideas, which could lead to adventures I'd never imagined and possibilities I'd never considered? I was standing in the arms of one such adventure I'd never dreamed I'd have after my heart had shattered, and I had seriously doubted that a right guy could exist for me.

"I loved this the first time I saw it, but it's even better the second time around," Quattro said, his eyes serious.

"That's because the second time around, you actually notice the details," said Stesha, walking toward us with her arms wide open. "You'll never guess who made the first donation."

"Grace," I said as she first enclosed me in an embrace, then Quattro.

"No, she was the second . . . along with her new honey."

"She's dating Henry?" I asked, grinning.

"Yes," said Stesha. "Helen was the first."

From the corner of my eye, I saw Christopher's head jerk up at the mention of Helen's name, and I smiled.

"The wedding's off," Stesha said, popping one of Ginny's miniature cookies into her mouth. "She's donating the entire catering budget to the cause."

"Whoa," I said, and then admitted, "I'm glad they're not getting married, but I feel a little bad for Hank."

"This might be the wake-up call he needed," Stesha said philosophically and shrugged. "We'll see." But now she nodded knowingly at me when everyone started promising to forward the link to the video to all their friends. That, as she said, is how a social revolution starts.

When everyone gathered around the dessert trays, Quattro

leaned over to me and said, "Which reminds me that you still owe me a modeling fee and a first date. You're racking up quite the debts."

"I still don't pay modeling fees, but I might make an exception for you." I smiled archly at him. "That is, if you're up for a surprise."

Chapter Thirty-Four

The morning after the party, I walked out to the front porch juggling two steaming mugs of coffee for my parents, who were chatting animatedly on the swing bench.

"What are you two plotting now?" I asked, handing them their Americanos, extra-hot the way they liked them.

Dad sipped the coffee with an appreciative groan. "It's time to retire the Fifty by Fifty."

"What? You can't!" I protested, ready to cheer Dad on in his own personal pep rally: Just because he was going blind didn't mean that he had to stop adventuring. Heck, as I had researched, there are plenty of blind adventurers. Look at Eric Weihenmayer, who summited Everest . . . blind! Not to mention blind archers. Archers! And blind artists, musicians, authors, and athletes.

Before I could slide behind my pulpit of peppiness, Mom said, "Who wants to cap it at fifty? We're voting for *daily* adventure."

Plan B, they told me, called for both of them cutting back the workweek to four days so they could hike together on Thursdays three seasons a year, and switch to snowshoeing in the winter. But they could only do this if Dad picked up vocational therapy to start adapting to his loss of vision.

"It's time to look this straight in the eye," Dad said, then shrugged with a wry expression that was wiped clean of any morbidity. "So to speak. I just need to figure out how to adapt."

"You will," I said.

"I will," he agreed confidently.

Mom added, "After seeing the video, we couldn't help but wonder if maybe you should apply to USC or NYU, too. Their film schools."

"But... aren't you going to need my help?"

"We're going to have to figure it out," Mom said.

"As much as we love you," Dad said, lifting his mug in a toast to me, "we don't want you living at home forever."

"We want you to have your own life," Mom said firmly.

One last protest bubbled up, but I stopped the words when it occurred to me that while my parents might welcome my help, they didn't *need* my help. This was no different from what I'd learned from Grace on the Inca Trail. Grace with her one leg, who tirelessly, relentlessly pursued the adventure she wanted. When she needed me, she'd ask. Otherwise, she wanted me to enjoy myself. And most of all, she wanted to enjoy herself, and that meant not feeling like a burden to anyone.

"Okay, I'll think about those schools, too," I told them, and basked in their blessing.

Before I left to pick up Quattro at his dad's downtown condo, I made one final pit stop with a gift for my parents: a fresh napkin, a blank canvas for their new dreams.

—ⵡ—

"So where are we going, you with that smug smile?" Quattro asked as he settled into the passenger seat.

"Smug? Who's smug?" I demanded, even though I knew perfectly well that I was exuding self-satisfaction that purified into sweet satisfaction after he leaned over the parking brake to kiss me. One strong hand cradled the back of my head, the other cupped my cheek. Cherished and respected, that's how I felt with Quattro, and my body must have let him know it, too, because when he pulled back from our kiss, let's talk about smug. His grin was all he-man glory. And I told him so.

"Yeah, well, when you've got it, you've got it," he said lazily. "So where are we headed?"

"A photo safari." I pulled onto the road. "My favorite spot in the city."

"The Gum Wall?"

"Nah, I'm on to the next thing."

"So where?"

"You'll see."

Behind the corporate headquarters of Starbucks is a building that's been set aside for young graffiti artists. With full permission from the owner to paint whatever they want, whenever they want, artists have turned the wall into an intriguing, ever-changing collage. Last time I dropped by the Graffiti Wall, I shot a portrait of Ginny under a painting of an enormous chocolate-brown-and-pink cupcake. The cupcake had long since disappeared under new images of a stack of books, a red skull, and a girl surfing a rainbow. And now, topping it all, was a very round, very pink doughnut.

"See? Stesha would say that we were meant to be here," I told Quattro before directing him to stand between the doughnut and a stylized word: "Dazzle." A better word would have been *sine qua non*, and that just might need to be remedied soon. "How are you with spray paint?"

"Now?"

"Later. We got time." I grinned. "So let's see what you got."

"What I got?"

I demonstrated—wiggled my hips, shimmied my shoulders, and struck the sultriest of sultry poses. "Voilà."

"You're killing me."

I snapped back into photographer mode. "So, Model Boy, your turn."

"Later. We got time." Quattro pulled me close and kissed me, long and scorching hot, oh, my. In the privacy of my own mind, I yelled silently to Grace's Wednesday Walkers: *Girls! Are* you listening? *Sexy. To. The. End.* Somehow, I managed to dredge up enough rational thought to step away from Quattro.

"Nope, time to work for your modeling fee." I held my cell phone up. There is a reason why people say creativity gets exercised when it works within tight constraints. Since I couldn't afford a new camera yet, I'd been playing with my old cell phone. What I found was that I loved this medium and had a couple of ideas that I wanted to experiment with today.

Five minutes, count them, that's all it took before I felt certain that I was about to get the perfect shot. The wind picked up, blowing Quattro's hair back. He looked straight at me, all focused intent, as if he were setting off to explore the last bit of uncharted rain forest left in the world. There was challenge in that expression and an undeniable hint of swagger.

"Done," I said, pocketing the cell phone.

"Already?"

"On to the next place."

"Gum Wall, Graffiti Wall. I can hardly wait."

"Oddfellows," I said.

He laughed as he followed me to the car. "Of course. Will your extraction crew be there?"

I reddened. "We don't need one."

One eyebrow lifted as his eyes twinkled. "You sure about that?"

"Well," I drawled. "You might need to convince me."

So he did, with another pulse-surging kiss. On the way to Capitol Hill, I told Quattro about my parents urging me to apply to USC and NYU, and he listened intently even as it spelled potential years apart from each other, one of the reasons I hesitated in seriously thinking about them. But he nodded and said firmly, "You've got to apply."

"I know, but..."

"Shana, it's over a year away. Who knows what could happen between now and then?"

"Are you saying we might break up?"

"Or maybe something better might happen—and we both end up in Oslo or at a fairy circle in Scotland."

"You're right," I said, laughing. "You're absolutely right."

Maybe that's just it. Maybe all we can do is grab hold of life as it unspools before us. I cast a glance over my shoulder to check my blind spot: all clear. With a quick grin at Quattro, I merged into the fast-moving traffic on the highway and headed for whatever adventure the next moment held for me, for him, for us.

Acknowledgments

Many people taught me how to see clearly as this book evolved.

Deepest gratitude goes to Alvina Ling and Bethany Strout, an editorial dream team if there ever was one.

Donna Francavilla generously shared her eyewitness account of the mudslides on the Inca Trail. And Ruben, raconteur and tour guide of Machu Picchu, regaled my kids and me with (harrowing) stories about the trail. I hope they and other trekkers understand that I needed to make a few geographic changes to that beloved trail for the sake of this story.

Meg Lippert is the best trekking partner a woman could have, leprechaun-green coat notwithstanding.

Annie Griffiths, photographer for *National Geographic*; Chris Linder; and Leslie Magid Higgins provided *veritas* and passion for their art form. And Eric Swangstu shared insights into the college portfolio review process and art that knocks your heart open.

Alfie Treleven of Sprague Pest Control, Tom Pleas, Susan Polzak, and May—quite possibly the most adorable bedbug-sniffing dog on the planet—thank you for teaching me about bedbugs, rats, and the pest control industry.

Dr. Bob Glaze, Dr. Kathy Vuu, and Dr. Mike Tam helped me understand some of the illnesses that lead to blindness—and, more important, the human emotions that accompany that process. All medical inaccuracies are mine and mine alone.

Karen Bonnell continues to teach me about insight and true sight.

And always, always, always, heartfelt thanks go to my children, Tyler and Sofia, who are especially patient when I live what I learn, even when I now insist on inspecting hotel rooms for bedbugs.